'I am more of a lady than you will ever be a gentleman! At least I have enough decency to know that it is quite wrong to make advances to the staff.'

Ross had the audacity to smile. 'Stop acting so shocked. I suspect that you are not truly as prim and proper as you would have me believe.'

Something about the way his eyes devoured her after those words made Hannah blush involuntarily, as if he could see through the fabric of the garment.

'Perhaps I should keep a very close eye on you—just to check that you are not up to no good. Would you like that, Prim?'

One hand curled around her waist possessively, then made a slow journey down the curve of her hip. Hannah had never been handled so... *intimately*. The twin emotions of outrage and exciteme—— —— —— ameless man war—— —— —— nes had she dream—— —— —— lonely bed?

His eyes—— —— —— promise...

3 8002 02283 932 0

Author Note

My husband is fond of analogies. One of my favourites is a story about two brothers. One is a successful doctor and the other a low-life drunk with no job. Their father is a cruel and violent man. One day the brothers are both asked the same question: Why have you turned out the way you are? Despite the vast difference in their lives, both brothers give exactly the same answer: 'It's hardly a surprise when you have a father like mine!'

It is an extreme example, I know, but the past shapes us all. That is a fact. Sometimes it makes us into better people, and other times it holds us back and stops us living life to the full.

In my novel *That Despicable Rogue* I have created two people who are shaped by their pasts. Ross Jameson has dragged himself out of the gutter and done everything possible to make sure he never has to go there again. Lady Hannah Steers has had her life destroyed by the past and feels that she has no future.

Once I'd created these two people and introduced them to each other they pretty much wrote their own story for me. At times I had no idea what they were going to do next! I hope that you enjoy their trials and tribulations as they seek their happy ending. An ending, incidentally, that they never told me about until it actually happened!

THAT DESPICABLE ROGUE

Virginia Heath

All rights reserved including the right of reproduction in whole
or in part in any form. This edition is published by arrangement with
Harlequin Books S.A.

This is a work of fiction. Names, characters, places, locations and
incidents are purely fictional and bear no relationship to any real
life individuals, living or dead, or to any actual places, business
establishments, locations, events or incidents. Any resemblance is
entirely coincidental.

This book is sold subject to the condition that it shall not, by way of
trade or otherwise, be lent, resold, hired out or otherwise circulated
without the prior consent of the publisher in any form of binding or
cover other than that in which it is published and without a similar
condition including this condition being imposed on the subsequent
purchaser.

® and TM are trademarks owned and used by the trademark owner
and/or its licensee. Trademarks marked with ® are registered with the
United Kingdom Patent Office and/or the Office for Harmonisation in
the Internal Market and in other countries.

Published in Great Britain 2016
by Mills & Boon, an imprint of HarperCollins*Publishers*
1 London Bridge Street, London, SE1 9GF

© 2016 Susan Merritt

ISBN: 978-0-263-91700-0

Our policy is to use papers that are natural, renewable and
recyclable products and made from wood grown in sustainable
forests. The logging and manufacturing processes conform to the
legal environmental regulations of the country of origin.

Printed an
by CPI, B

Coventry City Council	
CEN*	
3 8002 02283 932 0	
Askews & Holts	Apr-2016
ROM	£4.99

When **Virginia Heath** was a little girl it took her ages to fall asleep, so she made up stories in her head to help pass the time while she was staring at the ceiling. As she got older the stories became more complicated—sometimes taking weeks to get to their happy ending. One day she decided to embrace the insomnia and start writing them down. Virginia lives in Essex with her wonderful husband and two teenagers. It still takes her for ever to fall asleep…

That Despicable Rogue
is Virginia Heath's wonderful debut
for Mills & Boon Historical Romance!

Visit the Author Profile page at millsandboon.co.uk.

For Greg,
for encouraging me to follow my dreams and write.

For Katie,
who first read what I had written.

And for Alex,
who fortified me with tea and kept me sane.

Prologue

The crowd gathered around the card table signalled one of two things—either somebody was about to win a substantial sum or somebody was about to lose the shirt off his back. The spectacle drew Ross Jameson like a moth to a flame. At the card table sat the Earl of Runcorn, eyes wide and sweating profusely, as Viscount Denham idly gathered up the ridiculously large pile of banknotes he had just won from the middle.

Ross wandered to his friend Carstairs, knowing that he would clarify the situation perfectly. 'What's afoot?' he murmured as he took a sip of his drink.

John Carstairs copied the motion, his eyes never leaving the drama at the table. 'Denham has just cleaned Runcorn out. There is over a thousand pounds on that table.'

Ross was not surprised. Runcorn had been on the path of self-destruction for years and Viscount Denham did enjoy parting a fool from his money.

Denham stood and smiled smugly at his opponent. 'It has been a pleasure, Runcorn.'

The beaten man blinked rapidly, obviously in a state, and then reached into his jacket pocket with the air of a man about to do something completely stupid. He pulled out a large, official-looking document and practically threw it into the middle of the table.

'The deeds to Barchester Hall,' he announced with desperate zeal. 'It is unentailed and surrounded by excellent parkland and fine pasture— I will wager all I have lost against the house.'

The assembled crowd sucked in a collective breath.

'What sort of man comes to a card game with the deeds to his house?' Carstairs hissed under his breath.

'The sort who is fool enough to lose it,' Ross answered calmly. Runcorn was not the first man to gamble away the family silver, and doubtless he would not be the last.

The rest of the crowd were anxiously waiting for Denham to respond to the challenge. This was exactly the sort of thing that they lived for—the prospect of seeing one of their own ruined.

Denham had still not sat down again, but he was regarding Runcorn with open curiosity—to Ross it was obvious he was rejoicing in his own good fortune.

True to form, Denham was going to make the fool suffer. 'I seriously doubt that the property is worth much more than three thousand,' he said dismissively, 'but I am a reasonable man. Under the circumstances I will—'

Ross cut him off before he could finish. '*I* will take the wager, Runcorn.' He tossed an enormous bundle of banknotes onto the table. 'Five thousand against your house.'

The crowd gasped audibly at this interesting and totally unexpected turn of events. Excited words were exchanged and one or two men pointed out that Ross's challenge was poor form. This was Denham's game—he at least should claim first refusal. But such a vulgar upstart as Jameson would not understand the proper way things were done in polite society. Others simply marvelled at his apparent generosity. Five thousand against some old heap of bricks was well over the odds.

Ross ignored them. Instead he watched Runcorn eye the cash greedily and knew exactly what the blithering idiot was thinking—he could cover his losses and pay some debts with such a healthy purse. Gamblers like Runcorn could never see past the pathetic hope that their luck was about to change.

'Done!' Runcorn exclaimed excitedly, his gaze never leaving the money.

Ross watched Denham's pale eyes narrow briefly before he reluctantly stood aside to allow him to sit in the chair he had just vacated. 'What are we playing?' Ross asked casually, although he knew already that it was piquet.

Poor Runcorn really did not stand a chance. Many considered piquet less of a risk than hazard, but in truth it was much easier to cheat if one was so inclined. With hazard, chance and luck might scupper even the best player, but piquet was predictable for somebody with Ross's brain. He motioned for the cards to be dealt and took another sip of his drink before slowly picking up his hand.

The cards he had were good, so he discarded them and picked up five duds. It would not do to trounce the fellow completely from the outset.

Runcorn easily won the first rubber and visibly sagged in relief. The man really was a terrible player; it was no wonder Denham had cleared him out. He wore his emotions on his sleeve.

For the second deal Ross purposely played clumsily, and made it appear as if his final winning trick was a fluke. The third hand he played dead straight and won, but he threw the fourth for the sake of entertainment. The crowd and the atmosphere made it fun.

Runcorn was far too careless, and nerves made him sloppy. He was so grateful for each point that he lost track of the cards dealt and obviously had no concept of what was left on the table—a rash and stupid way to play such an easily rigged game. Hell, if he were so inclined as to feed in a few additional face cards, he doubted the man would realise. However, he just wanted to beat Runcorn—not meet him on Hampstead Heath at dawn.

As the penultimate hand was being dealt Ross caught John's eye. His friend made a show of checking his timepiece—an unsubtle reminder that they were due elsewhere—and Ross stopped toying with his prey. He played every card with calculation and took every trick. By the end of the *partie* Runcorn had begun to panic. Large beads of sweat rolled down the side of his face and dampened the high, pointed collar of his fashionable shirt.

That detail also spoke volumes about the man, Ross mused. It was well known that the Earl of

Runcorn had run up huge debts with every reputable tradesman in London—and some very *dis*-
reputable. He had long been spending above his
means, but instead of curbing this recklessness
Runcorn chose to affect a façade of wealth that
did not fool anyone—least of all Ross. He made
it his business to track fellows like that, so it was
difficult to feel sorry for him.

The final hand was dealt in silence as the onlookers tried to conceal their glee. At best, Runcorn needed thirty points to beat him. Such a
feat was possible for a skilled player, with a keen
awareness of the game. Unfortunately that was
not Runcorn. He lacked both skill and awareness.
In fact he lacked any prospect of basic common
sense as well, but—as with so many of his ilk—
he had no concept of his failings.

Ross decided to lull the hapless earl into a
false sense of security. Runcorn won the first
two tricks because Ross let him, and lost the third
badly because of his own stupidity. In desperation he played his one good card too soon. As a
result he won the fourth trick, but had nothing
higher than a jack left in his arsenal for the rest
of the game.

As Ross held two kings and a queen Runcorn's
defeat was not only inevitable but decisive. His
face took on a white, then an increasingly green

tinge as Ross's points rose past the number where he stood even the slightest chance of recouping his losses. When his final card was trumped by the King of Hearts, Runcorn buried his head in his hands as applause broke out around them.

Ross quietly picked up his five thousand, and the folded deeds, and put them safely into his inside pocket. Now would definitely be a prudent time to make a hasty exit.

Quietly, Viscount Denham came up behind him and whispered in barely audible tones, 'I see your luck continues to hold, Jameson.'

Ross nodded curtly. He had just ruined a man; he did not need to gloat. Nor did he need to spend one more second in Denham's company that he did not have to. The man made his flesh crawl.

At that moment the Earl of Runcorn lurched to his feet, unaware of the fact that he had knocked his chair over in the process. 'Well…well played, sir,' he stammered—out of ingrained politeness rather than respect, Ross assumed—and then he turned to the assembled crowd and inclined his head. 'If you gentlemen will all excuse me for a minute?'

Ross watched him stumble towards the door and his eyes flicked back towards his friend in unspoken communication. John nodded in understanding and slipped out of the crowd to follow Runcorn. He would know what to do.

'I wonder, Jameson,' Denham said silkily, 'is it the thrill of the game that draws you or is it merely the pleasure of thwarting *me* that you continually seek?'

The sound of a single shot ringing out prevented Ross from having to answer.

Everybody rushed towards the door that led out to the marbled hallway of the gentlemen's club. Before he even reached the hallway Ross had a premonition of what he would see, but he followed regardless. John, of course, was already there, and his shocked expression told the onlookers everything they needed to know.

An eerie silence settled over them as they took in the gruesome scene. The alabaster walls of White's were decorated with violent splatters of Runcorn's blood, which had already started to trickle in their journey downwards. A growing pool of crimson oozed slowly across the black and white marble floor around the body while the pistol he had used to blow his own brains out was still smoking in the earl's twitching hand.

Denham turned to Ross with a malicious gleam in his eye. 'Well, that should certainly give the newspapers something to print tomorrow.'

Chapter One

Just over one year later...

Lady Hannah Steers read the letter again with mounting excitement. If Cook was to be believed then this was finally her chance to set things to rights.

'What is that dear?' her Aunt Violet asked, curious to see any sort of letter, such were their rarity.

'It is a letter from Cook with news from Barchester Hall. That blackguard now intends to move in. Can you believe that?'

'Oh, dearest, I do wish that you would try to forget about that place,' said Aunt Beatrice with concern. 'It is time that you moved on with your life.'

Both her aged aunts were wearing twin expressions of pity, and Hannah felt her irritation rise at their continued lack of understanding.

How did they expect her to move on with her life when the single most important part of it had been stolen away? Barchester Hall was all she had left.

'Aunt Beatrice,' she stated, with as much patience as she could muster, 'I cannot move on until I see Ross Jameson swing from a gibbet. In the meantime, somebody has to expose his true character to the world.'

'Nonsense!' her aunt replied. 'He will get his comeuppance—but you are not the person to see that he does. You have five thousand pounds from your father sitting in the bank and you are still young enough to find a husband.'

Ha! As if *that* was ever going to happen now. After the scandal, no man worth his salt would touch her—regardless of her aunts' continued optimism. Nor did she want to put all her faith in one man again—any man for that matter. The last few years had taught her that she could function perfectly well on her own.

'You need to enjoy your life now. All this bitterness towards Mr Jameson is not healthy. In fact we know nothing certain about him at all. Are you even sure that he is as guilty as you believe? No charges were ever brought, after all.'

Hannah felt her blood begin to boil at that suggestion. 'Do not give that despicable rogue the benefit of the doubt. I can assure you that he does not deserve such kindness. All my enquiries and all the evidence I have gathered leads me to exactly the same conclusion. He is a villain and a swindler—make no bones about it. But he has covered his tracks well. Any man who can wheedle his way into society with such lowborn connections has a particular talent for deceit. Of course he is charming, and his fortune has bought him entry into some of London's finer homes, but there are still a goodly number of the ton who continue to turn their backs on him. They know what he truly is. The gossip columns are full of his salubrious exploits.'

'Need I remind you that your brother's exploits also made regular appearances in the scandal sheets?' her Aunt Violet pointed out. 'And we all know that George was not an angel. And most of society would still turn their back on *you*—not that you deserve it, of course—so I am inclined to ignore that particular point.'

Her two aunts shared a pointed look and Hannah sighed in frustration. She *had* featured briefly in the gossip columns too. Quite spectacularly, in fact—and none of that had been true either—but she would not let that distract her. The stories might have been false, but they had not been founded in fairytales. Everybody—her own fiancé included—had been convinced of her guilt before the cruel words had even made it to the papers. They had only printed the news.

'I know that you do not share my desire to have him brought to justice, but I cannot stand by and let him ruin Barchester Hall. It is my home and I love it. I have to at least try to get it back. And, whilst I do agree that in the main society is fickle and not to be trusted, there has been too much written about him for it all to be false. There is at least one story a week, usually involving either women or his dubious business dealings, and he never denies them. Why would he allow such things to be printed if they were not true? He would have grounds to sue for libel. Do you know that one newspaper even went as far to suggest that he killed his own father?'

'Surely not!' Aunt Violet covered her open mouth with her hand.

At her aunts' twin expressions of horror she clarified what she had read. 'Well, perhaps not directly. He surrendered his father to the authorities for the reward money and upon his testimony the man was transported to the colonies. He died on the passage over.'

'That does not make the man a murderer, Hannah,' Beatrice said in relief.

'But it *does* give us some insight into his character, Aunt. He betrayed his kin. He did not deny it. What sort of a person does that?'

Neither of the older women could think of a suitable response, which led Hannah to believe that they did actually agree with her on that score.

'Barchester Hall is his now,' Aunt Beatrice said kindly, and patted her hand. 'You must reconcile yourself to that sad fact. It is lost to our family for ever.'

'Not if I can prove that he came by it dishonestly,' Hannah countered vehemently. 'Perhaps then there is a chance that it can be returned to the family. If not, when Jameson is behind bars the Crown will sell it, and—as you rightly point out—I have five thousand pounds sitting in the bank to purchase it if such an opportunity presents itself.'

She was quite prepared to do whatever it took to go home again. She felt as though she were slowly dying here. Days, weeks, months, *years*— all had merged into one never-ending stream of monotony that left her so despondent that at times Hannah struggled to get out of bed.

Years ago she had been so vibrant—so full of life and hope and fun. Where had that effervescent girl gone? This prolonged period of exile had sucked all of the joy out of her heart and she was tired of feeling imprisoned. If only she could go home to Barchester Hall… Then perhaps she might once again blossom into the woman she had once been and live the life she deserved.

Aunt Violet shook her head slowly. 'But, dearest, we are in the wilds of Yorkshire and Barchester Hall is two hundred miles away. How exactly are you going to achieve all this from such a distance?'

Both her aunts still thought of her as a child. She knew quite well the futility of attempting such a thing from their tiny cottage on the moors. Hannah stifled the slow grin that threatened to spread across her face. She was no longer the green girl she had once been. Complete ruination had a way of hardening one's character, so she had every intention of pursuing any opportunity that presented itself—no matter how tenuous. But there was no way her aunts would support her if they actually suspected what she was up to. Cook's letter had thrown her a lifeline that she intended to grasp with both hands. This was her chance to have a different future.

'On a separate note,' she said after several minutes of silence, 'Cook says that Jane Barton has invited me to visit her for the summer.'

She had not spoken to the girl since the last ball they had attended together—just before Hannah had been banished to Yorkshire so spectacularly—but her aunts did not know that. None of her old London friends had spoken to her since that dreadful ball either. They had all taken her guilt for granted. Not that she would ever discuss those shameful facts with them… The lie would give her an excuse to get away for a month or two at least.

'That's nice, dear,' Violet said kindly as she picked up her embroidery. 'You s*hould* go and stay with her. It will be good for you to spend time with somebody your own age for once. You have been cooped up here with us old ladies for far too long.'

Aunt Beatrice heartily agreed. 'A good holiday will sort you out and take your mind off this silly revenge business. You might even meet a nice gentleman and be swept off your feet. Wouldn't that be nice?'

Hannah smiled politely at the familiar suggestion. Both women were convinced that the only route to her future happiness was with a man. Normally she would have set them straight on that score immediately. The very last thing she needed was a man in her life. It was thanks to men that she was in this predicament in the first place. However, if her aunts were hopeful that she would change her mind and be open to the idea of marriage they would actively encourage her to take a little holiday.

'I suppose…' she said a touch wistfully, and stifled a triumphant smile when she watched her aunts exchange a pointed look at her apparent sudden change of heart. 'Perhaps enough time has passed.'

'It has been seven years,' Aunt Beatrice said excitedly. 'It will all be forgotten. Besides, you are such a pretty girl, Hannah. You always did turn heads. And you are so thoughtful and caring—you deserve the chance of a family of your own. I firmly believe that once you meet the right gentleman he will not care one whit for silly gossip that is so many years old. But for that to happen you need to be with people of your own age—like Jane Barton. You should write to her at once and accept.'

'I shall make the arrangements, then,' she said, rising.

And now that she had the entire summer free she could take advantage of the very interesting information that Cook had told her. Not only was Jameson moving in to Barchester Hall, but he had asked Cook to advertise for a housekeeper. Finally she'd have an opportunity to study the beast in his lair. All applications were to be sent to Barchester Hall, and Cook had been given the responsibility of sifting through them and selecting the most suitable candidates for him to interview in London next week. Jameson did not want his busy lawyer to be burdened with such mundane things.

Hannah's application would be one of the few that he would see.

Hannah sailed out of the room without looking back. If she was going to make it onto the post in the morning she had much to do. Firstly she had a letter of application to write. Then she had references to forge. And at some point this evening she would also have to pack up her meagre possessions ready for the trip.

Fortunately her wardrobe was so dire already that she did not have to purchase new clothes to resemble a servant. Her existing clothes were drab and plain enough already. She probably did look a little too young to be a housekeeper, but she could scrape her hair into an unbecoming bun and perhaps affect some sort of disguise that would make her appear more suitable.

By hook or by crook she *would* be Ross Jameson's new housekeeper. It was her only real hope of getting some of her life back.

Ross folded his arms over his bare chest and stared at Francesca. What he had seen in her all those months ago he could not fathom. She was a selfish, self-centred, mean-spirited and manipulative wench with far too much to say for herself.

'You need to leave now—and this time I want you to leave the master key you charmed from the doorman.' For emphasis he stuck out his palm and waited.

'Oooh, Ross, we both know that you don't mean that,' she cooed as she lay back against his pillows and began to unlace the front of her low bodice. 'Come to bed and I will make you forget all your anger.'

Once upon a time he would have happily taken her up on the offer. Despite her intrinsic character flaws, Francesca had always been a good tumble. He had, of course, paid dearly for that privilege—but the harpy could keep the jewellery and the fripperies he had given her. It was the least he could do, he supposed, but facts were facts.

'I think that you are forgetting one *tiny* detail, Francesca, and it is one that I cannot overlook. Our arrangement was supposed to be exclusive for its duration.' And Ross knew she had been dallying elsewhere these last few weeks.

'I would never have strayed if you had taken more of an interest in me.' Her rouged lips pouted and she slowly pulled her bodice open.

Two very large, very round breasts stared back at him in open invitation. She did have a point, he supposed. He had lost interest in her. In the last few months he had been so busy with his work that he had scarcely had time for her. However, that did not give her carte blanche to seek entertainment from another benefactor before they had formally ended their arrangement. That was just basic good manners.

'I have it on good authority from Lord Marlow himself that he is more than happy to support you going forward,' Ross explained calmly. 'It will, I am reliably informed, suit you very well too—seeing as you have been inviting him over this last fortnight for a bit of a trial run. I do not actually have the time for a mistress at the moment, so let's just let bygones be bygones and leave it at that.'

Francesca bristled and stuffed her exuberant breasts back into her dress. 'You will come back to my door begging for it. You wait and see.'

The fact that he had not done so in over two months did not appear to have registered.

'Well, in the meantime I think you had better hand over that key and give it back to the doorman. I would prefer it if you did not turn up to my lodgings unannounced in the future. You gave me quite a scare.'

She had as well. One minute he had been enjoying a deep and dreamless sleep and the next he had felt her hand clamp around his privates. But then again Francesca had never been particularly subtle.

With a huff she fished the key out of her reticule and slapped it into his open palm, but she made no attempt to rise from her semi-reclining position on his bed.

'Are you sure you don't fancy one last ride, Rossy-Wossy? For old times' sake?' Francesca gave him her best come-hither smoulder and began to inch her frothy skirts slowly up her open legs.

'Here we are, mum.' The bedroom door crashed open and Reggie filled the frame with his enormous bulk. 'Your appointment is here, Ross,' he said, smiling, oblivious to the fact that he had not knocked and had brought a complete stranger into Ross's bedchamber without any warning whatsoever.

With a long-suffering sigh Ross walked towards the door. 'Thank you, Reggie. But do you remember I told you that visitors should be seated in the parlour and given a cup of tea?'

Reggie nodded his enormous mousy head and looked contrite. 'I remember, Ross. Sorry...' He turned towards the wide-eyed woman next to him and used one of his meaty arms to man-handle her out through the doorway. 'I have to sit you in the parlour and make you tea, mum.'

Ross closed the door and grabbed a fresh shirt. This was not exactly the way he had planned to start his day. First he had been forced to deal with Francesca, and now he had probably frightened off the only reasonable applicant he'd had for the job of housekeeper. He doubted the woman would even stay—she had looked so outraged at the scene she had just witnessed that she was probably halfway to Mayfair by now.

'Who is *she*?' Francesca snarled as she finally deigned to rise from his bed. 'Is she your new mistress?'

Ross heaved a long-suffering sigh. 'She *was* applying for the post of housekeeper at Barchester Hall—not that it is any of your business. But I should imagine she is already outside hailing a hackney, thanks to you and Reggie.'

Ross stalked to the door and headed towards the parlour. To his complete surprise the woman was in there. She sat primly, balanced on one edge of a chair, looking as though she was likely to bolt at any moment. Ross arranged his features into the most apologetic and friendly smile he could muster. Perhaps he could salvage the situation with his usual charm?

What was he thinking—of *course* he could salvage the situation with his charm. It was what he did best.

His search for a housekeeper thus far had been fruitless. Who knew that hiring servants was such an onerous task? Not having ever had a need for servants before, Ross had had no idea how problematic the process could be. He was offering a good salary, and more than the usual amount of time off, but so far every woman he had interviewed had been totally unacceptable. One had been obviously drunk, the second very peculiar and actually quite frightening, and the third had been so old and creaky she'd looked as if she might keel over at any minute.

Perhaps even decent servants were snobs? He had no title. He was not even a gentleman. And everyone in London knew that. Ross made no secret of his past because he was not ashamed of it. He might well have grown up in the gutter, but he had clawed his way out with determination. He had even taught himself to read and write. Now he had an impressive fortune and the reputation of being the canniest businessman in the city—a position that gave him both status and power, which in turn provided the kind of safety and security he had always craved.

He was a person to be reckoned with rather

than someone who lived at the mercy of others. It was gratifying to know that his services were in demand from the great and the good—it gave him a sense of satisfied achievement.

Apparently all that made no difference when one was hiring staff. This one was the last application he had received—there were no more candidates left—and even if she *did* look much too young to him, he was prepared to overlook a great many faults so long as she was even partially suitable.

If he did not have a housekeeper then he could not realistically begin renovating his new house. He certainly did not have time to hire all the tradesmen and servants himself, and somebody had to be around to supervise them. Especially now that the new ships were taking up so much of his time.

He could hardly go and find a butler. Reggie had got it into his head that *he* was going to be the butler, and Ross could not bring himself to shatter the oaf's dreams like that.

'I am so sorry for the way we were introduced, Mrs…er…' *Blast*, he had forgotten the woman's name.

'Mrs Preston,' the woman said tightly, and she peered at him coldly over the rims of her unflattering glasses.

'Yes, of course.' Ross gave her his most dazzling smile, but when it became clear that the woman had absolutely no intention of reciprocating it slid off his face despondently.

Already he was predisposed to dislike this woman. She was regarding him with complete distaste and ill-concealed disapproval. He hated it when people did that, and unfortunately it was an occurrence that happened far too often—especially since the newspapers had begun to immortalise his supposed exploits in print. However, somewhere in the back of his mind he quite liked the ruthless blackguard's reputation he had had foisted upon him. It portrayed the image that he was a force to be reckoned with—and surely that could not hurt in the long run?

The woman was still staring at him distastefully, as if he were the lowest of the low. This really was *not* a good start to the interview—although he did realise that the sight of Francesca sprawled on his bed might have shocked Mrs Preston, so he decided to give her the benefit of the doubt.

'I think we might have got off on the wrong foot,' he explained benevolently. 'What you just saw was not quite as it might have appeared.'

He grinned boyishly. That usually won over even the most hardened matron—but not this one. She stared at him levelly—a feat that was made all the more uncomfortable because her bright blue eyes were magnified in the thick lenses of her spectacles to such an extent that he was reminded of a frog.

'Really? How else should I construe what I just witnessed?' She was watching him so steadily that it made him feel like an errant child.

'Francesca arrived out of the blue,' he clarified, although why he felt the urge to do so was beyond him. 'Nothing untoward happened.'

'Perhaps not this morning,' she stated coldly. 'But I think it was plainly obvious that you and the lady have a…a special relationship. Am I correct?'

Ross felt his hackles rise at her sanctimonious tone. He certainly did not need to explain himself to this woman. Or to anybody, for that matter. He would be paying her wages. He certainly did not care whether or not she found *him* suitable.

'Mrs Preston, I am a single man and these are bachelor quarters. I am sorry that Reggie inadvertently exposed you to my bedchamber—but what happens in that room is none of your concern.'

He steeled himself for the woman to storm out, but she stayed resolutely where she was, chewing her bottom lip nervously.

The awkward silence was broken by Reggie, bumbling in with a laden tea tray. He smiled proudly at Ross and deposited the tray heavily on the side table. Hot tea sloshed out of the teapot and bathed the haphazard cups in brown liquid. Undeterred, Reggie poured tea into one of them and thrust it, without a saucer, at Mrs Preston.

'Here you are, mum, a nice cup of tea.' A large, hot drip fell onto her skirts, and she shrieked in pain and immediately stood.

'Oh! Let me help, mum!' Reggie began to use the hem of his own shirt to mop up the mess, rubbing it ineffectually over the woman's wet clothing, unaware that in doing so he was also— shockingly—rubbing her thighs.

To begin with she appeared mortified by this indiscretion, but then the most peculiar thing happened. Her features softened in sympathy and she allowed Reggie to try to help—even though he really wasn't. It was only then that Ross witnessed the look of stark panic in the big oaf's eyes—the look he had when he realised he had done something wrong but had no idea how to fix it.

'It is perfectly all right now. I was merely a bit shocked.' One of her hands came up and touched Reggie's enormous shoulder gently. Then she squeezed it for good measure, in a comforting manner that belied her previous cold expression.

Like an obedient sheepdog, Reggie stepped back and stood awkwardly. Then once again the harsh woman surprised Ross.

'I like one sugar in my tea.' This was accompanied with a genuine and kind smile that instantly made poor Reggie feel better about being such a clumsy fool. As if in an afterthought she glanced back at Ross, and her features froze again.

'Here we are, then,' said Reggie, proffering the second cup of tea to Mrs Preston as if it were the Crown Jewels and she was the Queen.

Mrs Preston glanced at Reggie's eager expression and her tense pout relaxed. Her lips curved in a lovely smile and she thanked him politely. 'This looks perfect. You clearly have a talent for making tea exactly the way a person likes it.'

Reggie beamed with pride and gave an embarrassed little chuckle—already won over by this strange conundrum of a woman.

The fact that she had shown such kindness to the big oaf made Ross soften towards her immediately. She was not all bad if she could do that—most people wouldn't. Reggie usually terrified them. Perhaps she was simply nervous. Or shy?

'You have excellent references, Mrs Preston,'

he said eventually, while taking the cup that Reggie proffered. 'Can you tell me what type of household you last worked in?'

Hannah tried to relax and formulate a sensible answer that sounded a tad more friendly. 'Nair House was not a grand residence, Mr Jameson, but I oversaw a staff of ten,' she lied.

It would not do to claim that she had vast experience of running a stately pile like Barchester Hall—such a falsity would be easily exposed—but she did want to give the impression that she was capable.

'I oversaw everything from menu planning and budgeting to dealing with disputes amongst the servants.'

Hannah schooled her features into a neutral mask to cover her disgust at being with him. She had heard that Jameson was a shocking libertine, but she had not expected to be confronted with such overwhelming evidence of his debauchery straight away. The sight of the rumpled bedclothes and that overpainted woman wantonly sprawled across them, skirts raised suggestively to her knees, had been bad enough—but then her eyes had encountered their first sight of Ross Jameson, and that had been frankly outrageous.

He was a huge bear of a man—showing far more exposed skin than a gentleman would deem proper. Of course a gentleman would not have the body of a farm labourer either. Jameson was solid and muscled—a sure sign of his coarse upbringing. Men of class were more willowy and less...*sturdy.* He probably looked ridiculous stuffed into a tailored coat. She supposed that less discerning women would describe his rumpled black hair and twinkling green eyes as handsome, but he used those good looks to his advantage. He appeared to Hannah exactly what he was—a charming, dangerous and duplicitous rogue. She certainly would not trust him as far as she could throw him—which, she conceded, was not likely to be very far.

It was also obvious that his minion—Reggie?—was severely lacking in intelligence... although she supposed that he had not been employed for his ability to think strategically. He had a wide, square jaw and a nose that had been so badly broken he looked as if it had simply melted into his face. But she had already realised that behind that frightening façade he was a bit slow and was desperately seeking approval. Poor fellow. It was obvious he just needed looking after. However, she was certain his main duties were to protect his nefarious master and to threaten or maim anybody who did not fall into line. How the authorities allowed Jameson to live freely within society was indeed a mystery.

'Would you tell me a little about your house?' Hannah asked, aware that she had not made the best first impression and keen to make amends. Everything hinged upon her getting this job.

'Barchester Hall is situated around twelve miles from London,' he replied with a smile. 'I am afraid that at the moment it is a bit of a wreck. Externally, the house is solid, and the grounds are lovely, but it has been shockingly mismanaged by the previous owner for many years and that shows.'

His glib condemnation of her brother and the home she loved so much rankled, but she managed to hide her anger. She could not properly gauge his expression through Aunt Beatrice's reading glasses, and the thick lenses were beginning to give her an awful headache.

'Obviously I need to make some urgent renovations. The whole interior needs remodelling, furniture and things will need to be bought to replace what is there currently, and I will need to recruit enough decent staff to run the place. Do you have experience of recruiting servants, Mrs Preston?'

Hannah nodded. This was one thing that she could talk about without lying. When she had lived at Barchester Hall they had had great difficulty retaining staff. This had been largely due to the fact that her brother had had a tendency not to pay their wages on time, if at all, and she'd constantly had to replace the never-ending line of servants who had refused to stay.

'Yes, indeed. I have had to recruit many suitable servants and I am well aware of the sorts of things that entice the best servants to work at a house.' Wages were their main priority. That she knew for a fact.

'You look a little young to be a housekeeper.'

'I am thirty-five, sir.' Hannah smiled tightly and hoped that she looked drab enough to be that age. The brown day dress was the most awful thing she possessed, and the lace cap, which she had bought as an afterthought yesterday, covered her wheat-coloured curls. 'I can assure you that I am eminently suitable for the position.'

'Hmm…' He had picked up one of her references and was reading it.

Hannah could feel her one chance slipping away. She opened her mouth to speak but Jameson spoke again before she could say anything.

'I think that I have heard—and seen—everything I need to. Reggie is already smitten with you. That is good enough for me.' He turned to Hannah with a friendly smile. 'Congratulations,

Mrs Preston—the position is yours. I will expect you at Barchester Hall next weekend. Please leave me the details of your lodgings so that I can send you the necessary formalities.'

He stood up and shook her hand vigorously and then walked her towards the door at a brisk pace.

Bemused, Hannah could do little but smile at her unexpected good fortune—although she was unsure exactly how it had come about. 'Thank you, sir,' she managed to mutter before she found herself standing alone again on the street as the door closed firmly behind her.

Not quite believing her luck, and just in case he retracted his offer, she decided not to tempt fate. She scribbled the inn's address on a piece of paper and popped it through the letter box before hurrying to the nearest waiting hackney. Finally, after seven long years, she was going home.

Chapter Two

Hannah arrived at Barchester Hall late on Sunday and was immediately engulfed in Cook's warm embrace.

'My goodness, my lady, you look well. You have barely changed in all these years.'

Hannah hoped that she had. It would be disastrous if one of the locals recognised her. She was overwhelmed with emotion. Happiness at finally seeing the house she had always loved warred with the humiliation and sadness that had led to her departure from it all those years ago.

'Oh, Cook—I have missed you.' Hannah happily sank into a chair around the large oak table and accepted the reviving tea that was thrust into her hand.

'The place has not been the same without you, my lady. Your brother never should have sent you away. We could have weathered the storm and restored your reputation. I just know we could have. When I think of how abominably you were treated—why, it makes my blood boil.' Cook dashed her sleeve across her eyes to wipe away more tears. 'If you had been here perhaps we would not be in this mess.'

Never a truer word had been spoken. There was no way Hannah would have allowed this shocking decline if she had been here. She would have been able to guide George and help him to make better decisions. She would have taken control of the accounts and managed the funds better—if George had relinquished them, of course, which was highly improbable in reality. George had never, *ever* listened to a single word she had said. He had probably forgotten she even existed the very same day he had put her on that coach headed to York.

'Never mind. I am here again now,' she responded happily, keen to change the subject away from her banishment. 'And I have no intention of ever leaving again. But if my deception is going to work you really must stop calling me "my lady". From now on I am Mrs Preston.'

The two women caught up on years of gossip over the course of several cups of tea. By the time Hannah finally hauled herself into her new bed she was feeling decidedly uneasy. She had not realised how dire things at Barchester Hall had become. There was a rag-tag group of four young maids and two very fresh-faced footmen. None of the old staff remained, apart from Cook. That was fortunate. The fewer people who knew her true identity the better—however, the village was still filled with familiar faces so she would have to avoid it at all costs. That would be a challenge, but not impossible.

It had grown too late for her to take a proper tour of the house, but Cook had painted a very grim picture as they had wandered around the ground floor. The gardens were decidedly unkempt and the pastures were long empty. All the tenants were now gone—largely because her brother had neglected the upkeep of their cottages and had then doubled their rents as a way to get more money.

George had also sold most of their valuable antiques, one by one, in a desperate attempt to keep the wolves from the door. However, any money he had raised had not been invested in the house but used to pay off his ever-rising gambling debts. Hannah had Jameson to thank for that. Now all that was left was a hotchpotch of old and dilapidated furniture that was barely fit for purpose and the shell of a once great house in bad need of some care.

The situation was dire. The way George had neglected the house was criminal and, had he still been alive, Hannah would have given him a piece of her mind—not that he would have listened.

Nobody apart from Cook and those few scattered maids and footmen had lived in the house since George's death, so the decline had continued unabated. A sad fact that was hardly their fault. None of them had known what was going to happen. Everybody had assumed that the house would be sold by its new owner, and the servants had received no clear direction. Then, out of the blue, Jameson had turned up a month ago and declared that he intended to live in it after all. Since then, as Cook had acknowledged, there had been *some* improvement.

He had already procured labourers to fix the leaking roof, and hired a head gardener and a gamekeeper who were both due to start work within the week to fix the grounds. The fact that he had also employed her as his housekeeper suggested that he meant business.

Her biggest concern was how she would react around him without giving herself away. How, exactly, did one conceal so much hatred and disgust? When she had first met him she had wanted to slap his face. She still did. Her brother

had always admonished her for her sharp words
and forthright opinions. Now she was to all intents and purposes a servant, so she would have
to watch her wayward tongue with Jameson or
risk the sack.

With any luck they would have little to do
with one another. Masters tended to stay well
away from the help unless absolutely necessary.
Surely she could manage under those circumstances? Especially as she was certain that it
would not take long to find conclusive evidence
of his crimes and take her rightful place as mistress of the house.

Ross tried to get some much-needed blood
into his long legs by stretching them. This was
no easy feat in the confines of the carriage, with
Reggie taking up most of the space.

'How much longer?' the big man asked, without taking his eyes off the scenery rushing by.
Poor Reggie was sometimes like a child, with
the attention span of a puppy. He had asked the
same question at least twenty times already and
the journey from London was less than an hour.

'We should be there in a few minutes, Reggie,' he said, smiling. 'When was the last time
you visited the countryside?'

The big man screwed up his face as he gave

the question some thought. 'I can't say I remember—but I'm sure that I *have* been.'

That sentence, in a nutshell, summed Reggie up. His memory was shot—thanks to far too many years in the boxing ring—so sometimes he recalled things and sometimes he didn't.

'Will there be food when we get there? I'm starving, Ross.'

Reggie's entire life revolved around food, and he could get quite unreasonable when there wasn't any, so Ross nodded. This appeared to placate the big man, who continued to watch the road as if his life depended on it. One of Ross's first jobs upon arrival, he knew, would be to make sure that Reggie knew exactly where everything was and how far he could wander.

Aside from the fact that the sight of him would probably scare the locals, Reggie panicked when he was lost or confused, and when he panicked he could be difficult to handle. Ross would also have to make sure that the rest of his motley crew of staff were made aware of Reggie's particular needs and peculiarities. He didn't particularly want any of *them* to be frightened either.

Just thinking about the prospect of having staff made him smile. Apart from Reggie, he had never had a servant before—and Reggie hardly counted as one of those. Ross gave him things to do because it made him happy to do them. In reality, he was far too clumsy to do more than fetch and carry effectively, and Ross was used to doing things for himself anyway.

But now he had a gamekeeper, a gardener, a rotund and jolly cook and a sour-faced housekeeper. In truth, he was not entirely convinced that the housekeeper would turn up. She had certainly not appeared to be particularly enamoured of him. He had only given the frog-eyed woman the job because she had shown a modicum of kindness to Reggie. He had a sneaking suspicion that even if she did turn up he and she would part company quite quickly.

'I can see a house!' exclaimed Reggie.

'That has to be Barchester Hall, then—we should arrive any minute now.'

Ross could not quite contain his own excitement. He was going to live in a proper house for the first time in his life, and as soon as it was in a fit state he would bring his mother and sister to live there with him. He had not told them about it yet. He was looking forward to seeing the looks on their faces when they entered such a grand house.

He owed them the security and safety of a proper home, where he would be able to keep a watchful eye on them. They had not lived together as a family in years. Ross had always taken care of them, but his business had demanded his full attention and he had neglected to find them all a home until he had accidentally found himself in possession of one. Even then he had not considered actually living in it, and still would not have unless his sister had declared an interest in leaving the quaint and quiet village he had moved them to in order to spend the season in London. And his mother was happy for that to happen. He still could not believe that.

After everything that had happened—all the years when they had both done their best to keep Sarah safe—his mother was now willingly going to let her loose in London again. The place was still filled with crooks, thieves and wealthy perverts who preyed on the vulnerable. His sister was a young woman, and despite her belief that she was all grown up she would need his protection now more than ever if she was to get through the season unscathed.

She was such a pretty thing. She always had been. He would never forgive himself if she was placed in danger again. The very thought made him feel sick to his stomach.

Therefore Barchester Hall was the perfect compromise. It was close enough to London for them to visit the place freely, but far enough away to keep his family out of harm's way. If everything went as Ross hoped it would he would finally be able to wave goodbye to the necessity of being in the city for every waking hour, and to the guilt he felt at not being around for his family to oversee their safety personally. Now there would be no more excuses. He could keep a very close eye on his sister or—more importantly—on anybody who came near her.

Hannah saw the shiny black carriage approach and assembled the small staff on the poorly maintained gravel drive, ready to meet their new master. As it came closer into view she saw his huge bodyguard, Reggie. He was smiling, with his face pressed up against the window. Two of the maids sniggered at the sight and she shot them a pointed look before the carriage came to a stop. Regardless of the peculiarity of the situation, they had no right to be so rude. Both girls coloured under her stern glare and looked down at their feet, and Hannah made a mental note to speak to them both later. Discipline had clearly been in short supply for far too long.

Reggie had the carriage door open before the tiger could get to it, and bounded out onto the drive and stared up at the house in awe.

'Blimey, it's big!' he exclaimed over his shoulder, just as Jameson poked his head out of the carriage and regarded the assembled group with amusement.

Hannah ignored the rising bile in her throat as she dipped into a reluctant curtsy and then stepped forward to greet him. 'Mr Jameson— welcome to Barchester Hall.' She could not quite bring herself to say *welcome home*. It was not his home, and if she had her way it never would be.

He looked her up and down and grinned. 'You came, then? I was not sure that you would. Especially after...' He left the rest of the sentence hanging awkwardly.

Hannah nodded in tight acknowledgement and then introduced him to the staff she had only met herself yesterday. He greeted all six of them with surprising good cheer and did a very good job of charming them all—including Cook. But Hannah had expected no less. Swindlers had to be charming. Manipulation was their stock in trade.

When she had dismissed the servants he sidled up next to her before she could escape into the house. 'Might I have a word, Mrs Preston?'

Hannah turned towards him and he gently took her arm and steered her away from the carriage. His big, overly familiar hand was warm, and it made her extremely conscious of their close proximity.

'I should probably tell you about Reggie now,' he confided in a hushed tone, a little too close to her face, 'because he is going to take a bit of getting used to.'

When they were well out of earshot he stopped walking and faced her.

'He's a good-natured sort, and keen to help, but he does not have the sense that you or I take for granted. Until he gets his bearings I would appreciate it if you could keep an eye out for him. Make sure he doesn't stray too far from the house and give him plenty of little jobs to do. Nothing that involves common sense, of course, because he certainly does not possess any—but he loves to help. Even if he is not being particularly useful I like to make him think he is. Could you also alert the rest of the staff to my wishes? Sometimes people can be cruel to people like Reggie. Let them know that I will not tolerate that in this house.'

'Of course, sir.' Hannah had certainly not been expecting this to be the first order that she took from her new employer. Despite his black heart he obviously had a soft spot for his poor servant. It was a great shame that he did not have the same concern for all the people whose lives he had ruined—of which she was sure there were many.

'I am going to take Reggie for a tour of the

house first—after I have fed him, of course,' he said with a smile. 'Perhaps we can have a chat this afternoon about my plans? I believe that we have a great deal to do, Mrs Preston.'

His po-faced housekeeper smiled tightly and then scurried off. She really was a most humourless woman, he thought as he watched her disappear back into the house. All the other servants appeared to be quite friendly, but Mrs Preston reminded him of an icicle—cold, hard and sharp. He hoped that the woman was at least good at her job; it might well be her only redeeming quality.

Well, that was not strictly true, he realised. Ross had always had a talent for spotting potential in things—especially things that were attractive in a woman. Behind the ugly glasses was quite a pretty face. With a little effort he suspected that she might scrub up quite well. There might even be a reasonable figure under that shapeless sludge-coloured dress as well. It was difficult to tell.

Her letter of application had stated that she was a widow, although she did seem a little young to be one. But he knew only too well that life could be hard, and that some people dealt with its harshness by becoming bitter. Perhaps her attitude would soften towards him in time. And, then again, perhaps not. He had not exactly made the best first impression on her. She probably saw him as a lecher—or worse. The shock on her face at the sight of Francesca reclining on his bed had been quite impressive. But in his experience people thought exactly what they wanted to—regardless.

'Come on, Reggie,' he called cheerfully. 'Let me show you around.'

Chapter Three

Several hours later Ross left Reggie washing pots happily with Cook and went off in search of his prim housekeeper. He found her hovering not far from the kitchen, notebook already in hand, and he ushered her into the large study and sat opposite her at the enormous desk he had brought with him from London.

'I think I should be brutally frank, Mrs Preston, and let you know now that I have absolutely no idea how to manage a house or staff. I am not completely sure, if I am honest, exactly what a housekeeper does. In that regard, I was hoping that you could let me know what exactly I need to attend to first.'

Ross watched her blink at his admission, but her face did not soften. Instead she pinned him with her scary frog stare, then tilted her head to one side.

The motion dislodged a curling tendril of golden hair from her lace cap, which she stuffed back in ruthlessly. The fact that it was such a lovely shade of blonde surprised him. He had not even considered that she might have hair. Not that he had thought her hairless, of course, but he had assumed that it would be nondescript and colourless—much as his housekeeper appeared to be. But now that he knew that she had such luscious-coloured locks he could not help wondering why she covered it all up in that dreadful mob cap.

Out of habit he smiled flirtatiously at her. Usually that garnered a faint blush at the very least. Mrs Prim-and-Proper Preston, though, was clearly made of granite, and she pursed her lips slightly in disgust at the overture. Then she launched into another lecture.

'The role of a housekeeper is to ensure the good running of all things domestic. I will need a budget to buy the necessary day-to-day supplies, such as candles, then there are costs such as staff wages, linens, brandy and wine, et cetera. Obviously all expenditure will be logged properly by myself, in the household accounts ledger. Occasionally, as you are not married, I will have to consult with you about menus and such things—usually a housekeeper would go to the mistress of the house for that. Unless there is a mistress I need to be apprised of?'

He could tell by the insolent raising of her eyebrow that that comment was meant to allude to Francesca or a similar type of woman. He did not care for her opinions on his morality.

'No mistress at the moment,' he replied with a wolfish smile. 'Married or otherwise. But I am always open to the possibility.'

He watched her lips thin and stifled a smile. He was actually enjoying irritating her. Something about disapproving people always brought out the worst in him, and as a self-defence mechanism he preferred to find humour in that disapproval rather than allow it to bother him. Mrs Preston was as prickly as a cactus. So far he knew that she disapproved of fornication and flirting, so he had plenty of ammunition already to use to rile her and he had only known her for a few hours.

'I think we should start by deciding upon the new household budget, sir,' she said, interrupting his thoughts. 'What figure did you have in mind?'

Ross did not have a clue. 'My solicitor advised me on costs when the property deed was stamped, but as I have never owned or lived in a grand house with a full staff before I shall have to defer to your expertise.'

The housekeeper blinked, and allowed herself the merest huff of exasperation before answering. 'That depends on how much you are willing to spend, sir. At the moment the budget really only pays the servants' wages and provides the basics. Some houses are run on a tight budget, and some of the grandest houses require vast sums of money—especially if the owner does a great deal of entertaining.'

'Mrs Preston, I work with numbers. Would you be so kind as to clarify, in pound notes, exactly what you mean by "tight" and "vast"?'

Her sandy eyebrows drew together as she considered this, and she chewed her bottom lip for several seconds. 'Realistically, with new servant costs included, the minimum yearly budget would have to be around five hundred pounds, sir. But that would mean that I'd have to be particularly thrifty. I suppose we could reduce that if we closed up part of the house in winter and reduced fuel costs. We could also purchase the cheaper cuts of meat.'

Ross screwed his face up in disgust. 'We do not need to be "thrifty", Mrs Preston. Give me a figure that will not leave me cold and chewing on gristle.'

She smiled ever so slightly at that, but quickly covered it. Underneath all that frost she might possess a sense of humour at least. Of course it might have been wind. The expression had been so fleeting he could not be sure.

'A sensible budget of around eight hundred pounds a year is probably more than enough—assuming that you do not want an army of servants, sir?'

'Heavens, no! There is only me—and in a few months my mother and sister will be coming to live here. I have no need of an army.'

Hannah could not hide her surprise. 'You have a mother and a sister?' She had not discovered that titbit in all her research.

He regarded her with amusement. 'Of course I have a mother. Did you assume that I had been created by some other miraculous method?'

'Not at all, sir,' she said hastily, 'but I had not considered the possibility that you had a family.'

A look of pleased affection crossed his features. 'I do—although they drive me to distraction and nag me incessantly. At the moment they both live in a lovely quiet village in Kent, but my sister is twenty and she is begging me to bring her to town for the season. Why? I have no idea. But for the sake of peace I will do it. I thought I would surprise them with this house when it is finished. I think my mother might actually be lost for words for the first time in her life.'

His admission made her curious. 'Why do they live in Kent?'

The moment the question popped out she regretted it. Servants were not meant to ask personal questions.

However, he did not appear to mind and answered happily. 'My business requires me to be in London, mostly at the docks, but that is not a particularly...*safe* place to live. This house is a good compromise. It is only an hour away from town, but far enough away not to be too close to all the dirt and danger.'

Danger? That was an interesting word for him to use, and it said a great deal about him, in Hannah's humble opinion. He must regularly mix with some shady characters indeed if he feared for the safety of his family in the city. Hannah had certainly never felt unsafe there. From what she remembered, Mayfair had been a charming place.

'One of your main duties will be to get this house shipshape, Mrs Preston. Many of the bedrooms are in a shocking state, and the whole place looks as if it needs a touch of paint. I take it that you have had a good look around the house? Tell me, what things do you think need doing first?'

His question startled Hannah, so she answered honestly, forgetting to be demure as a good servant should be. 'The main family rooms need to be sorted out first and foremost. The morning room and the dining room are looking very shabby.'

She had been shocked at just how shabby they had become in her absence. George had certainly run the house into the ground after he had banished her to Yorkshire.

'I agree,' he said, smiling. 'And I hate this room as well.' He waved his hand dismissively at the oppressive panelled walls.

Hannah had always loathed how dark the stained wood made this room. Even so, his criticism of it irritated.

'I think the panelling adds a certain gravitas to the study,' she countered, and watched his dark eyebrows draw together as he considered her words.

'But it is so *dingy* in here,' he finally ventured. 'It is far too depressing to work in.'

'What sort of work is it that you do?' she asked politely, wondering how he would answer. He would hardly admit to swindling people, robbing them blind and driving them to suicide.

'I make money,' he said matter-of-factly. 'I know that is considered a bad thing to confess in this day and age, but it is the truth. I make investments. I speculate—buy and sell. Whatever looks as if it has the potential for a solid profit I will dabble in. I was not born into money, Mrs Preston, so I appreciate its value and its power. And as I spend a great deal of my time poring over ledgers and papers I need a pleasant and *light* place to work in. This room, quite frankly, is *not* pleasant. Those ugly paintings need to come down for a start.'

He pointed to the ostentatious family portraits that her father had had painted and scowled.

'I presume that they are all long-dead members of the Runcorn dynasty?' They were—her brother, her father, grandfather and great-grandfather stared down at them haughtily from the walls. None of them had been particularly handsome men, she acknowledged. And it was difficult to remember any of them with any great affection.

'They look like a bunch of pompous arses,' he said disdainfully.

He took her expression of shock as outrage at his use of bad language, but he was unapologetic.

'Come on, Mrs Prim and Proper—surely you have heard the word *arse* before?'

Something about the way she bristled amused Ross. She was so easy to rile he decided there and then to do it often. If nothing else, it would make the days go quicker. He would start this very moment, by peppering his speech with a bit more colourful language and seeing how long it took her to bite back.

'Make a note to get all this blasted panelling painted a nice cheerful colour, and get those pompous arses shifted to the attic as soon as possible,' he said dismissively, and watched her scratch his instructions down in obvious irritation.

When she had finished she peered at him over the rims of her spectacles. 'What colours do you consider "cheerful", sir? Do you want something light and subtle? Like a pale primrose-yellow? Or would you feel more at home with something bolder—like bordello-red?'

Her blue eyes glared at him defiantly. The woman had spirit. Ross quite admired her cheek, but pretended to ponder. 'Hmm…perhaps we should save the red for my bedchamber, where it can be properly appreciated? I quite like the idea of pale yellow—but not for in here.'

She could picture the perfect place. 'The morning room would look lovely in pale yellow. It faces the gardens and catches the early-morning sun—' Stopping herself abruptly, Hannah stared at her notes. She was being much too presumptuous for a servant.

'Would *you* paint it pale yellow?' he asked, with an obvious interest that she found strangely flattering. The man was actually asking for her opinion on something.

'I would paint all the dark wood white and mix solid walls of primrose-yellow with some printed wallpapers. Flowers or vines or some such pattern—something that brings the garden into the room.'

Her favourite room would look stunning in such a sunny shade.

For several seconds he just stared at her, and then his face split into a devastating grin that made her pulse flutter in a most disconcerting way. 'I do believe that you have an eye for decorating, Mrs Prim. That is *exactly* how the morning room should look. But I want no spindly little chairs. I was not built for puny furniture—I want something more robust. Manly. And comfortable.'

'There is a lovely big sofa in the drawing room. If we had it reupholstered and found a pair of big wing chairs to go with it I think that might do quite well,' she answered wistfully as she imagined it, caught up in the vision.

She had always dreamed of changing the interior of the hall but had never, ever been consulted. She caught him watching her. Far from appearing annoyed at her presumptuousness, he looked impressed.

'Another good idea. Jot it down. I think I will put you in charge of picking out all the colours henceforth.'

This was a great responsibility he was delegating to her and one that she would relish. Hannah forgot herself, and grinned at his unexpected generosity. 'Shall I make a note of the bordello-red for your bedchamber too?' she asked cheekily, forgetting herself, and then blushed as his eyes twinkled flirtatiously.

What on earth was she thinking? He really was dangerously charming—and manipulative. Already he had briefly made her forget how much she disliked him.

'I am keen to get this house shipshape by the end of the summer.'

'But it is already May! Surely you cannot seriously expect it all to be done in such a short time?'

'I have quite set my mind to it—and when I set my mind to something, Mrs Prim, I usually get it. And I can be *very* persuasive.'

He winked at her saucily. In her entire life nobody had ever winked at her, and she felt her lips purse in consternation. If she had not been pretending to be a servant she would have given him a proper set-down. As it was, she had to settle for stony, disapproving silence.

'You can go through all the catalogues and then show me a selection of the most suitable wallpapers. I shall have to trust you to make a great deal of decisions in my absence, Mrs Prim. In the meantime, I will sort out your household accounts.'

She could tell by the way his eyes drifted to a pile of papers stacked haphazardly on the desk that his attention was already elsewhere, so she inclined her head and went to walk away.

'By the way, sir,' she said as an afterthought, 'my name is Mrs Preston—not Mrs Prim.'

A slow smile crept over his face. 'I am well aware of that, madam.'

Chapter Four

Ross was awoken by the spring sunshine streaming through his bedchamber window and decided that he needed to add thicker curtains to his growing list of things to buy. At the best of times he was not a morning person, but the sun in the countryside was definitely more invasive than it was in the city. It had a piercing quality that could not be ignored, no matter how hard he tried to.

To make matters worse, he could hear too many noises outside in the hallway again. In the fortnight during which he had intermittently lived at Barchester Hall, the sounds of Mrs Prim and her battalion of maids had woken him on a number of occasions, with their rattling buckets and clattering brooms.

Irritated, he threw the bedcovers back, dragged himself out of bed and trudged heavily towards the door. Clearly, if he was ever going to get

some rest, it was time he made them understand
that he really did not like being awake this early.

'What is all this blasted noise?' he barked as
he threw open the door.

Two young maids and his prickly housekeeper
dropped the linens they were carrying and stared
at him open-mouthed. Only then did he remember that he was only wearing his drawers. Now
that he no longer lived in bachelor lodgings he
should probably purchase a dressing gown, he
realised as the two maids giggled shyly behind
their hands at the sight of his bare chest. Out of
habit, he grinned wolfishly at them, well aware
that he looked pretty good in his birthday suit.
The maids happily grinned back.

'Mr Jameson!'

He could not help but notice that Mrs Prim-
and-Proper was *not* giggling at the spectacle. She
turned towards the two maids angrily, her face
glowing beetroot-red, and pointed at the pile of
sheets on the floor.

'Take those downstairs at once.'

They nodded in unison and scurried away,
leaving Ross alone with the woman on the landing. To rile her, he braced his arms on the doorframe above his head and smiled innocently
while she did her level best not to meet his eyes.
Those same eyes kept flicking to his bare chest,

though, he noticed, and he was prepared to bet money that she liked what she saw.

'Good morning, Mrs Prim. How are you today?' he asked cheerfully, still braced against the door to show his biceps off to their best effect.

'Mr Jameson.'

She was all pink, outraged and flustered, and the spectacle made him smile.

'It is not *proper* for you to wander around so freely in your underclothes.'

'Is it not?' Ross responded as he idly scratched his stomach and watched her eyes lock on to that spot. 'I do apologise. But seeing as I was rudely awoken by all the noise you were making I do think that I should be excused. I am never fully *compos mentis* at the crack of dawn.'

Immediately, her gaze shot back to his face and she stared at him accusingly over the rim of her glasses. She did that a lot, he realised— and always *over* the rims of her thick lenses, never through them. If she did not need the awful spectacles for distance he had no idea why she would wear them. They were an abomination on her face.

'Mr Jameson, this house is, as you have rightly pointed out, in a shabby and neglected state. We are presently doing our best to clean out the bed-chambers, ready for the tradesmen to begin their renovations. That requires the maids to work in them. Already it is past midday—*not* the crack of dawn, as you claim—and we waste several hours every day waiting for you to be awake. Perhaps if you kept more *regular* hours then you would not be so tired in the mornings.'

For emphasis, Hannah folded her arms across her chest and stoically held her ground. She would *not* allow the sight of his naked body to distract her.

Although it *was* quite distracting... He had interesting muscles all over the place. And hair. Fine dark hair dusted his chest, and a thin trail of it bisected his navel and disappeared into his drawers. To make matters worse he had crossed his own arms, mirroring her posture, and this caused the muscles in his upper arms to bulge significantly in a way that made her breath hitch.

'You dare to lecture me on my bedtime, Mrs Prim? Have you been keeping track of the hours I keep? I did not know that you cared.'

He raised his dark eyebrows suggestively and she felt a hot, guilty blush stain her cheeks. She *had* become a little preoccupied with his nocturnal activities.

His voice dropped to a silky whisper. 'Do you disapprove?'

'The hours that you keep and how you choose

to spend them are not my concern, sir,' she finally bit out. 'But the hours that the servants keep are. The maids start at six o'clock. Are you suggesting that I pay them for standing idle for hours on end while you are still abed? That is not going to get this house finished by the end of the summer.'

His green eyes narrowed in assessment and then he cheerfully shrugged in surrender. 'You are right, as always, Mrs Prim. I am still working to town hours. Now that I am intent on rusticating for the summer I should make more of an effort to get up in the morning. Add a cockerel to the list of things I need to buy. I shall endeavour to drag myself from my pit the moment that he crows.'

Hannah nodded curtly, refusing to be amused by his roguish charm. The man was a snake, after all. She needed to remember that. 'As you wish, sir. I shall also add a dressing gown to the list.'

Clearly the woman was a mind-reader. 'Does the sight of my near nude body bother you, Mrs Prim?'

He was laughing at her—she could hear it in his voice despite her resolutely avoiding his eyes. Of *course* the sight of his naked body bothered her. Hannah had never actually seen a man without his clothes on—not that she could admit that

as a supposed widow. Nor could she admit that
the sight of his fascinated her far too much—although she suspected he knew that already.

'On the contrary, Mr Jameson.' Her eyes
locked with his defiantly. 'I find your shameless displaying of it to all and sundry crass. A
gentleman would never behave in such a manner.
He would have more respect for the impressionable young maids in his employ.'

He sighed and pretended to be contrite. 'You
are quite right again, Prim. Thank goodness I
have you here to correct my errant ways. Sometimes I can be a *very* naughty boy.'

Hannah glared back at him, unfazed. 'So I
have read, Mr Jameson. In fact there is another
story about you in the newspapers this morning.
Something about a vicar's daughter, I believe,
although I could not be bothered to read it all. I
suppose we should be thankful that your indiscretions are kept in London and that none of the
maids can read.'

Then she turned and scurried down the hallway before he could use his abundant charm
again. That was the problem, she conceded. He
was charming—and surprisingly affable. So far
none of the servants had a bad word to say about
him. He had already memorised all their names,
knew about their families and backgrounds, and

happily chatted away to them in a manner that made them feel comfortable around him.

And she found his cheeky humour entertaining. More than once she had been tempted to laugh at his irreverence or a witty turn of phrase, especially as his comments so often mirrored exactly what she was thinking. The fact that he was also very pleasant to look at did not help. More than once she had found her traitorous eyes flicking towards him in admiration. At times, the only way she could stop herself was to list silently all the reasons why she disliked him in her head, like a mantra.

Of *course* she had been keeping a close eye on his routines and whereabouts. Most days he disappeared in his carriage, allegedly headed back into London or to Kent to visit his family, and did not return until late. Then he usually worked in the study for several hours, scratching in big ledgers by candlelight or writing lists of things to attend to. His handwriting was an abomination. It was legible, but it lacked the form and discipline that came from a proper education. In actual fact it looked as if he had dipped a nest of spiders into his inkpot and then allowed them to walk unchecked all over the paper.

She had been searching through his private papers while he was away, although so far she had found nothing of any use. Even his post was disappointingly mundane. As soon as it was collected every day she carefully sliced through the wax seals and read his correspondence. It was all either genuine business letters, outlining investments, profits and speculations, or surprisingly jocular missives from people from all levels of society, usually thanking him for investing money on their behalf.

All she really knew about the man, so far, was that he was apparently well-liked and was in possession of an impressive fortune. Once read, she meticulously resealed the letters with a small blob of wax, so that to all intents and purposes they appeared unopened, and left them on a tray in the hallway.

Jameson was also annoyingly even-tempered. He did not shout or snap, even at Reggie—although goodness only knew that man would try the patience of a saint. His lovable henchman was an accident waiting to happen, and was so clumsy that he left a trail of destruction in his wake wherever he went. She had lost count of the number of plates and cups he had broken already. But Jameson simply rolled his eyes like a long-suffering parent and said, 'Never mind'.

In fact, to anybody who did not know better, the rogue appeared on the surface to be a thoroughly decent sort—nice, even, if you ignored his frequent appearances in the gossip columns and constant shameless flirting.

That irritated Hannah more than anything. Every time he flirted with her she found herself feeling a little off-kilter. He had a way of looking deep into her eyes, as if he could see into her very soul. It made her feel nervous, awkward—and very, very special. But when he flirted with the maids in her presence it was worse. She did not *want* people to like him. She wanted them to see the truth about him. As she did. And she certainly did not want to feel that possessive pang of jealousy when he bestowed his ample charm on another woman. That was happening a little too frequently for her liking. Clearly, the memories churned up by this house were more unsettling than she had given them credit for. As if she could be *jealous*!

Hannah was so deep in thought that at the bottom of the staircase she almost collided with Reggie. He had a large wooden chest in his arms, which obviously weighed a considerable amount, although he carried it effortlessly in his meaty arms.

'What's that, Reggie?' she asked as curiosity got the better of her.

'Some of Ross's papers, mum. The carriage has just brought them all from his office at the docks. I'm to put them in the study, where they will be safe.' He smiled his lopsided smile and trudged past her.

With nothing better to do, Hannah followed him. Six large chests were already stacked against one wall.

'Mr Jameson must have a lot of papers,' she said with renewed interest. And she would bet her entire five thousand pounds that those very papers held the key to Jameson's downfall.

'You have no idea, mum!' Reggie exclaimed good-naturedly as he hoisted the chest he carried onto the pile. 'There's deeds and contracts, ledgers and letters...I reckon Ross has enough paper here to light all the fires in this house for a year.'

He smiled proudly at his own joke, then shuffled back out of the study to fetch another box.

Hannah wandered over to the pile of chests and tried to open one. It was locked, but that did not surprise her. He would hardly leave important and potentially damning documents unsecured during transit. But at least they were now here!

She would have to bide her time and wait for an opportunity to go through them properly. Jameson's business interests intrigued her more than anything. He was obviously successful and rich, as far as she could make out, but she doubted that he had come by the bulk of his riches honestly. Especially as it was no secret that he had hauled himself out of the gutter. Guttersnipes did not, as a rule, make the transition from squalor to high society quite so seamlessly.

Aside from the fact that he had told her that he 'invested', she had no clear idea what he did. He always claimed he had urgent business in town, but what sort of business brought him home so late at night? The banks and the Stock Exchange were closed by six, and the journey back to Barchester Hall was only an hour—she really could not think what else he might be doing.

Unless he was out whoring and gambling. She already knew that he indulged in both those vices with regularity.

Also surprising was the fact that he rarely took his henchman into town with him. This led her to conclude that he probably had other cronies in town who fulfilled the role of protector.

Reggie approached, huffing and puffing with another trunk, so she slipped out of the study. Fortunately, thanks to Jameson's peculiar hours, she would have plenty of opportunities to rummage through his precious papers. In the meantime, it would not hurt to practise picking a lock or two with a hairpin in the privacy of her own room, just in case the chests remained sealed. Every good spy needed to be able to pick a lock.

Chapter Five

By the end of May the heat had become uncharacteristically oppressive in London, and the
majority of those who could afford it departed
the city much earlier than usual. This meant that
Ross did not really have much cause to visit there
quite as often. The stock market was so slow that
it was almost stagnant, and he could manage his
other businesses quite effectively from home.
The only thing he needed to go to town for concerned his new ships—but even they were nowhere near ready.

He found this enforced hiatus unnerving. He
had never really experienced the concept of free
time—he had always been too busy building his
little empire and consolidating his power. Becoming important, and respected, took a great
deal of time. However, he was beginning to feel
at a bit of a loose end with so much free time

on his hands and it had only been two days. He feared he might actually die of boredom.

'Are you going to eat that?' Reggie asked, looking covetously at the last sausage on the sideboard. Before Ross could reply he had already speared it on his fork and taken a huge bite.

'Tell me, Reggie, what do you do with your days when I am in town?' Ross was genuinely curious—perhaps he was missing something that he might enjoy.

The big man chewed thoughtfully for a moment before replying. 'Well, let's see. I have me breakfast, then I chop some wood and fetch and carry stuff for Cook. Then I usually help Mrs Prim with whatever she needs doing. Prim says that she would be quite lost without me.'

The fact that Ross's little nickname had taken root in Reggie's brain must really rankle the housekeeper, but he was glad that she put the big oaf to use.

'What things does Mrs Prim ask you to do?'

The big man smiled. 'Yesterday we was stripping all the curtains out of the back bedrooms ready for the painters to go in. Today she wants me to help lug some old furniture up to the attic.'

Reggie looked remarkably pleased to have been asked to do it, and then he said something that shocked Ross.

'I like Mrs Prim. She has a lovely laugh.'

Ross gaped at Reggie in astonishment. 'Are you sure, Reggie? You must be confusing her with one of the maids. Prim doesn't *laugh*.'

'She might not laugh around you,' Reggie said sagely, 'but she laughs around me. And I ain't so dense as not to know the difference between Mrs Prim and one of the maids. When we work together she makes it fun.'

'Fun? *Prim?*' The very concept was laughable.

Reggie actually grinned at that. 'Yesterday she wrapped one of the velvet curtains round her shoulders and stuffed a pillow under her skirt and pretended to be the King George for the whole morning. Made me bow to her every time I said something.'

Ross snorted. That sounded about right. 'I doubt that was a joke, Reggie. She is so bossy I imagine she *expects* you to bow to her. You must have got the wrong end of the stick.'

'She even knighted me,' Reggie boasted. 'I was Sir Reginald Hamfisted of Hackney all afternoon. What's that if it's not a joke?'

He had him there. It certainly sounded like a joke.

'Like I say, Ross—Mrs Prim is lovely when you get to know her.'

Well, this was an astounding and interesting piece of news. Prim-and-Proper possessed a sense of humour and a pair of lips that *did* curl upwards? He would have to test that theory. All he had witnessed so far was outrage tinged with barely disguised hostility.

That was not strictly true, he conceded. She was also kind and thoughtful. The way she looked after Reggie was admirable. The pair of them were constantly to be found in each other's company. Ross rarely collided with her, and he had the distinct feeling that was deliberate. They corresponded through the maids, or little notes that she left atop his desk in the surprisingly flamboyant sloping handwriting that did not suit her repressed and dour character in the slightest. It was far too…*effervescent*—too devil-may-care for such a repressed and formal woman.

Despite her lack of sociability, he could not complain about her work ethic or her common sense. As a housekeeper she was a marvel. In the last fortnight Mrs Prim had made great inroads into transforming Barchester Hall from a wreck to a home. Pretty soon it would be a suitable home for his sister and mother. A nice, snug place where they would be safe for ever.

Parts of the house were beginning to look much better already. The morning room had been stripped, the paint and papers had quickly been selected for the walls, and a great deal of the shabby upholstery and rugs throughout the house had disappeared. He actually looked forward to coming home. Instead of the dank and musty smell of neglect, his house smelled of polish—and increasingly of fresh paint. It was beginning to have a cosy feel that was most comforting, thanks to Prim, and he made a point of taking a keen interest in each new change.

Why didn't she like him?

Ross must have been scowling, because he noticed Reggie grinning at him smugly.

'What's so funny?' he asked as he stood up from the table.

'You are.' Reggie pointed at him with his fork. 'You've got the hump because Mrs Prim don't like you.'

'Hardly,' he replied peevishly, irritated that Reggie was a little bit right. Women were *always* charmed by him. He had the knack. Usually. 'I could not care less either way.'

Why the devil did she not like him? Had he inadvertently done something to upset or offend her since he had moved in to Barchester Hall? And what on earth made her prefer Reggie to him? That was just insulting. Much as he liked the big oaf, he was certainly not as likeable and definitely not as handsome or charming as Ross was himself. Surely the woman was not still holding a grudge about their first meeting?

Ross marched out of the breakfast room and went off in search of his housekeeper, determined to make her re-evaluate her opinion of him. It had become a point of personal pride. People *always* liked him—well, *most* people liked him. He worked hard to ensure that they did. His business depended on it. If his housekeeper did not, then he simply had to change her poor opinion of him. It would give him something to do, if nothing else.

He spied her in her little office near the kitchen and marched towards her. The door was slightly ajar and she had not yet noticed him, but something about the way she sat made him stop and loiter in the passageway.

For a start, her floppy cap was not stuffed on her head and he got his first proper look at her. Her hair was thick, with an obvious natural wave to it, and, although it was secured in an austere knot at the back of her head, there was no disguising the fact that it was quite lovely. It seemed to run the gamut of shades of blonde. The fine tendrils that sat at the base of her swan-like neck were pale golden, the rest was a swirl of honey, wheat and bronze.

Stranger still was the fact that her unattractive

spectacles had been carelessly discarded, despite the fact that she was busily recording numbers in a large ledger. She clearly did not need them for close work either, it seemed. All in all she was a very tidy little package.

Ross leaned against the doorframe with his arms folded. 'Morning Prim,' he said cheerfully, and watched her nearly jump out of her skin and hastily turn towards him.

Without the glasses and the lace cap she was a very pretty woman indeed. Her pink lips formed a startled 'O' as she blinked at him in surprise. Her eyes were not even slightly frog-like. They were large, though, deep blue, and framed in lovely long lashes.

He gave her an assessing half-smile. 'Somebody has been hiding their light under a bushel,' he drawled appreciatively, and then he smiled again as she grabbed her cap and plonked it ruthlessly on her head and scrambled for her glasses.

'I think we both know that you don't need those,' he said, and at the same time he reached out and plucked the wire frames off her small nose. He held the offending glasses up to his eyes and then put them on. 'Good grief, these *are* thick. Did they belong to a blind person?' He tentatively took a few steps around the small office, his flailing arms outstretched for comic effect. 'No wonder you always look over the top of them. Do they give you a headache?'

They did. Hannah had taken to removing them at every opportunity—hence her current predicament. 'Give those back!' she hissed, and she could feel a virulent flush of embarrassment sweep over her face.

'You do not need them to read,' he responded suspiciously, 'and you constantly peer over them—never through them. In actual fact, I suspect that they are not even yours.'

She was glowing beetroot-red now, and clearly flummoxed. Obviously he had sailed dangerously close to the truth. Ross leaned over her and peered through the glasses. 'Why do you wear them? Are they a disguise?' He wiggled his dark eyebrows, as if greatly intrigued by the mystery.

His canny comment left her momentarily speechless. Her mouth opened to issue a denial, and then closed as she realised that she had been caught red-handed. 'Yes—I suppose they are,' she finally whispered, certain that the game was up. But he was still smiling… Then an idea struck. 'I did not think you would employ me if you realised how young I actually am.'

His dark head tilted to one side and his mouth curved slightly in amusement. 'Why would you think that?'

'Most housekeepers are well into their fortieth or fiftieth years. I am not yet thirty.' If she was going to keep her position she had to tell him some of the truth. It was not as if he did not have concrete evidence of the fact staring back at him.

'Is that why you wear the ugly cap as well?' he asked, glancing at the top of her head. 'Because if it is you should probably take that off too.'

Hannah reached up guiltily and pulled the mob cap off and placed it on the table. Then she stood primly facing him, with her hands folded in front of her. He was still wearing her aunt's reading glasses and was peering at her over the top of them with a friendly smile on his face. He should have looked ridiculous—instead he appeared handsome. Her stupid heart gave a little flutter as he regarded her thoughtfully for a few moments.

'You are very good at your job, Prim, so you have nothing to worry about. Already this house is beginning to look significantly better, and I should probably thank you for that. I have been very remiss in not doing so sooner. You have done a splendid job of organising the staff and the tradesmen—so much so that I am more than happy to let you get on with it despite your obvious lack of years.

'I quite admire your tenacity. You saw an opportunity and you seized it. I cannot be angry at that—I have done it a time or two myself, in fact. You have proved yourself to be more than capable of running this house, despite your lack of age. Not to mention your obvious talent for choosing the correct colours and furniture for each of the rooms. It is a relief to be able to delegate that task to you and trust in the outcome. You seem to instinctively know what is best for this place—far better than I do. I am quite clueless, really. I could not ask for a more competent housekeeper, and already I feel that I would be lost without you.'

He could have dismissed her on the spot, she realised. He had caught her out in a blatant lie—and yet he had instantly forgiven her for it, as if he understood and accepted her reasons for lying. Bizarrely, she felt he almost respected her for being enterprising in order to get the job. And he had praised her work. It was such a lovely compliment that Hannah blossomed—she could actually feel her shoulders rise and her mouth curve upwards at the unexpected flattery.

He was an unusual man. He had noticed all the effort she was putting into the house. He valued her opinions. Trusted them. All at once she felt ashamed. She was truly enjoying the opportunity to turn the house she had always loved into the home that she had always dreamed of. A place where she could finally live free of the shackles that had always bound her. A place where *she* was going to be the mistress—free from any master to spoil it for her. And now she was able to make that transformation unhindered. Using *his* money, lies and deception.

As guilt curdled in her chest she steeled herself against it with some pertinent facts. This man used lies and deception all the time. It was about time he had a taste of his own medicine. And wouldn't that just serve him right?

'Thank you, sir,' she said awkwardly, without meeting his eyes. 'It is good to know that my work is appreciated.'

'I also appreciate your kindness towards Reggie. He speaks very highly of you.'

Hannah beamed at that. 'That is no bother. Reggie has been a great help to me and to Cook.'

Despite his clumsiness and outwardly menacing appearance, Reggie was the sweetest and most trusting man. Already she felt great affection for him.

'Is Reggie a relation?' she asked tentatively, in the hope of changing the subject and assuaging the sudden bout of unexpected guilt that kept niggling. She *had* begun to wonder exactly what the man's place in the household was.

'Not really,' he answered as he took off the thick spectacles and tossed them on her desk. 'I sort of inherited him.'

'How does one inherit a *person*?'

'I bought a building and Reggie came with it. That is probably the best way of explaining it.' He crossed his arms and leaned against the wall casually, clearly content with this limited explanation.

'And now Reggie has a seat at your table and one of the best bedrooms in the house? You must think me very gullible, sir.'

A devastating grin split his face and made her all fluttery inside again. She grinned in return, despite her better judgement, her lips curving of their own accord, as if he were a puppeteer and she just a marionette.

'I can assure you that I am telling the truth— Reggie *did* come with a building that I bought and I have been stuck with him ever since.'

'I do not believe you.' Hannah folded her own arms cheekily. 'I will have to ask Reggie for the truth.'

'Ask Reggie—he will tell you the same. I am an open book, Prim. You, on the other hand, are not—and it has not escaped my notice that you have changed the subject on purpose to avoid being asked questions about yourself. Now that we have established that you are *not* a dour-faced middle-aged woman, I am rather intrigued to know what other little lies you have told me. For instance, are you really a widow—or was that part of the disguise as well?'

Hannah chewed her bottom lip nervously, and then plumped for the truth. 'I have never been married, sir.' And never would be. 'I thought I might appear more believable if I said I had misplaced a husband at some point. I am sorry for that too. I just wanted this job so very much.'

He appeared vastly amused. 'Did you misplace him in some tragic and gruesome way?'

A rogue giggle escaped. 'He went quietly in his sleep, sir. I barely noticed his passing.'

When he laughed at her humour she felt a burst of triumph. So many people did not understand her ironic wit.

'I am sorry for your loss. Tell me, does *Miss* Preston have a better wardrobe than Mrs Preston? Or do you both prefer to walk around in shapeless brown wool?'

His dig rankled and her good mood soured instantly. She had a few decent dresses, but not many. Thanks to scheming men like him her brother had been bled dry, which had always left her with very little.

'Whilst the renovations are going on shapeless brown wool is perfectly suitable for a servant, sir.'

Ross sighed as prickly Prim returned with a vengeance. Her cornflower eyes had narrowed and her plump pink lips had thinned again. 'I did not mean to sound insulting, *Miss* Preston, so lower your hackles.'

He watched her face colour and her shoulders stiffen and regretted his words instantly. Their brief accord was clearly over. Stating the obvious was hardly going to get her to think better of him—although why he cared about that he could not quite fathom. Even without the spectacles and mob cap she was still a difficult and humourless woman.

He had managed to make her smile twice, though, so he supposed that was some achievement. She lit up when she smiled. Unfortunately it did not appear that it was an event that would happen particularly often—much like an eclipse or a double rainbow.

'I am sorry that I have lied to you. I can assure that it will not happen again,' she said crisply.

Ross did not believe a word of it. She certainly did not look particularly sorry. In fact she looked positively hostile again. The corners of her mouth had already begun to turn down as she glared at him in her customary disapproval.

'Will that be all, sir?' she asked flatly, and he realised he had been dismissed. In his own house.

More than a little peeved at her attitude, and confused as to why she disliked him so intensely, Ross shook his head in exasperation and headed to his study.

Chapter Six

Hannah had been going through Jameson's chests for over a week now and still had not found anything even slightly incriminating—despite having endless opportunities to search through his papers unhindered. Yesterday he had gone to London and had still not returned.

The candle she was using had almost burned itself out and her eyes had begun to droop. A quick glance at the clock on the mantel told her that it was an hour after midnight and long past time she went to bed.

She gathered all the documents together and carefully replaced them in the trunk exactly as she had found them. She had to give him credit for being thorough. Each one of the eight trunks she had already sifted through contained every bill, deed or ledger he had ever owned. At least she assumed they did. He might well have destroyed any damning evidence, but how he could ever have found it in such a disorganised mess was beyond her. There was no rhyme or reason to his filing system at all. Tailor's receipts were mingled with deeds and share certificates.

However, her search *had* given her a greater insight into the man. He had not lied when he had told her that he made money. Each nocturnal visit to his study had unravelled a little more about his finances and how he had made his fortune. He had a talent for backing profitable ventures and he had stocks in all manner of businesses—from shipping to poultry. It was really quite impressive, and a part of her could not help feeling a little respect at his achievement.

Everything was frustratingly legitimate, and he also made money by investing other people's fortunes for them and charging ten per cent of the profits made. There were several grateful letters from the great and the good, complimenting him on his astuteness on their behalf.

No wonder he had gained passage into the exclusive gentlemen's clubs and ballrooms of the ton. A goodly number of them owed him a favour or two, and probably did not feel they could refuse him—and their letters… Some of them were so affectionate in tone that she did wonder if he had made real friends amongst the powerful men of the ton, despite his humble beginnings.

He certainly had more friends than she did. You could count hers on one finger—Cook. Or perhaps two now that she had Reggie.

Hannah sighed in exasperation. It was becoming increasingly difficult to stick to her purpose. She simply had to expose him as a fraud and a cheat, yet at times he was so...*honourable*. He had even been gracious when he had seen through her disguise. The only real proof she had that he was *not* a hard-working, generous and admirable fellow was the nefarious details about his antics that had been printed in the newspapers and the one scandalous experience she had had of seeing him with his mistress.

On that score she accepted that most gentlemen had mistresses. Her brother and father certainly had. George had been a hedonist, so she expected that his mistresses would have been as abundant in their charms as Jameson's. Her own attributes were nothing compared to that woman's, although why that had started to bother her she could not say.

The thought of him with such an obvious floozy rankled.

He deserved better.

That thought *really* irritated her, and she

groaned in annoyance. What in heaven's name was the matter with her even to think so benevolently about that man? His manipulative charm was truly dangerous.

A noise in the hallway alerted her to the fact that she was no longer alone downstairs and she quickly closed the lid of the chest and hurried from the study. Jameson stood at the foot of the stairs, looking the worse for wear, but he had not yet noticed her.

'Mr Jameson,' she said calmly. 'Welcome back, sir. I trust you had a good trip?'

He stared back at her with slightly bleary eyes and grunted in response. 'Hello, Prim.' Then he rubbed his forehead and briefly closed his eyes.

He had clearly been drinking. And probably gambling and enjoying the company of loose women as well, she realised with disappointment. Images of his shameless buxom mistress sprawled across his tangled bedcovers sprang immediately to mind and she pursed her lips in annoyance.

'I suggest you go to bed, sir. You are obviously completely foxed.'

He was carrying his coat and his waistcoat was undone. His shirt looked decidedly rumpled. He looked at her for several moments before shrugging his broad shoulders. 'How like you to think that, Prim,' he said flatly. 'But I will take your advice. Could you send me up some hot tea? It might help me feel a little better.'

'Certainly sir,' she muttered through clenched teeth. 'Tea is well known as the perfect antidote to a night's debauchery.'

Hannah turned on her heel and headed towards the kitchen herself. It was hardly fair to wake up one of the maids to furnish his unreasonable request. It was hardly their fault that he had chosen to come home in the small hours in such a state.

After setting the kettle to boil, she arranged crockery on a tray and poured fresh milk into a jug—he liked his tea very pale and very sweet. Occasionally she had even seen him sneak a third spoonful of sugar into his drink. The man really did have a ridiculously sweet tooth. As an afterthought she added a plate of biscuits to the tray, in case he was hungry, and waited for the kettle to boil.

Ross started up the stairs wearily. With his head still pounding he carefully made his way towards his bedchamber, massaging his temples. He really should not have spent his entire journey from London reading reports and writing letters, especially after the light had started to fade. Close work like that always gave him dreadful headaches, but he rarely took heed of the warning signs until it was too late.

Of course, typically, *she* had assumed he was drunk and that had got her dander up—although why she felt she had the right to be quite so sanctimonious towards him when he had been so understanding about her ridiculous disguise, he had no idea. In fact he found her attitude two-faced and frankly outrageous. How dared she treat him as if he was the one with loose morals when it was hers that were questionable? He had never done anything untoward to her, and he had always treated her with the utmost respect—sort of. Even though she did not deserve it much of the time. *She* was the liar.

It had not occurred to her to ask him what he had been doing for the last few days. If she had, then she would have realised that he had spent most of it with lawyers, signing the final papers and transferring funds for the new ships he would soon take ownership of. He had barely had time to eat dinner, let alone partake in the sort of 'debauchery' that she had just accused him of.

But she did read those blasted newspapers, so no doubt her opinions of him came from those sordid pages. Did she not realise that almost everything written in those scandal sheets was created specifically for the purpose of selling more newspapers? And nothing sold better than a bit of light titillation.

But, then again, why was he so surprised by it? From the moment he had starting to make serious money certain people—usually dyed-in-the-wool aristocrats—had become offended by his success, and had justified their reaction by embellishing it with colourful stories about his weak character.

To begin with he had tried to deny them, and then he had tried to win them over. He had been charming, generous and helpful—all to no avail. The harder he'd worked at making those people like him, the less disposed they'd been to do so—until he'd realised that the reasons they disliked him had nothing whatsoever to do with his character and everything to do with the circumstances of his birth.

People born into the higher orders felt distinctly uncomfortable around men like him. It threatened their ingrained view of the world. If a man like him—an upstart from the docks—could go around making money, mixing freely with his betters and increasing his influence and power, then society was surely in grave danger. Whatever next? Interbreeding? Revolution? Anarchy?

Ross smiled at the irony despite his headache.

It was a good thing they did not realise that it had been the innate power of the aristocracy that had motivated him to seek his fortune in the first place. Not because he envied it, but because he feared it. The great and the good in society wielded so much power that they could do whatever they wanted to the people below them and get away with it. He knew that from bitter experience. So did his sister.

Ross never, ever wanted to be that powerless underling again.

So now he ignored all the criticism and lies levelled against him. Let them think exactly what they wanted. In his experience people always did anyway, and a bad reputation might actually work in his favour. It was *good* that some people feared him. If they had not he would never have been allowed to join White's.

One newspaper had got wind of his application for membership and written the most ridiculous story about how he intended to ruin anybody who obstructed his membership financially. For weeks he had wandered around town, giving certain people his 'death glare', and it had worked. His membership had been approved without a single black ball, and White's had proved to be an excellent place for him to do business.

Yet here he was again, trying to win Prim

over when he had done nothing wrong. It was a pathetic character flaw that he could not seem to overcome. He apparently still needed people to like him. Why, he had no clear idea.

His mother claimed that he did it to avoid being compared to his father. She had constructed an entire theory around it and convinced herself that Ross had made it an almost evangelical mission not to possess any of the man's character traits. It was a ridiculous notion. Why would he even bother with such ludicrousness? The traits he shared with his unfortunate sire were physical. The dark hair, height and square chin were the only similarities he was prepared to concede. His father had been a selfish, devious and nasty human being who had not given one whit for anybody else—even his own children. The man had lived solely for his own pleasure.

Much as his blasted housekeeper had just accused *him* of doing just now.

Ross was still smarting when he reached his bedchamber. Perhaps he should start behaving like the libertine she clearly believed him to be? She had already found him guilty of the charge. It would serve her right to find out what it would be like if she had been employed by a lecher. If nothing else it would be amusing.

And pleasant. She was such a pretty thing—if

you ignored her belligerent personality—and he had not engaged in anything more than a little mild flirting in weeks. Maybe he should have a little fun at her expense? It might teach the wench a lesson.

As soon as the thought took hold Ross could not stop it. He stalked over to the brandy decanter that stood on a little side table near his bed and poured some of the amber liquid into his hands. Then he patted it liberally around his neck like cologne. If she thought him a drunk then he might as well *be* one.

He quickly pulled off his shirt and mussed his hair with his fingers. She would certainly disapprove of the sight of his bare chest as well. She had before—although she had also had a good look, he remembered with satisfaction. Prim had *liked* the sight of him half naked.

A quick check of his reflection in the mirror made him smile. He looked positively rogue-like and totally disreputable. Even his head was not giving him as much grief now that it was occupied with something else. Poor old Prim was in for a bit of a shock.

Hannah balanced the tea tray on one hand and knocked quietly on his bedroom door. With any luck he had already fallen fast asleep.

'Come in.'

His deep voice sounded a little muffled, and as soon as she gingerly opened the door she could see why. He was face-down on his bed, bare arms flung carelessly above his head on the pillow.

'I have your tea, Mr Jameson.' She deposited the tray on the table smartly and turned to leave.

'Could you pour me a cup, Prim, and bring it here?'

He did not even raise his head from the pillow, so she doubted he would actually even drink it. Hannah rolled her eyes in annoyance and stalked back to the tray. Not caring whether or not it bothered him, she noisily poured him a cup of tea, heaped in three sugars and stirred it furiously before plonking it unceremoniously on the bedside table.

'Your tea, sir,' she said snippily, but before she could walk away he rolled over and grabbed her arm.

'Why don't you like me, Prim?' he slurred as he rose to a sitting position.

The dim candlelight made his bare skin glow golden and emphasised the powerful corded muscles in his arms and across his broad shoulders.

'It is not my place to either like or dislike you, sir,' she replied carefully, while trying to extricate her wrist from his firm hold and not look at his distracting body.

Up close, she could see the dark stubble on his chin. She should have found it unappealing—further evidence of his dissipation—but bizarrely it suited him. Hannah started to feel a little warm and off-kilter when she should have been outraged.

He laughed with drunken derision and leaned a little closer towards her, as if about to impart some great secret. 'Come now, Prim, we both know that you are lying—although I have to say you are quite dreadful at it. If you did not dislike me so intently then you would be much... *friendlier*.'

His dark gaze held hers. There was no mistaking his meaning, especially when his thumb began to caress the sensitive skin on the underside of her trapped wrist—something that made the nerve-endings in her arm tingle with awareness. She forced her mind to be angry. The wretch was flirting with her. Shamelessly. Even drunk he was trying to manipulate her own body into betraying her.

'If that is all, *sir,* then I should like to retire. It is very late and I must get up early in the morning to attend to my duties.'

Unfortunately her request fell on deaf ears, although why she had expected anything else she did not know. The gentle rhythm of his thumb circling that small patch of her skin was having an odd effect on her. It had been so long since anybody had intentionally touched her that she was keenly aware of every movement. She could feel her heart fluttering, and her flesh begin to tingle in a most unwelcome way.

The knowing stare he gave her through half-hooded eyes did make her feel a tad nervous. It was as if he was fully aware of the effect his ministrations were having on her.

'Come now, Prim. As your employer I am more than happy to allow you to sleep in, should you need to. I do believe that you might have other duties to attend to tonight that are far more pressing.'

Hannah could not quite believe her ears, even though her pulse quickened at the suggestion. Had he *really* just made completely improper and outrageous advances towards her?

She stiffened her spine in outrage and roughly snatched her wrist away. 'How dare you? You are drunk, sir. This is *not* the way a gentleman behaves towards a member of his household.'

She swiftly spun round and marched to the door in righteous indignation. She did not care if her words *did* threaten to compromise her employment here. In fact she did not care if he dismissed her on the spot—she would not allow him to treat her as if she were some lightskirt. Even if society believed that about her she would never demean herself by allowing another man to treat her that way.

As soon as she got to the door he was behind her. 'Not so fast, Prim,' he whispered, close to the back of her head, planting his arms upon the wood on either side of her, preventing her from leaving.

Despite the drink he was unbelievably swift and light on his feet. She had not even heard him rise from the bed, let alone dash across the floor of his bedchamber. That made her feel even more nervous and exposed. Even in the state he was in he was a force to be reckoned with.

She turned in the confines of his arms and folded her own arms across her chest in defiance. It would not do to let him see that she was rattled. 'What do you intend to do, sir? Keep me here against my will? Force yourself upon me?'

Her chin lifted as she stared up at him. Goodness, he was tall—and imposing at such close quarters. Her eyes barely came level with his chin. And he smelled so...*masculine*.

A low, intimate chuckle emanated from somewhere deep in his chest and resonated through her body. 'Dear Prim, I can assure you that I have never, *ever* had to force myself upon a woman. They all come quite willingly, in my experience—so your precious virtue is quite safe. I merely want a proper answer to my question. Why do you dislike me so very much?'

He was so close to her that she could feel his warm breath brush across her face. The unmistakable smell of brandy was surprisingly faint, but the heady aroma of bay and spice from his cologne was more prominent—and far from unpleasant.

'I don't dislike you,' she finally said cautiously, and then realised that those words were not so very far from the truth. She *wanted* to dislike him. She was desperately trying to find the evidence to do so. 'I disapprove of the great majority of your morals and behaviour.'

'Give me examples,' he whispered, quite lucidly, and he stared covetously at her mouth in a way that made her lips warm with awareness. 'What do I do, specifically, that you so thoroughly disapprove of?'

Hannah involuntarily licked her lips and saw his expression turn a little smug as she did so. He knew she was not completely immune to his charms, the devil, and he leaned a little closer in an attempt to fluster her further. Their faces were inches apart and his braced arms still formed a cage around her.

'I disapprove of your shameless flirting!' she spat, and positively glared at him. 'And I disapprove of your drinking, gambling and whor...'

Hannah allowed her angry outburst to trail off, too embarrassed to accuse him of whoring as well. Oh, how she hated that word.

'Most gentleman drink, gamble and fraternise with women, Prim. I am not unique in that respect.'

He lifted one finger and used it to loosen a tendril of hair at the side of her face. When it refused to budge from her severe coiffure he plucked out the hairpin that prevented it and smiled as the curl bounced to her jaw. Lazily, and to her great consternation, he wound it around his index finger possessively. It felt wonderful.

'You are no gentleman, sir. That fact is well reported.' It was a spiteful thing to say, but the truth none the less. She needed him to give her space. His close proximity was scattering her wits.

Unfortunately her insult amused him more than it offended. 'I have never claimed to be a gentleman, Prim. And you are right. That fact *has* been widely reported—you do seem to love the gossip columns, don't you? But the newspapers do not know the half of it. My background is far worse than even they realise. I am the son of a forger and a tavern maid. There is not a single drop of aristocratic blood in my common veins. We lived in one room next to a brothel when we could afford it. Once or twice we slept on the streets. Do not let my ruthlessly trained accent fool you. I come from the gutter, Prim. That is certainly not the background of a gentleman. Why on earth would you expect me to behave like a one?'

His tone was reasonable, as if she were expecting the impossible.

'I expect it, sir, because you pretend to be one. You rub shoulders with them, dress like one of them—that is when you can be bothered to put on a coat—and now you live like one. As owner of this house you should at least attempt to act like one.'

At some point during her lecture she had begun to point her finger into the solid wall of his ribcage.

'And what about *you*, madam?' he replied as he simultaneously removed her accusing finger from his breastbone and laced his own through her wayward hand.

The motion seemed to make their position even more intimate—if such a thing were possible when they already stood touching from chest to thigh.

'You have such great expectations of me but make no effort to comport *yourself* properly. A good servant, I am told, should be seen and not heard. *You* throw around your lofty opinions as if you have a right to be so high and mighty. Get off your high horse, Prim. Need I remind you that you are no lady either?'

Hannah bristled at that charge, because it had been said before—and worse. 'I am more of a lady than you will ever be a gentleman! At least *I* have enough decency to know that it is quite wrong to make advances to the staff.'

He had the audacity to smirk. 'Stop acting so shocked. A woman as lovely as you should be used to the improper advances of men. And I suspect that you are not truly as prim and proper as you would have me believe. In fact, I believe all the little lies you have told me are only the tip of the iceberg. You have already been caught out in one deception. I wonder what other rebellious traits you hide under that sensible, drab dress?'

Something about the way his eyes devoured her after those words made her blush involuntarily, as if he could see through the fabric of the garment. Goosebumps sprang up all over her body at the thought, and the urge to get away doubled, but he was not finished.

'Perhaps I should keep a very close eye on

you—just to check that you are not up to no good. Would you like that, Prim?' One hand curled around her waist possessively, then made a slow journey down the curve of her hip.

Hannah had never been handled so…so intimately. The twin emotions of outrage and excitement at being desired by this shameless man warred within her. How long had it been since any man had looked at her with anything other than disgust? How many times had she dreamed about such things in her lonely bed? Of a faceless saviour who would want her regardless? A man who would love her regardless?

His eyes held such forbidden promise…

Common sense won out. 'You are drunk, sir, and will no doubt regret this behaviour tomorrow. Now, unhand me if you please.' Again she stared defiantly at him, ignoring the fierce attraction she felt.

For the merest second he paused, and then he grinned wickedly. 'As you have quite rightly pointed out, Prim, I am no gentleman.'

Before she fully understood his intent, his dark head had dipped and his mouth fastened on hers boldly and feasted.

Her initial response was to flatten her hands against his chest in order to push him away. She clamped her lips firmly shut at the impertinent onslaught. But then her rebellious body rejoiced at the contact. His mouth moved sensually over hers with such skill and tenderness that she forgot her outrage and began to soften against him and her own better judgement. It had been so many years since anybody had stolen a kiss from her that she had forgotten quite how pleasant it could be.

This kiss was more than simply pleasant, though. It lit a fire within her that she had not known existed, and for a few moments she let it to burn unchecked, allowed herself simply to feel rather than think. Oh, how she had yearned for someone to want her again. It felt so very, *very* good.

In a second she would stop this silly experiment. She was overcome, that was all, and surprised to have been kissed. Nothing more.

But one second turned to two, then two turned to five.

Under her splayed hands she felt his heartbeat, sure and steady under the warm, silky skin of his chest. It felt decadent to touch a man like that, and without knowing it her fingers began to feel the shape of the muscles and ribs under her palms. When one of his hands gently cupped the side of her face she forgot that she hated him and kissed him back. Just once. Just because it felt so wonderful.

It was all the encouragement he needed. He trailed hot kisses down her cheek until he reached the place where her jaw met her neck. Then he used his teeth and tongue to nuzzle the tender pulse that beat there, before nipping and licking his way back to her ready mouth.

When he kissed her again she welcomed it like a starving man welcomed food, and moaned when his tongue tasted her mouth in the most scandalous joining of lips she had ever experienced. Her fiancé had never kissed her like this. And still she allowed him liberties with her person, let the passion build inside her. It made the tips of her breasts throb, and a dull ache began to form deep between her legs. Her breathing became unsteady. Uneven.

The powerful sensations and her needy re-action to them made her panic, and that emotion brought her crashing back to reality with a thud. She was kissing the man who had stolen her home and pushed her brother to suicide. What the *hell* was she thinking?

That, she realised with a jolt of disgust, was the problem. She had not been thinking at all. Only feeling.

With one decisive push she broke the contact and slipped out from under his arms, more than a little dazed and confused. To be fair, judging by the way his breathing was also laboured, he appeared as shocked as she by how quickly their brief kiss had turned to sheer carnal desire.

He stared at her dumbly for several moments, with a startled expression on his face. Then he finally stepped away from the door with a gloating smirk and folded his arms across his annoyingly distracting bare chest.

'As I suspected,' he drawled. 'Not as prim and proper as you would have me believe. And, despite your disapproval, you are clearly not as averse to me as you pretend to be either. I know that you thoroughly enjoyed what I just did— didn't you, Prim?'

'You flatter yourself,' she hissed, ashamed that he was correct, and grabbed the door handle forcefully.

After wrenching it open she turned and fled to her own bedroom, not caring that he could clearly see that she was running as fast as she could to get away—both from him and the inconvenient passion that had bubbled so unexpectedly between them.

When she got to her room she bolted the door—just in case. He had been right—damn him—she *had* thoroughly enjoyed what he had just done to her.

And that would not do at all.

Chapter Seven

❦

Hannah spent the entire morning worrying. Fortunately nobody else was aware of the outrageously improper kiss they had shared last night. Just thinking about it made her blush to the tips of her toes. It had not been her finest moment. One minute she had been happily disgusted at his behaviour, and the next she had been swept away in the throes of unwanted passion. Clearly she had been too deprived of male contact in the last few years if her traitorous body could respond with such uncharacteristic fervour.

He had taken advantage of her, she reasoned self-righteously. If she had not been taken so completely by surprise she would have slapped him for his impertinence and admonished him for abusing his position. Surely?

That was the problem, however. In the cold light of day Hannah knew that the only reason she had ended the kiss was out of fear. Her intense, needy reaction to Jameson had frightened her, and all she'd been able to do in response was flee. Worse, all night she had not been able to forget about how glorious it had felt. Her mind kept flitting back and remembering the unfamiliar sensations he had elicited.

He had been deliciously solid under her fingers. Her body had rejoiced at the pleasure of being held in his arms, and her lips had tingled with need hours afterwards. Even now her body craved more of the same, and appeared to be oblivious to the stark warnings from her head. She had been positively wanton—after accusing *him* of living his life in pursuit of carnal pleasure. How on earth was she ever going to face the man again without dying from embarrassment?

Feeling very silly, Hannah had hidden away upstairs, instructing Reggie and a particularly timid footman on which pieces of furniture needed consigning to the attic. Worn down by Reggie's complaining, she had finally relented and broken for tea. Now the pair of them were sitting around the kitchen table, cooling off.

'Can I ask you a personal question, Reggie?' she said carefully as she sipped the cold lemonade Cook had pressed into her hand.

'Ask away, mum,' he replied cheerfully, through

a mouthful of bread and cheese. It was quite staggering the amount of food he could consume in a single day.

'Mr Jameson told me that he inherited you when he bought a building. Is that true?'

Reggie laughed and sent a fine spray of crumbs shooting across the table. 'Sort of, I suppose. He does have a funny way of explaining things. Ross bought out a warehouse at the docks—lock, stock and barrel—and as I lived there he said I could stay. Been with him ever since.'

'You lived in a warehouse?' Such a prospect sounded terrible. 'Why did you live in a warehouse?'

Reggie's eyebrows drew together as he thought about the question and she sat quietly while he did so. In the short time she had known him she had learned that his memory was better if he had time to recall things. If put on the spot, he remembered nothing.

After almost a full minute he smiled in recollection. 'I was a fighter. 'Course, them sorts of fights is illegal, so they happen on the quiet. The guvnor had the warehouse because it was a good venue, with plenty of space for the Fancy.' He popped another chunk of cheese into his mouth.

'The Fancy? What is that?'

'Well, that's the name we give to the punters who come to watch and bet on a fight. Some of them are from the gentry, and dress right posh, so we call them the Fancy.'

'You used to engage in illegal boxing matches in a warehouse and you lived there as well?'

Reggie nodded and began to carve off another slice of bread from the loaf that had been left on the table. His explanation raised more questions for Hannah than answers.

'Men go to Gentleman Jackson's all the time—what was different about the boxing matches you took part in at that warehouse that made them illegal?'

Reggie did not need to think about his answer. 'Jackson's has proper rules and things. We didn't. When you fought at the warehouse you had to keep going till you either won or was knocked unconscious. Especially if the fight was fixed—which it usually was. The Guvnor would tell me to keep going for as long as I could as the punters bet more money on the fight then. 'Course, I was one of his favourites because I could take a punch. Sometimes I could go for twenty or thirty rounds before I was knocked out.'

This went a long way to explaining why Reggie's mind was damaged. 'Did you ever win, Reggie?'

'In me prime, I did. But as I got older I had to throw the fights. With me being so big the punters always bet on me to win—but I let the other fella win, the Guvnor raked in the cash and I got me board and lodgings for free.'

And his skull battered for the privilege.

The reality of what he had endured was awful. Reggie had been grossly taken advantage of because he'd lacked the intelligence to know better or the power to do anything about it.

'And Mr Jameson bought the illegal boxing ring and you with it?' Poor Reggie had been a means of making money for Jameson as well. The man had the morals of an alley cat.

'Yes, he did,' Reggie confirmed happily. 'I was part of the deal because Ross said he needed my services. I thought he meant as a fighter, though, so I was a bit surprised when he stripped the place out and turned it into a proper warehouse.'

The last piece of bread disappeared down Reggie's gullet and he sat back in the chair with his hands resting comfortably on his now full stomach.

'What do you mean? Did he close down the boxing ring or simply move it?' Surely he'd moved it. Such a spectacle would have created an easy source of revenue for a person who fed off others like carrion.

Reggie chuckled and sighed. 'Ross ain't got no appetite for boxing. He closed it completely and put me in charge of guarding the warehouse.'

Hannah sat forward in her chair, staggered by this news until she realised that there was obviously something even more lucrative and illegal than bare-knuckle boxing going on there.

'What sort of things did you have to guard in that warehouse, Reggie?'

He had to think about that, and she had to hide her impatience while he did so.

'Mostly silk,' he said after an interminable age, 'although sometimes there was fancy pottery as well. Ross gets a lot of things from the Orient, and quality ladies do love nice frocks.'

This information could not have been more disappointing, and Hannah felt her spirits plunge. If Reggie was to be believed—and he really did not have the intelligence to lie convincingly—then Jameson had saved him from a life of extreme violence and potential death, closed down a lucrative underground gambling den and instead traded in fine silks for the gentry.

That made him sound almost noble!

'Does Mr Jameson ever need your fighting skills for other things, Reggie? For example, have you ever had to threaten people for him, or collect debts owed to him?' Surely he had to do that at least?

The big man shook his shaggy head. 'I ain't thrown a punch in five years, mum—honest. Now I just look after Ross, on account of him needing someone to fetch and carry for him, so I moved out of the warehouse a few winters ago and moved in with him. Mind you, it was proper cold that year, so I can't say that I minded.'

With a sinking feeling Hannah just knew that the cold winter had had a great deal to do with Reggie's promotion. 'Does Mr Jameson pay you well, Reggie?'

Not that Reggie had any need for money—he was fed at the master's table and slept in one of the best family bedrooms in the house—but it would give her some consolation to know that he treated his personal servant badly in at least that respect.

'I ain't got no need of money!' Reggie exclaimed in outrage. 'I keep telling him that, but he don't listen. Ross puts me wages into investments. He says money makes money. Do you know, I get yearly dividends on it? I must have close to five hundred quid in the bank.'

Hannah's spirts sank further. To listen to Reggie, Jameson was a candidate for sainthood. Depressed, and more than a little confused, Hannah finished her lemonade. At this rate she would be a very old lady and still merely a housekeeper in her own house.

Ross felt the first sign of a headache beginning to form behind his eyes and realised he had been staring at his ledgers for hours. Not that he minded the work. The columns of numbers were his friends. They made perfect sense to him, and he loved to see his profits rise exactly as he had predicted they would. However, the headaches were always a sign that he had done too much and needed some air and a change of scenery.

He should have stopped when the tea tray had magically arrived. It did that a great deal of late, he had noticed, thanks to Prim, and it was always timed to break up his work—as if she realised he was doing too much.

The woman appeared to have clairvoyant tendencies at times. Ever since the day she had shed her disguise she had taken the trouble to fuss over him a bit. More often than not she bustled in with her usual disapproving expression on her face, yet she brought him fresh fruit in the mornings and his favourite cakes in the afternoons. If he worked late in the evenings she would bring in a light snack with the tray, and then wordlessly go about the study lighting all the lamps and admonishing him for squinting in the dark and potentially ruining his eyesight.

All around the room were little feminine touches that had her name written all over them. He knew that the vase of fragrant roses on the mantel, for instance, were refreshed every few days because he had casually mentioned that he enjoyed the smell of the ones she had put in the hall.

It was those little thoughtful, personal touches that had him baffled. On the one hand she could be brusque and formal, but apparently she could not stop herself from doing little things that made him feel happy. She could be as cold and brittle as a brisk north wind one minute, then burn hot with fiery passion the next. Last night had proved that.

She exuded so much confidence sometimes that she could be a little intimidating, and then she would retreat into herself like a timid mouse as she had today. He had expected her to come and give him a sound telling off for kissing her yesterday evening, but she had avoided him quite deftly instead, as if she were embarrassed rather than outraged. Everything about her was so conflicting he found her oddly intriguing. He had certainly never encountered another woman quite like her.

With a contented sigh he closed the big leather book and stretched, before heading towards the convenient French doors that connected his study with the garden. His new gardener had already begun to clear the flowerbeds from the choking weeds that had overtaken them. Next year there would be flowers everywhere, he promised himself, and cheerful new benches would be set in secluded parts of the gardens, so that he could sit and think in tranquil peace—master of all he surveyed and at the mercy of no one.

That thought made him smile as he stuffed his hands in his pockets and headed outside. The early-evening air was less oppressive, and he traipsed towards the wooded area at the back of the formal gardens and found a suitably sturdy tree to sit against...

Ross must have nodded off, he realised with a start, because he was no longer alone. A very skinny, pathetic excuse for a dog had plonked itself on the ground next to him and was watching him with interest. The animal was of no discernible breed, and was neither large nor small for a hound. Its fur was a dull shade of beige, but his eyes, ears and tail were ringed with black. Ross stared back at the ugly canine and then tentatively reached out a hand to stroke it. The dog stood and pushed his knobbly head into his open palm, and let out a small doggy sigh of contentment when he scratched behind one of its flea-bitten pointed ears.

A quick glance to the left confirmed its sex. 'Hello, boy,' Ross whispered. 'Where is your owner?'

There was not a single person in sight. The creature panted in response and the sour aroma of dank dog wafted up Ross's nostrils and made him pull a face.

'Pardon my forthrightness, Dog, but you stink.'

His hand felt decidedly unpleasant, and he immediately regretted petting the mangy thing. He wiped it on the grass and then hoisted himself to his feet. The dog sidled up next to him and looked up hopefully.

'Shoo! Go away!' He started to walk towards the house and the dog trotted alongside. Just what he needed—another stray to blight his life. 'I mean it, dog—*go away*!'

The animal paused and Ross made a break for it. Decisively he marched out of the woods, and did his best to ignore the sound of the mongrel's panting as it continued to trot behind his heels. The blasted animal had latched on to him. Annoyed, he stopped dead and turned to face it, with his hands planted on his hips. But then he saw something else move through the edge of the trees in the distance and forgot about the mutt. If he was not mistaken that was Prim he had just spotted—no doubt she was still fuming about the kiss.

A smile crept over his face as he remembered how enthusiastically she had kissed him back. Kissing Prim had been a bit of a revelation. Usually, kissing was a bit of a means to an end—a way of getting a woman into bed. Kissing Prim had been a wholly enjoyable activity in itself. Ross could have carried on and on. When she had abruptly ended it he had felt bereft—and more than a little bit stunned. He had certainly never experienced that before—and certainly not from just a kiss. Would it have the same effect on him again? he wondered.

There was only one way to find out.

Quickly, he slipped back into the woods. She was walking at some speed in the opposite direction to the house and was clutching a bouquet of freshly picked wild flowers. Curious, he kept in the cover of the trees and followed her. Soon she had inadvertently led him to a part of the grounds he had not yet seen. There was a small area enclosed by a low wall that had been almost completely obscured by weeds and meadow grass. From a distance it appeared to be a small cemetery. He could just make out the tops of one or two of the headstones.

Prim opened the gate and let herself in, then he watched her separate the flowers into three small bunches, which she placed next to the stones. Oblivious to his hiding place, she knelt down and began pulling up the weeds.

Chapter Eight

Hannah felt guilty as she tidied up her brother's grave. Up until now she had not even seen it. Word of his death had arrived in Yorkshire only after his funeral. Their solicitor had informed her that Jameson, in an unexpected show of decency, had allowed her brother to rest with the family and his remains had been buried quickly. Since her return to Barchester Hall she had not been able to bring herself to come and see him. There were too many bad memories. She could not even bring herself to forgive him for sending her away.

'I am sorry I have not come sooner,' she said aloud, 'But you must understand, George, that I am beyond angry at you.'

She tugged at a stubborn dandelion and sighed.

'What were you thinking? You lost everything

George. *Everything.* How could you gamble away our home on a game of cards? Although I suppose I should not have been surprised after you had gambled away everything else first.'

She felt tears prickle her eyes and let them fall. There was nobody here to see her and she was truly miserable.

'Do you know what was worse?' She spoke directly to the gravestone. 'You kept the truth from me. I had no idea how dire the situation was until after I had learned that you were dead—and by then it was far too late for me to be able to do anything. The house was gone. There was nothing left in the bank. How could you *do* that to me?'

She did not expect an answer and sat back on her heels to survey the graves of her parents. They were in an even worse state, and had obviously been neglected since George had banished her to the North.

'I shall have to come back with proper tools to get rid of those brambles,' she muttered as she swiped at her eyes with her sleeve. Crying was not going to make things right. It would not bring back her reputation or her chance of marriage and children. 'At least Father saved some money. I have the five thousand he kept in trust for my dowry to buy back Barchester

Hall—although I should not have to do it, and I doubt I will be able to forgive you for that either.'

The hall represented the very last vestige of what she had once been—before she had been jilted, publically shamed and exiled. If she lost that, then she was truly left with nothing. All that would lie ahead of her were more empty years in Yorkshire, living with two old and timid maiden aunts, her future as bleak as the landscape on the moors in the winter.

That prospect terrified her more than anything. If she had learned one thing in the last seven years it was that she simply had to be in control of her own destiny. She had had enough of banishment and isolation and obeying another's commands. When she got the hall back things were going to change for the better.

'Perhaps I will feel differently when I find something on Jameson,' she continued, forcing optimism into her voice. 'That is proving particularly difficult as well—but I am determined. So far I have found nothing untoward. Of all the people to lose the house to, you had to choose *him*. He is far too clever. Any evidence of his wrongdoing is well hidden. Obviously I shall be persistent, and I am sure that I will find something, but I think it is going to take far longer than I had originally hoped. At least I am home…'

Hannah glanced back towards the house wistfully.

'The truth is, Jameson does appear to have some decent qualities. He is kind to Reggie and the servants, and quite generous with his money. The house will look as good as new after we have finished. Aside from his loose morals and libertine lifestyle, I cannot help but admire him—he was born with nothing and has worked tirelessly to amass his great fortune—which makes this predicament all the more difficult. He appears to be very personable and is very easy to work for.

'He even asks for my opinion. Imagine that. I can never remember either you or Father asking me what I thought about anything. *Ever.* I was always expected to adhere to your edicts without question. And he listens to my advice. Genuinely listens. He has this way of looking at me intently when I speak, as if he actually wants to know what I am going to say—which is surprisingly flattering. He has even let me pick the colours for the morning room and the hallway, and he trusts me to simply get on with things. Which is nice… More than nice, actually. It makes me feel special in a strange sort of way—like I belong here.

'It's quite an odd feeling, not to be considered a burden or an obligation for once. He is quite charming, really. And handsome, in a rough sort of way. Well, not so rough, now that I come to think about it. He has lovely green eyes that sparkle when he smiles. Under different circumstances, and if I did not know better, he would probably turn my head. I only hope that I find something nefarious about him soon, George, because I find myself in danger of *liking* the scoundrel. He can be rather…intoxicating at times.'

Hannah still could not stop thinking about the kiss. Even here, at her brother's grave, she had to concentrate hard to avoid revisiting the way it had made her feel.

After carefully standing, she tipped all the weeds over the wall out onto the meadow. As an afterthought she wandered back to her parents' graves and stood for a moment contemplating them. It seemed to be the respectable thing to do, although she had very little memory of her mother. She had died while Hannah was very young.

Her father had passed away when she was twelve. She recalled him as an aloof and self-indulgent man. Like George, he had set great store in his own comforts and pleasures, and had paid little attention to his only daughter. After her mother's death he'd hardly spent any time at

Barchester Hall, preferring the entertainments of town, so with George away at school, and then later at university, Hannah had grown up virtually alone. Alone save for Cook, who had been the one constant in a sea of ever-changing servants and governesses.

It was no wonder she had been so bowled over by the first man who had courted her—right up until the moment he had cruelly cast her aside in that ballroom.

Hannah felt fresh tears threaten and turned back towards the grave again. 'What I don't understand, George, is why you never sent for me. When I was bundled off to the middle of nowhere you promised me that it was only temporary. You promised me that you would sort it all out and restore my reputation. Why would you not let me come home? I wrote to you time and time again, begging you to let me, and you never replied. Did you actually *believe* all the lies he told you? Did you think that I *deserved* to be jilted?'

Ross could not work out exactly what she was doing, but found the image of her tending the Runcorn family graves to be a little odd. He watched her from a distance for a little while, until curiosity got the better of him and he bounded over to the little plot.

'Hello, Prim,' he said, and watched her jump out of her skin.

'Hello, Mr Jameson,' she replied, a little too wide-eyed for his liking. 'It is a fine evening for a walk.'

'Yes, it is,' he responded cheerfully. 'What are you doing?'

She blinked, and licked her pretty pink lips nervously before answering. 'I saw that this little graveyard was in dire need of some care and decided to tidy it up. I think that it is important to be respectful of the dead. Don't you?'

Ross glanced at the headstones and then back at her face, so that he could gauge her reaction. 'This must be the Runcorn family plot.'

'Is that the family who lived here before?' she asked, with just the right amount of uninterest, so that he was almost convinced that she was unaware of that fact.

'Yes, it is.' He pointed to the newest stone. 'I won this house from the last Earl of Runcorn in a card game.'

She did not look surprised by this statement, but her face was just a little too blank. Such information should at least cause her to raise an eyebrow.

Instead she stared at him levelly. 'I read about

that in the newspapers. He died shortly afterwards, did he not?'

'Come now, Prim. If you read about it in the newspapers then you already know that he blew his own brains out.'

He detected the smallest of winces at that, but she covered it quickly.

'Perhaps he felt he had no other choice,' she said after a beat of silence. 'He must have been quite desperate to do such a thing.'

'I think he was actually being quite selfish. He had just gambled away his house. His fortune was already long gone. Suicide gave him a way of not having to explain all that to his family. He should have avoided being so reckless with the only thing he had left.'

Hannah could not argue with him because she felt much the same way about her brother's actions herself. However, to agree felt disloyal—especially as George was lying beneath her very feet. Jameson had happily entered into a card game with her brother and had taken the house. That fact had led to George's death. Jameson might not have held the gun that had killed him, but he had certainly provided the ammunition. That detail did not appear to give him a moment's regret. However, that was not something that she could take him to task about yet.

'Do you win many houses in card games?' She felt it was a fair question.

He smiled ruefully. 'This is the first. I once won a ship, though. And a tiara. I gave that to my sister, although she has never had any cause to wear it. I usually play cards for money.'

'Does it not bother you that in doing so you might be causing the ruin of others?' Hannah tried to make her tone inquisitive, rather than accusatory, but a hint of the latter sneaked in nevertheless. It made his expression harden slightly.

'I suspect that question is loaded, Prim—especially as you obviously read the newspapers enthusiastically and know full well that they have accused me of the ruination of many good men. But, to answer your question, all I will say is that I did not ask any of them to sit down at the card table with me. Nor did I encourage them to risk their entire fortunes on the turn of a card. The simple truth is, a fool and his money are soon parted. Therefore if it had not been me who relieved them of their purses it would have been somebody else.'

Hannah had not considered that—but it still did not excuse his cavalier attitude. 'But when they run out of money you allow them to be reckless and stake things of far greater value. The Earl of Runcorn, for instance. When he ran out of money why did you continue to play with him? Surely the decent thing to do in such a situation would be to decline?'

'That idiot came to White's with the deeds to this house in his pocket! Who *does* that? He had every intention of gambling it—if I had not relieved him of it then somebody else would have. He was an atrocious card player—the more he lost, the more transparent and sloppy he became. One way or another, Barchester Hall was doomed to have a new owner that night. It might as well have been me.'

Hannah felt the bile rise in her throat at the sheer reckless stupidity of her brother. He had purposely and wilfully taken the deeds to their home to the club! She had not known that pertinent detail before. It beggared belief.

His voice penetrated her thoughts. 'Some men find the lure of Lady Luck too great to resist, Prim. Gambling becomes an addiction to them, and the more they lose the more they are prepared to risk.'

There was a slightly wistful expression on his handsome face as he looked at her brother's grave.

'It is a disease, and it makes them become desperate. Sometimes they do terrible, abhorrent things—which seem perfectly reasonable to them when they are in the grip of the addiction—and they do not even consider the dire consequences their actions might have for others. Poor old Runcorn did not only bring the deeds to White's—he also brought a loaded pistol. Why would he do that? There are no footpads or murderers loose in White's. I believe that he had every intention of ending his life if he lost again. It is sad, but he chose his own destiny.'

Hannah had the urge to stamp on her selfish brother's grave. She had not realised that it was possible to be more angry with him—but she was. And as for Jameson…

'But you benefited from his stupidity,' she said quietly, willing herself to stare at her feet when she wanted to scratch and claw at him instead.

'As did you, Prim.'

His words were like a dash of cold water and her head snapped up.

'If he had not lost the house to me, then you would not be housekeeper. You would be working for somebody who does not see past your age or your lack of experience. I doubt there are many employers daft enough to keep on a servant who has fed them a complete pack of lies and who continues to disapprove of her benevolent employer quite so openly.'

Although he was still smiling, there was a

challenge in his green eyes that made her nervous. She was alienating him at a time when she needed to build his trust—especially as she still had no tangible evidence to prove any wrongdoing on his part.

'You are quite right, Mr Jameson. I doubt many other employers would entertain such a difficult servant and I am grateful that you do.' She flashed him her best friendly but shy smile. 'I need to keep my forthright opinions to myself. It has always been a character flaw. You are a decent man, Mr Jameson. Please do not take my impertinent questions as evidence of my disapproval. I am simply curious about the motives of the Earl of Runcorn. He must have been a very troubled man.'

Initially he stared at her warily, and then his mouth quirked up in acknowledgement of her apology.

'Are you aware that you appear to have acquired a dog?' she asked, as a means to change the subject.

'We are merely walking in the same direction,' he said dismissively. 'If we ignore him he will go away. Shall we walk back to the house together, Miss Prim, or would you find the prospect of that too distasteful?'

Hannah forced another smile. She would

rather walk over hot coals, but under the circumstances she had no other option. 'That would be pleasant, sir. Thank you.'

She sailed through the gate he held open for her and he offered her his arm. Hannah stared at it in surprise.

'I see,' he said in amusement. 'You feel that it is improper for me to offer you my arm?'

Hannah nodded, more than a little relieved when he shrugged and dropped the offending limb back to his side. 'I am your employee, sir. Employees do not, as a rule, take their employer's arms under any circumstances.'

'Or kiss them?'

Hannah felt a hot blush stain her cheeks. 'Indeed. You most definitely overstepped the boundary last night. But you were drunk, so I will forgive you.'

'I could not help noticing that you were *not* drunk, Prim, and yet you kissed me back.' He winked at her and smiled smugly.

'I most definitely did not! You caught me by surprise with your outrageous behaviour! You cannot go around manhandling the staff,' she declared, sounding a great deal like a schoolmistress reprimanding an errant pupil.

Once again she was telling him off—not that

he did not deserve it—but she really had to make an effort. Her whole future depended on it.

Hannah decided to change the subject tactically. 'I spoke to Reggie this afternoon. He confirmed that you did indeed inherit him with a building—although he tells the tale a little differently from you.'

'Does he? What did he say?'

He had stuffed his hands into his pockets—something a gentleman would never do—and she could not fail to notice his casual attire. The light breeze moulded the soft linen of his shirt to the hard planes of his chest and shoulders, emphasising his lean and muscular body. She now knew a little of what that body felt like, and it was not at all unpleasant.

Despite her disapproval, she could see what other women found appealing about him. He was irritatingly handsome. His dark, almost black hair was ever so slightly ruffled, and it curled a little at the nape of his neck and around his forehead. His sea-green eyes always seemed to be twinkling with amusement, as if he found the whole world and everyone in it one big joke that only he understood.

'Reggie told me that you rescued him from a life of mindless violence—like a hero.'

He stopped and stared at her astounded. 'He

did? That sounds positively gushing.' Then he grinned. 'But I suppose there is no point denying the truth. I am, in actual fact, a saint.'

Hannah could not help smiling at the self-deprecating way he dismissed the praise, as if it was of no matter. 'He also said that you moved him out of the warehouse during a particularly harsh winter.'

'He most definitely did not say that, Prim. For a start I have never heard him use the word "particularly". It has far too many syllables in it. And, secondly, he firmly believes that I needed him to look after me.'

'But you do not deny that the cold winter had a bearing on your decision?' she teased. 'Therefore I have to believe that you have a charitable streak buried under all that charm and bravado.'

He turned towards her and did his best impression of a man affronted. 'Hardly. The cold winter notwithstanding, I could not keep him in the warehouse. It was filled with Chinese porcelain at the time and I feared that he would break it all. You must have noticed how clumsy he is. I was simply protecting my investment.' Then he grinned boyishly. 'And now I am stuck with him.'

'Of course you are. That is why you have moved him into one of the family bedrooms here at Barchester Hall.' Hannah was intrigued to see how he was going to get around that particular fact.

He stopped momentarily and glared at her with his hands on his hips. 'Have you not seen the *size* of the oaf? He is built like an oak tree! The beds in the servants' quarters would shatter into matchsticks if he rested his enormous bulk on one of them. I put him in that room because it has the sturdiest bed.'

His amused eyes locked with hers, and for a moment she basked in their warmth, then he shrugged, stuffed his hands back in his pockets and started to walk again—as if he knew that she could read the truth in his eyes but admitting the truth about himself made him feel uncomfortable.

'Now that I know that you are not a widowed hag I am a little intrigued about your background. Tell me a little bit about *you*, Prim.'

Chapter Nine

~~~~~~~~~~~~~

Hannah felt a jolt of nerves and tried to brush him off with banality as she quickened her pace. 'There is nothing interesting to tell. The decorators will start work on the morning room tomorrow. We should probably discuss how you would like the hallway to be done, so that I can order the materials. I was thinking green would look good—not so dark as to be oppressive—perhaps a sage-green would be appropriate?'

'Oh, no, you don't,' he said, wagging his finger in admonishment and purposefully slowing his gait. 'I will not allow you to change the subject. If you will not volunteer information about yourself I shall have to ask you questions—and as your employer I will demand that you answer them honestly. For example, you are such a pretty girl—why are you not married?'

Hannah felt her smile instantly slip and struggled to retain it. She was not entirely sure of the answer herself. A version of the truth would be easier for her to remember, she realised, feeling a little sick as memory assaulted her.

'I think those years passed me by, sir,' she admitted, hoping that it sounded convincing. 'When my parents died I went to live with my aunts for a while. After that I had to seek employment.' She kept the small lie to a minimum and hoped he would not probe her story further.

He digested this for a moment or two. 'Then why not become a governess? Surely your age and marital status would not be an issue with such a position? And at least you would have more free time and less responsibility.'

Another innocent question that reopened old wounds. Children were one more thing that would not be in her future now. 'I lack the patience required to look after other people's children, sir. Also, I lack some of the finer skills that many good families insist upon in a governess. My piano-playing is abysmal, at best, and I have no talent for languages.'

He appeared a little confused, and then shook his head. 'How peculiar,' he said finally. 'I would have thought that the most important thing to do for a child is to love it.' He stopped walking and turned to her. 'I am not sure I will ever fully understand the gentry, Prim. I am trying—but half of what they do truly baffles me.'

'I think you must give specific examples, sir. What baffles you?'

'Too many things to list now. But there are quite a few that you might be able to shed some light on, seeing as you have worked for them. Why, for instance, is it considered poor form to introduce yourself to somebody? Why must I wait an age for somebody *else* to introduce me when I am perfectly capable of doing that for myself?'

'I am not sure that I know,' she replied with a smile, 'except that it is the proper order of things.'

He pulled a face. 'And why is it improper to dance with the same lady more than once at a ball?'

'I can answer *that*! To dance with a woman more than once declares to everybody that you have a particular interest in her.'

'Surely that is the whole point of dancing with her in the first place?' He looked outraged. 'Why else would a man prance around the floor like an idiot unless he wants to let the woman know he has a particular interest in her?'

Hannah sighed dramatically. 'But you would be announcing your interest in *public*. People would get ideas.'

'Where I come from we *want* people to get ideas. It lets them know that they should back off. I wouldn't want some other fella going after my girl.'

It was the first time his diction had slipped in her presence, alluding to his coarse roots, but she found it strangely charming instead of repulsive.

'And why on *earth* is a man judged by his ability to ride a horse?'

'Good horsemanship is a skill that all gentlemen are taught almost from the moment they can walk,' she said in response. 'Ladies embroider and gentlemen ride.'

'Then I shall *never* be a gentleman,' he declared resolutely. 'I do not care for horses.'

'Why ever not? Most horses are gentle beasts who like people.'

He glared at her for a second, and then shrugged his broad shoulders. 'Horses do not like me. They have a tendency to evacuate their bowels whenever I go near them.'

Hannah laughed derisively at this ridiculous statement. 'I think you are being a tad overdramatic, sir.'

'I am not. I speak from experience. My first job was as an ostler at a coaching inn. I only lasted two days! Every single horse I came into contact with soiled my boots. And I tried riding once. It frankly terrified me.'

He looked so aggrieved that she could not help sniggering. 'What was it that frightened you?'

He thought for a moment, and then gave her a rare glimpse of the man beneath all the bravado.

'In hindsight…nothing. I suppose it was being at the mercy of the animal. I need to be in control of things. If I am not I feel uncomfortable.' He was starting to look a little uncomfortable at this admission too, but he quickly covered it with another boyish grin. 'We are talking about me again. You are very good at distracting me. Where were we? Ah, yes—you and marriage. You are still young, Prim. Perhaps…'

'There is no "perhaps". I have no intention of getting married now.'

He appeared genuinely bemused. 'Why ever not?'

'The older I get, the more I appreciate my independence, sir. If I was married I would have to live my life at the mercy of my husband's whims and edicts. I prefer to be in control of my own destiny—much like you do, apparently, so you of all people should understand.'

His dark eyebrows drew together and he frowned. 'If you don't mind me saying, that is a very cynical attitude, Prim. I like to be in control of my business and my life, but I have no intention of behaving like a tyrant towards my future wife. I should imagine that marriage is a very pleasant state to find oneself in—so long as it is with the right person.'

'Why, then, are you not married, sir?' she responded sarcastically.

'I am not averse to the idea. I just do not have the time to go hunting for the right woman yet. Once my sister is happily settled with a decent man then I will. I believe I shall settle down to marital bliss quite happily. Until then I prefer to keep my options open.'

'I thought your sister was much younger than you? Why would you put off your own wedding until after hers?'

'I should like to know that she is well taken care of before I divert my attention from her welfare. She is young and impressionable, and therefore ripe for fortune-hunters or scoundrels to take advantage of her.'

Hannah regarded him sceptically. 'I see. And your current lady-friend—does she know that you do not consider her an "option", as you put it, for being the future Mrs Jameson?'

He threw back his dark head and laughed. 'You really are quite forthright, aren't you, Miss Prim? Francesca was never an "option"—and, to be fair, she was well aware of that fact. Francesca was merely a…dalliance…a convenient outlet for a little while.' At her bemused expression he clarified. 'Lust. I know that you are quite familiar with the concept, Prim.'

He climbed over a stile briskly, and then took her hand as she stepped up, artfully grabbing her around the waist and slowly lowering her down, his hot gaze raking over her and making her far too aware of him. He paused for a moment before releasing her, and then tugged her closer instead, his eyes darkening as they fixed on her lips, his face inches from her own.

Hannah held her breath at this unexpected physical contact, and blinked back at him in confusion as her body began to hum with need even as she desperately willed it not to. Slowly she brought her hands up to rest on his chest, ready to push him away. She could not let him overwhelm her senses again.

'So now am I a convenient "dalliance", sir? How demeaning.'

Instantly he took a step back and released her. Then he sighed. 'You make me feel ashamed, Prim, but I am only human. Lust is nothing more than a basic animal instinct—much like needing food or air. But you are right. It is unfair of me to direct it at you.'

They walked on a little further in silence.

'Why do you want to get married one day?' Hannah could not help being curious. The idea of him settled with one woman when he was such an outrageous flirt was difficult to imagine.

'I have every intention of filling this house with a large and noisy family.' He shot her a look that suggested he was looking forward to *making* the children. 'And I happen to think I will make a good father.'

His self-confidence was quite astounding, and Hannah snorted. 'Really. And what has led you to make that conclusion?'

'I had a good role model,' he countered quickly.

She snorted again. 'You told me your father was a forger!'

'Exactly! That made him a perfect role model. I firmly believe that you can learn just as much— sometimes more—from other people's mistakes as from their successes. My father taught me how *not* to do things. So long as I never do anything he did then I know I am on the right path. Aside from that, I do not want to be lonely when I am an old man. Surely you don't want that either?'

Once again he had turned the tables on her and put her on the spot.

Hannah shrugged. 'I am used to being on my own.'

The house in Yorkshire was very remote but

she had managed well enough—even if the days had dragged and the nights had felt interminable and at times she had wanted to weep from loneliness.

'I think that is a shame,' he said after a pause. 'But I suppose it is your choice. If you do not want to get married, what *are* your hopes for the future?'

'To own my own home,' she said without hesitation, and gave him a reluctant smile. 'I want a place where I can live out my days according to my own whims. Like you, I want to be in control. Not being makes me feel uncomfortable too.'

'It will still be a lonely place with nobody to share it. You will end up like poor old Runcorn in his untended grave. Who will put flowers down for *you*?'

His words hurt her—not because he was being deliberately cruel, but because they were a hard dose of reality. If everything went the way she wanted it she might well be buried in that same plot, next to a mother she did not know, an indifferent father and a reckless and neglectful brother. That was a very dire prospect indeed. Was that *really* all her future held?

There was something about this man that had her questioning her own strongly held beliefs and making her doubt them.

'Are you aware of the fact that the dog is still following you?' she asked in desperation.

He stared straight ahead. 'Ignore him. He will go away.'

She turned back to the filthy, panting animal trotting along happily in their wake. 'I doubt it,' she said. 'He has been following us for ten minutes now. Did you do anything to encourage him?'

'Of course I didn't. Do I *look* like a soft touch? The blasted animal has just latched on to me. As soon as he realises he is not welcome he will go away.'

But the animal did not. It trotted behind them all the way back to Barchester Hall, his long tongue lolling happily out of his mouth and his eyes fixed stoically on Jameson's legs.

Hannah entered the kitchen first, and left him to deal with the mongrel alone.

'Right, Dog,' he said decisively. 'This is where we part company.'

The fact that he was trying to reason with the mutt using conversation made her smile.

Reggie wandered into the kitchen and watched Ross quizzically. 'What's he doing?' he asked Hannah as he munched on an apple, unaware of the fact that he was spraying juice all over the place.

'He is trying to tell a stray dog to go away,' she replied laughingly. 'Although he is not doing a particularly good job of it.'

'Huh! He won't get rid of it,' muttered Reggie with resignation as he took a look at the animal for himself. 'Ross is too kind-hearted.' Then he shouted to the man in question. 'Shall I give it a bath and a bit of dinner, Ross?'

Hannah watched Jameson roll his eyes in a manner that she recognised as his *I am so put upon* expression, and then he sighed.

'Yes, Reggie. Do that.'

As he turned and stalked into the kitchen he paused briefly in front of her with a playful look in his eyes.

'And I will thank you not to say anything, madam.'

'I would not dream of it, sir,' she said to his retreating back, and felt her lips twitching with amusement. He really was kind-hearted. And nice to talk to. And to kiss.

Immediately she checked herself. Good grief, at this rate he was going to charm her thoroughly too. At some point during their walk back to the house she had forgotten that she hated him. And perhaps she did not any more. But she still certainly disliked him. Quite a bit.

Chapter Ten

Ross ran his fingertip over the seal again thoughtfully. It was definitely not right. The embossed pattern bore a small crack through its centre, and had been repaired with wax that was an ever so slightly different shade of red. If the letter had not been from his friend John Carstairs, a man totally convinced that they were being spied upon by the East India Company, he probably would not have noticed. But it *was* from John—so he had.

His friend believed that the East India Company were put out by the fact that the pair of them were undercutting them considerably and would try and put a stop to it by using fair means or foul. Ross had always laughed it off. Their growing trade in silk, porcelain and spices from the Orient had never been a secret and was completely above-board. All the duties were paid and the cargos were sold on legitimately to the growing list of merchants who clamoured for them. Although they made a very healthy profit from it, the amounts were a drop in the ocean compared to the mighty Crown-licensed corporation.

Ross had always severely doubted that the East India Company were bothered. Now, looking at the correspondence that had clearly been tampered with, he was not so sure. Their imports from Siam had quadrupled this year. That amount would triple again soon, when his new ships came into service. Perhaps the East India Company *was* a little upset at the prospect of growing competition... But were they upset enough to send a spy to delve into his business affairs?

It was a trifle far-fetched, but not out of the realms of possibility.

One thing was for certain: if there was a spy in his household the main suspect had to be his disingenuous and changeable housekeeper Prim. Nobody else had the wherewithal to do such a task. Prim was very intelligent, and had already been caught out in one lie. He supposed that it might explain her latent hostility towards him. She might well be an emissary from the East India Company. It did make sense in a peculiar sort of way.

Then he chuckled to himself. He was being paranoid—probably because his sister was determined to revisit London and would not be talked out of it. It had him on edge. Talk of Sarah and London in the same sentence always got his heart racing and his mind whirring. As if Prim was actually a *spy*! The prospect was really quite funny. Prim had already proved herself to be lacking in the talent necessary for true espionage. He had seen through her stupid disguise quite quickly.

But, then again, it *would* explain why she was being standoffish. She had avoided him like the plague for over a week now, and despite the initial thawing of relations after their kiss they only collided when she wanted to consult him on the rapidly proceeding restorations. Each time she blushed furiously and struggled to meet his eye. She had even stopped delivering his tea tray herself. It still arrived with pleasing regularity, at just the right moment, but she had delegated the responsibility now and he missed her.

When he did see her, Ross went of his way to remind her of their transgression, though. He might well have instigated it, but she had kissed him back. Quite enthusiastically too. Just thinking about it made him feel amorous... Occasionally, because it amused him, he would shoot her a saucy wink and a knowing smile and then enjoy the sight of her turning bright pink and totally flustered. He especially enjoyed watching her retreating bottom sway temptingly as she scurried away. The woman *did* have a lovely arse.

She was also very good at being a housekeeper. She was a spectacularly good organiser, with a keen eye for exactly what the house needed. She had the servants and the tradesmen working like a well-oiled machine. At this rate the house would be like a palace well before the summer finished.

Surely Prim was not a spy?

On a whim, he went to find her.

'I think somebody has been opening my letters,' he said without preamble when he found her in her little office.

Two red spots instantly bloomed on her cheeks and she briefly looked as guilty as sin.

'Surely not, sir!' she replied quickly. 'What makes you say that?'

He handed her the letter and pointed to the seal. 'It looks wrong. As if it has already been broken and then hastily repaired. See there—the wax in that crack is a slightly different shade of red.'

She peered at it and then looked back at him, fully composed once again. 'Is there a chance that the postmaster might have noticed it was open and resealed it before it was delivered?'

It was certainly a reasonable explanation, and he might have believed it except that she was blinking just a little too rapidly.

'Perhaps,' he said. 'But I would appreciate it if you could keep an eye on any future letters, Prim. Just in case.'

She nodded serenely. 'Of course, sir.'

She said nothing further. But her lovely blue eyes were still blinking furiously. Something was off.

Ross turned and headed back to his study and sat down. With a sigh, he cracked open the letter and scanned the contents. John was in Portsmouth with their latest cargo of Siamese silk and would remain there for a few days to oversee some repairs to the ship. He was keen for him to join him there.

Ross had not seen his friend and business partner for several months and was looking forward to catching up with him, and to showing him Barchester Hall. John would find the sight of him as a respectable land-owner hilarious.

Laying the letter on his desk, he could not dispel a feeling of uneasiness. It would be good to discuss his new suspicions with his friend. It might also be prudent to do a little investigating into his suspicious housekeeper's background. It would be fascinating to see if Miss Preston was exactly who she claimed to be and if he was indeed being paranoid.

He sincerely hoped it was the latter. But if she *was* working for the East India Company then it would be prudent to keep her at Barchester Hall for the time being. At least here he could keep a watchful eye on her. To do otherwise would merely tip off the East India Company—that might well open him up to further scrutiny, and their next spy might not be quite so clumsy or as obvious as Prim.

By early evening all the preparations for his trip were made and he was ready to set off in the morning. Ross closed a ledger decisively and stood. He stretched and wandered to the open window of his study, in search of some air, but was disappointed. Even now, at well past six in the evening, the heat was ridiculous. He could not remember a time when the beginning of June had been quite so hot.

Dog yawned and rose from his usual spot under Ross's desk, and toddled over to keep him company at the window. Idly he gave his ears a scratch, at which the dog sighed and promptly rolled over onto his back, so that Ross could tickle his mangy belly.

'What do you think of your new home, boy?' he asked. 'It's a bit grand for the likes of you and me, isn't it? Us low-born mongrels are not used to all this luxury, are we? But we shall bear it.'

Dog's eyes rolled back into his head in ecstasy and Ross allowed himself a moment of indulgent satisfaction. Then he spotted a sudden movement in his peripheral vision that made him turn his head.

Skirting the edge of the lawn, clutching a large basket, was Prim. He slunk back to the side of the window so that she would not see him and watched her for several seconds. She was certainly in a hurry, and kept glancing furtively over her shoulder as if she was up to no good—which, he now realised, she probably was. When she darted on to the little path that he now knew led towards the cemetery he decided on a whim to follow her, certain that he was a better spy that she was.

He hoisted himself onto the window frame and the blasted stray danced excitedly at his feet. 'Not you, Dog,' he said firmly. 'You are not coming. You will give the game away, for sure.'

He secured the window, to prevent the animal from following, and dashed across the lawns. As he had before, he kept to the trees, but she did not stop at the cemetery. Instead she plunged further still into the parkland, crossing the overgrown meadow and disappearing into another copse of trees further ahead.

Ross had to wait until he'd lost sight of her before he jogged across the meadow, and for several minutes he struggled to locate her. Just as he was about to give up and head back to the house the trees thinned and he saw her again. He had never been to this part of the grounds, and was surprised to find a large natural pond surrounded by colourful bulrushes and weeping willows. How had she discovered this secret little place?

Prim sat underneath one of the willows, rifling through her basket.

Ross edged around the water as best he could without exposing himself and hovered behind a dense bush, feeling a bit of an idiot. The woman had clearly come to enjoy the early evening weather—not to have an illicit assignation, as he had allowed his wild imagination to suggest.

She was leaning back, her pretty face bathed in sunlight, with her weight braced upon her hands. Her boots sat next to her and he watched her wiggle her bare pink toes and sigh. She had well-turned ankles, he thought admiringly, and probably had a lovely pair of legs under the shapeless brown skirts that covered them.

Slowly she sat upright again, and her hands

went to the ties at the back of her dress. In no time at all she had undone it, and had shimmied out of the sleeves before standing up. Frozen on the spot, and feeling a trifle guilty for watching such a private moment, Ross stared mesmerised as she stood in only her shift. The thin material was almost translucent in the hazy sunshine, so he could clearly see the gentle curves and contours of her body beneath as she stood in profile.

When her hands went to the ribbons that closed the bodice of her shift a gentleman would have looked away. Fortunately, having been born and raised in the London slum of Whitechapel, Ross reasoned that he was as far away from being a gentleman as it was possible to be, so such expectations excluded him.

His throat went dry and his eyes devoured her as she worked the ribbons loose and then turned her back to him. She eased the cotton straps from her shoulders and let the garment slither to the ground, giving him the wonderful sight of her gracefully arched back and a peach-shaped bare bottom. Two delightful dimples graced the top of each cheek, and she really did have lovely legs.

Ross grinned. He really could not believe his luck. Miss Prim was not half as proper as she made out. Because currently she stood as naked as the day she was born in broad daylight.

He willed her to turn around, so that he could get a proper look, but she did not. Instead she began to walk into the inviting water, and did not stop until she was immersed right up to her armpits. Then she swam out of sight for a few minutes, leaving Ross sweating in anticipation of her return and feeling as eager as a schoolboy.

It did not occur to him *not* to wait. At some point she would have to retrace her steps and retrieve her clothes, and his patience would be rewarded with the sight of her elusive bare breasts upon her return. That was certainly something worth hanging around in the heat for.

Ross made himself comfortable on a sturdy-looking tree root that lay conveniently close by and kept watch through the branches. For a moment or two he considered the idea of joining her in the water and then hastily discarded it. If she saw him he would *have* to be gentlemanly—although he was sure he could convince her that he had innocently come for a swim and accidentally stumbled across her. Good manners dictated that he would have to avert his gaze and allow her to cover herself.

By staying hidden he could gawp openly and she would be none the wiser. That would be much better all round—especially as she had reprimanded him for treating her like a 'dalliance'.

If he could not dally he could at least look, he reasoned selfishly. He was only human, after all.

Prim came back into view a few minutes later and then dived under the water. When she emerged a heavy lock of her wet hair fell from its pins and trailed over one shoulder as she started to walk slowly up the low bank. Ross inhaled and held his breath, keen not to make a single sound that might alert her to his presence. Unfortunately at the crucial moment the blasted woman doffed her hat to propriety and wrapped her arms around her interesting bits, denying him the opportunity of finally seeing them. The air escaped in a whoosh, nonetheless, as she turned and gave him another glorious view of her bottom.

She had certainly kept a lush figure hidden under all that brown serge—Ross was as hard as iron and in a state of aroused discomfort. For a brief moment he felt guilty at this intrusion into her privacy. Then he remembered the fact that she was blatantly intruding into his with her spying—if indeed she *was* a spy—and the guilt lifted slightly.

Prim scurried to the spot where she had left her clothes and pulled a towel out of her basket. She sat with her back to him once again. As if to torture him further, she subjected him to several painful minutes when he had to endure the sight of her thoroughly drying every single inch of her soft, creamy skin, before unpinning her wet hair.

Like a siren, she wrung out the long, curling ponytail, then spread the towel on the ground and sat gloriously naked upon it. Unaware of her audience, she obviously wanted the remnants of the sunshine to dry her body, so made absolutely no effort to cover herself. He caught a glimpse of the side of one of her breasts. It jiggled a little as she pulled a hairbrush out of her basket, which she then proceeded to draw slowly through her hair.

He stifled a groan. Who could have known that Prim was, in actuality, a temptress? Ross could not remember ever being so aroused in his entire life—and by the mere sight of a bare back and bottom and all that perfect alabaster skin.

When she finally dropped the brush and pulled on her shift ten minutes later he felt bereft. Then she twisted her lush hair into a savage knot and pinned it ruthlessly at the nape of her neck. She rolled on her stockings, laced her boots, and stepped into her ugly brown dress last of all.

Ross made no attempt to follow her when she eventually set off. Frankly, he did not care where she was going or who she was going to see. If she was about to pass all his secrets to the East India Company she could do so unhindered, as far as he was concerned. It was not as if he was physically capable of following her. He was still as hard as iron and positively dripping in sweat.

Once the coast was clear he exploded out of the trees, ripped off his own clothes and stalked towards the pond. Cold water had never looked so appealing. Or been as necessary.

Chapter Eleven

Hannah tapped her chin thoughtfully. This letter was slightly different from every one she had read before, and hinted at something that might prove useful. It was short and to the point and had been written by Viscount Tremley.

She remembered him from her brief time as a debutante as a handsome fellow with a dashing smile. They had danced once or twice at various balls almost a decade ago—it had been such a long time since she had last danced that it felt like a complete lifetime. There was no point in churning up that unhappy memory now, though. It would change nothing. She would never be invited to another ball.

She had a vague recollection that Tremley had been involved in some sort of scandal involving money—much as her foolish brother had been—but he had not been seen in society for a couple of years. For a little while the newspapers had been filled with stories of his financial disgrace. Hannah could not remember the exact cause of his downfall, but seemed to have a vague recollection that gambling debts had been instrumental in his reduced circumstances.

The letter alluded to this. Tremley thanked Jameson for his patience in repaying his debt, and assured him that he would visit soon to *'pay off my marker in full'*. Hannah had a basic understanding of what a marker was, and could only assume that Ross Jameson had taken Tremley's during a card game as collateral—in much the same way as he had taken the deeds to Barchester Hall. Like her brother, Tremley had been left ruined. But Jameson had clearly profited. The man made money the way King Midas made gold.

Carefully, she dripped a fresh blob of wax under the disc and resealed the letter. Now she had evidence that at least two men had been shockingly misused by Jameson. Unlike her brother, however, Tremley was still very much alive. Perhaps he might be willing to share some information with her? In the meantime she needed to find his gambling marker. It might be tangible proof of deception that could be used as evidence in court.

After weeks of searching she had still found nothing that would get her home back apart from this one letter. What if the letter was actual proof that he was exerting undue pressure on silly men who were hell-bent on losing their fortunes? If it was, could she really hand him over to the authorities now that she knew him?

Just the thought of it left a bitter taste in her mouth. Hannah had already abandoned her belief that Jameson was responsible for her brother's suicide. He had not killed her brother, nor truly been the cause of his ruin. George had managed that all by himself. Probably Tremley had as well. All Jameson had done was take advantage of the situation and see it as a chance to make money—something that by his own admission he was not ashamed of doing. And why should he be? He had dragged himself up from nothing, built a successful business, and he provided decent employment for numerous people—herself included.

He was a kind and generous employer. Barchester Hall had felt empty without him this last week. If the truth be told, *she* also felt a little empty without his teasing presence.

In his absence, the renovations in the morning room, hallway and study had all been finished, and she was inordinately pleased with the way they had turned out. He had entrusted the task to her, and she was eager to see his reaction to the changes. Especially in his study. She was particularly proud of the bright, airy and practical space she had created for him there.

As he had complained that the room was dingy, she had instructed the decorators to cover the top two thirds of dark panelling with a muted cream colour. Only the lower panels remained as the natural dark wood. Rather cleverly, she had set the carpenters to making a bank of cupboards along one wall that appeared to all intents and purposes to blend into the panels as if they had always been there. This gave him a long surface to spread things out on, and storage to move his many documents into. The large leather Chesterfield and matching wingback chair she had found were now arranged around a small table near the window, so that he could read whilst looking out onto the gardens, and the heavy oak desk was now closer to the other window, so that he would have plenty of natural light while he worked.

There was nothing dingy about the room now. Even the ugly Runcorn family portraits had been consigned to the attic. It had been quite therapeutic to banish her brother's smug face to that dull, forgotten place to rot. It some small way it had felt a little like revenge.

Hannah glanced back to the potentially damning letter in her hand. It was odd that she did not feel the same little thrill at finding her first piece of evidence against her employer as she had on exiling George's likeness to the loft. If she was ever going to expose him then she needed to harden her heart and double her efforts, rather than allow herself to be waylaid by renovations and wayward thoughts as she had been all week.

The trouble was, Hannah had too many things cluttering her mind. For a start, a week on and she was still mulling over that kiss. Her head might well be warning her to resist his charms, but her body—and perhaps a tiny forgotten piece of her heart—kept urging her to go for it. And that one single kiss had apparently scrambled her wits to such an extent that she had started dreaming about it. More than once she had relived the experience in her sleep—except in her dreams she had not pushed him away and fled. In her dreams things had gone much further, and she'd woken feeling restless and agitated, with her body craving things she had not realised she needed.

One particular dream had been most unsettling. It had started innocuously enough, with images of Barchester Hall pictured in her mind's eye. Every room had been finished and the gardens had been filled with colourful flowerbeds stuffed with beautiful fat blooms. Hannah had been sitting on the lawn, enjoying the peace of it all—and then the garden had been filled with childish laughter. Two chubby green-eyed cherubs with dark hair and mischievous grins had raced across the manicured lawns, with Dog yapping at their feet, while Hannah had been sitting with a man, drinking tea and laughing at the children.

In her dream she had not seen his face, but he had called her Prim and the sound of his voice had made her insides melt and warmed her heart. And then she'd woken up, lectured herself on how silly and ridiculous dreams could be, and tried to convince herself that it did not matter. But it did. His warning that she would die alone had resonated, and now she found that she could not stop yearning for more than just a home of her own.

Irritated at her odd, melancholy mood, Hannah sighed. This was most unlike her. She was allowing silly thoughts and emotions to cloud her purpose. If she was going to get her home back she needed to concentrate on exposing Jameson, the sooner the better, not on yearning for things that she could not have.

Filled with a new sense of purpose, Hannah

marched into the hallway and dropped Tremley's letter on the mounting pile of post on the tray. With her despicable employer gone to Portsmouth, followed by a quick trip to see his family in Kent, there was no better time to search through another locked chest. She headed to his study and closed the door behind her, then quickly removed a hairpin from the knot at the back of her head and twisted it into the shape that she now knew worked best. A few clicks and turns later and another of his chests was opened for her scrutiny.

Hannah had probably already worked her way through half of them and found nothing. This current chest held large rolled documents tied with ribbon. She picked up the first one, undid the bow, and opened it out on the floor. The unravelled parchment showed a meticulous plan of a sailing ship. She had begun to roll the thing back up when she heard Reggie call her from another part of the ground floor.

'Miss Prim!' he bellowed. 'I can see Ross's carriage coming down the driveway.'

Hannah panicked and hastily stuffed the untied plan back into the chest and closed the lid.

Then she realised the strangest thing.

She was actually looking forward to seeing him.

All the signs were there. Her heart was beating a little too rapidly and she had excited butter-flies fluttering in her tummy, not to mention the overwhelming urge to primp a little in front of the mirror to check that she looked pretty enough to greet him.

She sat back on her heels and absorbed this new development. Was that why he plagued her dreams every night? With a brisk shake of her head she dismissed the thought. In this heat it was a wonder that she managed to enjoy *any* un-disturbed sleep. Hannah had never known a sum-mer quite so hot—and besides, she had long ago sworn off men. Every single one she'd known had let her down, one way or another, and she would certainly never be foolish enough to offer her heart to one—especially Ross Jameson.

She was out of sorts. That was all. And just because she was not interested in *any* form of ro-mantic attachment, it did not mean she was dead, either. It was only natural that her mind should occasionally wander in that direction. Jameson had said lust was simply an animal instinct, much as hunger was. At the time she had not under-stood what he meant, but now she did. With no other suitable man to fantasise over, it was per-fectly reasonable that her mind should latch onto him. His was merely the face that her brain had attached to her lustful dreams—whether those dreams involved kissing or darling little green-eyed babies—it certainly did not mean anything more than that.

Equilibrium restored, Hannah smoothed down her dress and hurried out of the study, ready to greet him. By the time the glossy black coach had pulled up at the front door she had pasted a respectful smile on her face.

Jameson's dark head appeared the moment the horses came to a stop. 'Hello, Prim,' he said.

And her insides melted.

It was only then that she realised she might just be in a bit of trouble.

Prim stood quietly, looking as if butter would not melt in her sinful mouth, and he could not resist riling her just a tiny bit. 'Did you miss me?' As he'd expected, her upturned lips flattened, and then pursed in consternation. 'I can see that you did, as your mouth is already puckered for a kiss.'

That did it. She huffed and spun on her heel, and then he was treated to the sight of her swaying bottom retreating into the house at speed.

'She ain't never going like you if you keep treating her like that,' Reggie chastised. 'She's a *nice* girl.'

Ross held his tongue. His trip away had been most enlightening. He now knew for a fact that all her references were patently forged. There was no Nair House. Nor was there any record of a Hannah Preston within ten miles of where she had claimed to be for all those years.

Of course that anomaly might well be easily explained because she had lied to get the job in the first place, so it stood to reason that her references would be fake. It did not mean that she was a spy for the East India Company.

However, Carstairs had made a valid point. Until they could be certain that she *wasn't* a spy they had to err on the side of caution and keep a close eye on her. A spy in their midst would leave the business vulnerable. The East India Company might benefit from knowing the names of their suppliers and the prices they bought things for. They could make things extremely difficult for them if they wanted to.

He was not prepared to let his libido undermine that. If he understood exactly what was going on he could control it—and perhaps benefit in the long run.

Reggie gave him a pitying look as they wandered back inside. 'You just don't know her like I do. Perhaps you need to make a bit more effort to soften her up?'

Now, that *was* an intriguing thought. He would quite enjoy softening the woman up. Even after he had uncovered more of her deceptions he still had not been able to stop thinking about her this past week. Granted, in most of those thoughts she was naked and floating in the pond, or he was wondering if she was indeed not quite what she seemed.

He had never been so flummoxed by a woman in his life. Prim was hot and cold. Fire and ice. Thoughtful and disapproving. Completely competent whilst perhaps being disingenuous and threatening everything he had built. She was maddening and addictive all at the same time. He did not understand her at all—and nor did he understand why he wanted to.

Usually Ross was able to compartmentalise the women in his life. There were three distinct categories: those he had a responsibility to care for, the ones he wanted to bed, and the ones he had no interest in bedding. At the moment he could not stuff Prim into any of them. She was intrinsic to his household because she was making the old ruin a home for him, so in that respect he was coming to care for her. Sort of. But he definitely wanted to bed her as well.

His dreams ever since that night in his bedchamber had been filled with her soft sighs as he kissed her—both her mouth and all those intriguing naked bits, the image of which was now apparently seared onto his brain for ever. Not that he was complaining. Some memories were worth keeping. However, he was also duty-bound *not* to bed her, because she was an excellent house-keeper and deserved more than being a passing dalliance—a fact that she herself had reminded him of—and he was certainly not in a position to offer anything more. Not yet at least.

So pursuing the attraction properly made him feel guilty. And there was also the slight prospect that she might be a spy.

Ross was so confused it took him several seconds to realise that his study was barely recognisable. And perfect. How typical of Prim to get it exactly right. At times she seemed to know what he wanted better than he did himself—as if she could read his mind.

His old trunks were stacked against one wall, no doubt waiting for him to unpack and organise as he wished. If the sun had not been streaming through the window he would not have noticed the tiny piece of metal wire protruding out of one of the locks on a chest. But it glinted slightly so Ross walked towards it. It looked like… Was that a hairpin?

On closer inspection, he saw it *was* a hairpin—which meant that somebody was going through his blasted business papers! He could still smell the vaguest hint of her perfume, rose tinged with jasmine, so he knew she had been in here. Prim always smelled of flowers. The blasted aroma had haunted his dreams for a week.

He muttered a few coarse words under his breath, but left the hairpin exactly where it was. 'Reggie—can you get Prim for me? I have to thank her for the splendid job she has done in here.'

'I knew you would,' Reggie replied cheerfully as he stomped off to do as he'd been bade.

'And tell her to bring in some tea!' he shouted to the man's back. 'I'm parched.'

A few minutes later the object of his musings appeared in the open doorway, followed by a young maid carrying a tea tray laden with cakes.

'You wanted to see me, sir?' she asked politely, and he smiled and gestured for her to come and sit with him.

She chose the wingback chair and perched on the end of the seat while the maid arranged the tray on the little table next to them, then she shooed the maid away and started to pour herself. He found himself smiling as Prim fussed over his tea, making small talk about his trip. She knew exactly how he liked it—two sugars and lots of milk. As always, his favourite pastries were on the tray. He had missed her thoughtful little touches this past week. He would miss them dreadfully if she had to leave.

But there was no point beating around the bush. If she was a spy then she had to go—no matter how much that fact bothered him. He and Carstairs had agreed that the quickest way to find out if she was up to anything was to give her the opportunity to get caught by putting temptation in her way.

'I have had an idea for the upstairs bedchambers, Prim. I thought that the beds and windows would look good covered in silk. To that end, I should like you to accompany me to my warehouse tomorrow and select some. You have such a good eye.'

It was time to see if the East India Company was up to no good. If Prim was a spy, then he would ignore his noble feelings of guilt and use her shamelessly to his own advantage until he sent her packing. At least he would be the one in control, and he would lead the East India Company a merry dance.

Chapter Twelve

Ignoring her better judgement, Hannah had not been able to bring herself to put on her serviceable brown work dress that morning. For a start, the sun was already heating the air and it was barely past seven. She did not want to boil in the close confines of Jameson's fancy carriage. Secondly, for once she wanted to look nice. She was going to London, albeit briefly, and in London there were certain standards—even for a trip to a warehouse by the docks.

The sprigged blue muslin, although several years old, was a particular favourite of hers. It was light enough to withstand the summer heat and just smart enough that she would not feel like a pauper. She certainly had not put on a pretty dress for *him*.

Her initial nervousness at his unexpected request had quickly evaporated. This visit was an opportunity to find out more about his business dealings and might well provide her with something useful to use against him. She had just one dubious letter so far, after over a month of diligent searching, and that was hardly going to get her the hall back.

Besides, she had been so pathetically grateful to see him yesterday that it had got her worried. He was obviously manipulating her with his deadly charm—she just had to find the wherewithal to continue to resist. She was now resolved to double her efforts to expose him. The sooner the better.

Reggie called her to say that the carriage was waiting outside. 'Don't you look pretty?' he exclaimed as he looked her up and down. 'If Ross has half a brain he could do a lot worse than you. I think you make a fine pair.'

Hannah stopped fastening the ribbons on her bonnet and stared at him, flabbergasted. 'What a ridiculous thing to say, Reggie. Mr Jameson is my *employer*.' And a rogue and a scoundrel to boot.

'What's that got to do with anything?' the big man replied, confused. 'You're young, he's young, you're both single... You could do a lot worse than Ross, Prim. That's all I'm saying. You should give it some thought.'

Hannah turned to her friend and rolled her eyes in exasperation. 'Tell him, Cook, all the reasons why his suggestion is ridiculous.'

But Cook simply smiled. 'You certainly would make a handsome pair. It might also be the answer to all your problems.' The older woman gave her a pointed look and wiggled her grey eyebrows suggestively. 'I think Reggie is right. You should give it some thought.'

Irritated, Hannah snatched up her reticule and glared at the pair of them. 'You are both daft,' she muttered, even though in her dreams she clearly had been subconsciously giving it a great deal of thought. 'Whatever has got into the pair of you? Mr Jameson is a shameless flirt who is interested in every single female in possession of a pulse. You know that. Look at all the carousing he does in town. When I first met you, Reggie, he was entertaining his *mistress*, for pity's sake. The man is a shocking libertine. Lord only knows what scandalous things he gets up to— especially with the hours he keeps. Do you seriously expect me to believe that he shows *me* any particular regard? Even if he did,' she added for good measure, 'I certainly would not be interested in anybody who engages in such drunken debauchery.'

Reggie laughed at her. 'Drunken debauchery?

That *is* funny. For a start, that morning Francesca had turned up out of the blue and he was trying to get rid of her. I live with him, remember? And I can tell you he ain't had that much debauchery of late. As for the drunken bit—well, Ross don't even drink.'

He looked so convinced by his statement that she felt sorry for him. Poor Reggie really did lack brain cells if he believed that, so she patted him kindly. 'He most certainly does drink. I have experienced his behaviour under the influence of drink at least once.'

Cook eyed her with interest. 'Oh, yes? And what did he do?' she asked wickedly, and wiggled her stupid eyebrows again.

Hannah felt a blush stain her cheeks under the woman's scrutiny, and Cook grinned as soon as she saw it.

Reggie, thankfully, was oblivious to the undertones in the room and was still ready to fight for Jameson's honour. 'Ross don't drink, Prim. He never has. His dad was a drinker, and he put him off the stuff for life. When was the last time you had to refill all them fancy decanters that you pulled out of the attic and put around this house?'

That brought her up short—because the answer was *never*. She had ensured that each and every one was filled before he had arrived at

Barchester Hall and then locked away the rest of the alcohol in her cupboard. Nobody had ever asked her for the key. That did not mean he did not partake of the demon drink when in town, though…

'I have to go,' she muttered in exasperation. 'I do not have time to discuss all this nonsense now.'

Hannah hurried out of the kitchen and found Jameson waiting for her in the hallway. He made a great show of looking her up and down and whistled.

'You look pretty, Prim. I do wish you would burn that ugly brown dress. Shall we both do it later? I could get Reggie to build a bonfire and we could say a few respectful words before we toss it onto the pyre. *Dearly beloved, we are gathered here today to say goodbye to the shapeless sack that once swamped a beautiful housekeeper…*'

She smiled tightly and stalked towards the carriage. She really did *not* need his flirting after the comments she had just received in the kitchen.

Politely, he helped her up and she sat on the bench, facing forward out of habit. Ladies always faced front. She carefully undid the ribbons of her bonnet and placed it in her lap.

When he hoisted himself in he did not sit

opposite her, as a gentleman would have. Instead he dropped heavily on the bench next to her, stretched out his long legs and crossed one booted foot over the other. As an afterthought he leaned forward and shrugged out of his jacket and casually tossed it on the other bench before settling back again.

'It's so hot,' he muttered. 'Do you mind if we keep the windows open?'

'I suppose so,' she replied, wishing she had not spent such a long time dressing her hair. With the windows open it would be a disaster in less than ten minutes.

Reggie came huffing out of the front door and stuck his head into the carriage, beaming. 'I was right. You *do* make a pretty pair. Give it some thought, Prim.'

He tapped the side of his flattened nose as if he had just imparted some great secret. To make matters worse he then winked at her before he slammed the door shut and told the driver to get going. Hannah felt her face redden, but stared straight ahead regardless.

They set off, and had not even left the drive when he turned to her. 'Am I missing something?' he asked with a half-smile as his green eyes burned into hers with interest.

'Reggie thinks we should get married,' she announced, with as much dignity as she could muster under the circumstances. 'He has quite set his mind on it.' From his expression he thought the idea was as ridiculous as she did, so she smiled back. 'I have told him that it is a ridiculous notion—but you know Reggie.'

'Ah, yes, I do. When he gets an idea into that thick skull of his it is difficult to get him to drop it. I suppose that we should be grateful that his ideas are few and far between.'

'He means well, though. And he thinks the world of you.'

'You cannot blame him,' he said in mock seriousness. 'I am easy to love.'

A giggle escaped her lips. She had missed sparring with the rogue. 'And so modest. But poor Reggie has put you on such a high pedestal that he refuses to see any faults.'

'I have *faults*?' he asked incredulously. 'Do enlighten me?'

In for a penny, Hannah thought as she faced him. 'For one thing, he is convinced that you do not drink.'

She smiled a *we both know he's wrong* smile and he shrugged.

'He's right. I don't.'

Hannah raised her eyebrows at this obvious lie and fixed him with a disbelieving glare. 'We both know that is patently *not* true—' Then she coloured, unable to finish her sentence as thoughts of their kiss swirled in her mind again and reminded her that he was sitting just a few scant inches away in a confined and private carriage.

'If you are referring to the night that *you* kissed me, then I have to confess I was as sober as a judge. As always.'

He was staring straight ahead but his lips had curved into a satisfied smile. He was clearly enjoying teasing her.

'Excuse me, but as I recall *you* kissed *me*—and I could smell the brandy on you.'

Still facing ahead he peeked at her from the corners of his eyes. 'You accused me of being drunk. And, if I recall correctly, of whoring as well. In actual fact I had a headache. I get them when I spend too long reading. I thought that if I was going to be accused of a crime and be the recipient of such hurtful censure then I might as well do it. So I dabbed a little brandy on my neck, made myself look disreputable, and *then* I kissed you.'

He looked very pleased with himself indeed.

'If you were not drunk then why did you kiss me?' Her tone was a little high-pitched—but, really, he was being outrageous.

'Oh, Prim—that's easy. I kissed you because I wanted to.'

His green eyes darkened as he gazed back at her boldly. It was hypnotic, and she could not tear her own eyes away. At times she was certain he could see into her very soul, and knew that she would likely surrender without much of a fight if she allowed his lips to touch hers again.

His face was edging closer to hers. There was no mistaking his intent. He wanted to kiss her again. All at once she felt tempted and terrified at the same time. Tempted to let him, and to hell with the consequences, and terrified that if he did kiss her she would be lost. He had scrambled her wits. Again.

'Stop!' The word came out hoarsely and without much conviction.

'I don't want to stop,' he whispered, and grazed his fingers gently over her arm, making all her nerve-ending stand to attention in anticipation. 'I don't think you want me to stop either.'

His eyes dropped to her lips and she licked them involuntarily. A lazy smile curved his mouth as his eyes locked with hers again. He knew she was tempted.

Hannah scrambled upright. 'Mr Jameson, I have told you repeatedly not to flirt with me.'

'I can't help it.' He slowly raked his gaze over

the length of her body before his eyes settled hotly on hers. 'You are a very attractive woman, after all, and I find that I cannot stop thinking about you. You have consumed my thoughts and my dreams for the last week, Prim. I keep wondering what it would feel like to kiss you again.'

Hannah's jaw hung slack for a moment. She was both scandalised at his words and thrilled by the fact that his thoughts had mirrored hers, but he did not appear to be the slightest bit sorry.

'We have an hour to kill…if you want me to.'

If she had been anywhere but in a moving carriage she would have turned on her heel and marched away. Or, more likely, run away as fast as she could from the insistent yearnings he created within her heart and her body. That meant that the only recourse available to her was to stand up as best as she could and throw herself unceremoniously onto the opposite seat with a huff.

'Shall I take that as a no?' he asked in wide-eyed innocence, and she glared at him.

The man was incorrigible. She certainly did not have a response to his shocking suggestion yet—but when she did she was definitely going to give him a piece of her mind. Unfortunately her mind was still reeling with unrequited passion, need and confusion, so Hannah stared resolutely out of the window and watched the world fly by instead.

Typically, he decided to ignore the fact that she was ignoring him. 'You do realise,' he said conversationally, 'that the more prim and proper and outraged you become, the worse I behave? I cannot seem to help myself. It has always been the same. It is my one and only character flaw.'

She said nothing.

'I can tell by your silence that you agree with me, or you would be listing all my other flaws by now.'

'There are not enough hours in the day to list your flaws, sir,' she muttered, and watched him smirk triumphantly.

'And there she is! Prim and Proper is back with a vengeance. I was starting to miss her. For a moment or two there we were almost having a civil conversation.'

'It is impossible to have a civil conversation with you because you never take anything seriously and you take every opportunity to say or do outrageous things to me,' she muttered quietly, fully expecting him to spear her with another silly retort, or pin her with his smouldering gaze.

But he sighed, and then groaned. 'That is fair. If I promise not to flirt outrageously today, do you promise to make an effort to be less prickly?

After all, we shall be stuck in each other's company for hours.'

He had a valid point, so she conceded with as much dignity as she could muster. 'I think I can manage that.'

'What shall we talk about, then? And please don't say the weather.'

He sat forward on his seat with his wrists loosely resting on his knees. Hannah tried to think of safe and inert topics but came up blank. 'Perhaps you should tell me about your business interests,' she offered after a few moments. 'I still do not fully understand what you do. For example, what are you most involved in now?'

She had asked it so innocently he had to give her credit for her acting. Ross wondered how much to tell her, and decided he had nothing to hide just yet.

'My shipping company takes up most of my time at the moment. I have three ships already, and a business partner. His name is Captain John Carstairs—you will probably meet him today—and he oversees all the shipping and purchasing parts of the venture. I sell the cargo here, for the best price possible—mostly silk, but also spices, tea, and porcelain from Asia. It has been so profitable that we have just commissioned three new ships to be built from scratch.'

Her next question surprised him.

'Isn't it terribly expensive to build ships? Why did you not buy older ships? Surely second-hand ships would be cheaper and mean that you'd achieve greater profit?'

'In the short term you are right,' he agreed slowly. 'But competition is now fierce, and modern ships are much faster and hold more cargo, which means that they can do more journeys. More journeys means significantly more profit. These new ships will have paid for themselves in three years. By then I hope to have doubled the fleet again.'

Ross watched her carefully as she considered this, knowing that what he had just told her would be of great interest to the East India Company. If they were concerned about how he would undercut them with three ships then they would be scandalised to think about how much he would erode their monopoly with more. However, there was nothing in her reaction that hinted at this.

'Goodness! I had not thought about it like that. For investment purposes it does make sense to purchase an entirely new and modern fleet. It will give you an advantage over other companies in the future. It is no wonder so many gentlemen entrust you to invest their money for them. You obviously have a talent for it.'

She had clearly not realised that she had just let slip the fact that she had been going through his papers—because he had certainly never told her that he speculated on behalf of others. She really was the most useless spy.

Ross schooled his features into a nonchalant mask and ruthlessly buried his wounded feelings. 'They would not give me their money unless I made a healthy return,' he stated calmly, 'and I have purposely built up a good reputation for improving people's fortunes.'

Her eyes narrowed slightly, as if she doubted his word, and then she was all politeness again. 'Why have you purposely built a good reputation? How does that benefit you?'

Ross shrugged his shoulders, amused at her lack of business acumen. 'I believe I told you once that I make money? This is how I have been able to do it so quickly. I take a commission from the profits that my clients make. The more people who entrust me with money to invest, the greater the investment I am able to make. If I know that I can double my money somewhere, I will get a much bigger return from a thousand pounds than I will get from a hundred. It is simple mathematics. The profit is multiplied.'

She was concentrating on his words so intently that a tiny furrow had appeared between her wheat-coloured eyebrows. 'But surely there are times when there is no profit? What happens then? Do your investors get angry?'

Ross leaned a little closer and lowered his voice a little so that she could not move away. 'They go into it on the understanding that nothing is guaranteed—but I am very good at what I do. I rarely lose money from a speculation.'

She snorted derisively at that, and sat back on her seat. 'I doubt you are that infallible. Call it what you will, but "investment" and "speculation" are just fancy words for gambling. What you really mean is that you rely a great deal on luck, and so far you have been very lucky indeed.' There was a malicious gleam in her cornflower eyes that suggested she felt she had just summed him up perfectly.

'Luck has a minor role in it, that is true,' he conceded. 'But to be very successful with investments, speculations and gambling you need to have a great talent with numbers.'

'And you have such a talent?'

Ross wondered how much he should admit, and then plumped for the truth again. It was hardly a secret. 'I do, as a matter of fact. In the same way that being a great artist or a great musician requires you to have been born with a gift, I believe I was born with the ability to *think* in numbers and to remember them. It is quite logical, really. I see the patterns and can make fairly accurate predictions as a result. Of course I also have to keep a close eye on new ideas, prices and demand—but in reality it is all just mathematics.'

His words appeared to anger her, although he had no idea why.

After a few moments she tilted her pretty head to one side and speared him with a cold look. 'If what you say is true then that means you would have a distinct advantage in…let's say a card game, for instance.'

'There are only fifty-two cards—it is easy to keep track of them.'

'Then surely it is morally wrong for you to enter into a game with a gentleman who does *not* possess your particular talent?' She appeared to be positively outraged and leaned forward again, her face filled with challenge.

'I am not a cheat, Prim, if that is what you are accusing me of. I keep track of the cards, and I can speculate on what my opponent holds in his hand, but I have no control over how he plays it. Strategy is just as important in most card games. That is why I never play hazard. With dice there are no patterns—and definitely no strategy. It is a game of pure chance.'

'You only indulge in gambling that brings you a profit!' she blurted out. 'Isn't that how you stole Barchester Hall?'

Hannah regretted the words as soon as they came out of her mouth.

'I am sorry, sir. Sometimes I say things that I do not mean.'

'Oh, I think you meant it, Prim,' he replied curtly, 'So now we can add "cheat" and "thief" to the list of character traits that you attribute to me. They go quite nicely with "drunkard", "libertine" and "debaucher". It's a wonder you agreed to sit in the same carriage as me. You should write for the newspapers, Prim. They paint me as quite the scandalous fellow as well.'

Hannah could not think of a response straight away, and was already swamped with guilt for saying what she had, but he did not appear to expect one. Instead he leaned back against the bench, rested his head on the leather and closed his eyes.

Whether or not he actually slept she could not say. But he remained like that for the rest of the journey.

Chapter Thirteen

When they arrived at the warehouse he left her to her own devices. He pointed vaguely in the direction she needed to go and instructed a burly-looking man to carry whatever she selected to the carriage and then he disappeared into an office at the back of the huge building without another word.

Regardless of the fact that he was probably a cheating, thieving libertine, Hannah felt strangely guilty at having so bluntly let him know how much those things disgusted her. His feelings were hurt. She knew that with a strange certainty.

She had seen it briefly flicker on his face when she had issued the barb. First hurt, then anger and disappointment had shimmered in his green eyes, as if he had expected more of her. But still he had refused to deny her accusation—nor confirm it, she was forced to note. He had merely extricated himself from further discussion and let her think exactly what she pleased—as if it did not matter to him one way or the other what she thought of him.

But she now knew that it did—and it bothered her that she had made him feel that way.

With less enthusiasm than she had expected, Hannah sorted through the hundreds of bolts of fine silk that were stacked on the far side of the warehouse.

She had not expected the building to be quite so large; the sheer size of it and the amount of material and boxes within it were astonishing. Neither was the fabric or the porcelain gaudy. Jameson had more taste than she'd given him credit for. Why she had expected less, when he was so outrageously successful, she could not say. Except that she had hoped he lacked such genteel instincts. He was easier to cope with if she could continue to label him a vulgar, uneducated and uncultured social climber.

She ran her fingers lightly over a bolt of the palest eggshell-blue fabric with delicate navy and white embroidered flowers. It would look perfect in one of the bedrooms.

'Hello, there!'

The arrival of a very handsome blond gentleman startled her, and she blinked at him in confusion.

'I am sorry—I can see I have given you quite a fright. Let me start again. Hello, I am Captain John Carstairs, co-owner of this wonderful warehouse, and you must be Miss Hannah Preston—Ross's housekeeper?'

He held out his hand and she politely shook it.

Captain Carstairs was nothing like she had envisaged either. He was not coarse or common, as she had imagined a merchant seaman would be, and judging by his cultured accent he was from the ranks of the aristocracy.

'Yes, I am Miss Preston. I am pleased to make your acquaintance, sir.'

'I did ask Ross to come out and make the introductions properly, but something has put him in a foul temper and he is refusing to tear himself away from the ship's manifest.'

Captain Carstairs had such an open and friendly smile that she instantly felt comfortable in his presence. 'I am afraid that I might be the cause of his ill mood, Captain Carstairs. I spoke out of turn to him and he has every right to be angry with me.'

'Really?' The captain could not hide his curiosity. 'What on earth did you say? He is not usually one for sulking.'

Hannah felt the knot of guilt tighten and sighed. 'I might have inadvertently accused him of cheating and stealing a house in a card game.' Saying it out loud made her feel even worse, although she knew it to be partly true anyway.

Carstairs was visibly surprised, and then chuckled. 'Well, I suppose that would do it. Although it is quite unfounded. I was with him that night and he most certainly did not cheat. Ross won that house fair and square. He even approached the family afterwards and offered to return it to them, but they did not want the responsibility of such a rundown estate. So he definitely did not steal it either. He would never do something like that.'

Hannah fought to stay calm at this blatantly false revelation. How dared he claim to have offered the house back to the family? She could state with absolute certainty that nobody had ever approached her about Barchester Hall after her brother's death. However, she supposed such a lie legitimised his right to live in the house, so it should not surprise her.

'I am sure you are right Captain Carstairs. I will apologise to Mr Jameson for my outburst. He had just explained to me that he has a particular talent when it comes to numbers and I put two and two together. It was unfair of me to make such an outrageous assumption.'

Hannah did her best to look contrite, and must have done a reasonable job because Carstairs grinned.

'I am sure if you apologise to him he will get over it quickly enough. Allow me to give you a tour of the premises.'

He held out his arm politely and she took it.

Ross gave the ship's manifest a cursory scan but his heart was not in it. He was still smarting from Prim's hurtful accusation and he could not shake the thought that he had expected better from her. Yes, she was dishonest, and had probably been planted in his house by the East India Company, but she had also lived under his roof for over a month and seen first-hand the kind of man that he was.

At times, he had even thought there was something akin to friendship blossoming between them. That was what had initially hurt his feelings. Now he was just angry with her. Had it not been for the fact that John wanted to keep a close eye on her, he would have stopped the coach there and then, ordered her out and left her unceremoniously on the side of the road. At least he would like to think he would have done. He was not a soft touch, after all.

But why did the blasted woman continue to think ill of him when he had given her no cause to? Did she actually think him capable of those things?

The sad fact was that it was all so unfair. Thanks largely to the newspapers, he now had quite a dastardly reputation that was ill-deserved and so far from the truth that it beggared belief. She should have seen beyond that—but she hadn't. People did believe all the rot that was written about him. And that was the problem, he supposed, if his own staff believed it. Not all of them, he rationalised, just Prim. Anybody would think that he had personally wronged her, the way she carried on. Or wronged her real employers.

John sauntered into the office and sat opposite him. After propping his crossed legs on the desk he regarded Ross levelly across its scarred surface. 'I know her,' he stated flatly, causing Ross to sit up straighter in his seat.

'Who the hell is she, then? *Is* she from the Company?'

John shrugged and shook his head. 'That's the problem. I am not sure how I know her or where I have seen her—but I recognised her lovely face the moment I clapped eyes on her. It has been a long time since I worked for the East India Company—I might have seen her there.'

Ross stood and paced the tiny office in agitation. 'That is not much use, then, is it? If you cannot place the blasted woman then we are still fumbling around in the dark. I will not accept a Trojan horse and put in jeopardy everything I have worked for. I have a good mind just to give *Miss Preston* her marching orders and to hell with it.'

He ran a hand through his black hair in frustration. John let him rant and pace until the urge to rant and pace began to pass.

'We cannot do that, and you know it. Not until we know what she is up to. The East India Company are capable of resorting to all sorts of dirty tactics—if they discover our supply chain they may well offer a better price just to put us out of business. But do not worry. I have already started to soften her up with my charm.' John grinned wolfishly. 'It is only a matter of time before she tells me all her secrets.'

Ross felt a surge of jealousy. If anybody was going to soften Prim, with her delectable naked bottom, it was going to be him. 'No need,' he stated firmly. 'I am already working on her myself.'

'Do I detect the merest hint of jealousy? Have you developed a bit of a *tendre* for your lovely young housekeeper?'

Ross resumed his pacing. 'Hardly. But as it is *my* house that she is ensconced in, if anybody deserves the pleasure of softening Miss Prim and Proper then it is me. The woman irritates me intensely. Where is she now?'

'I left her on her own and have instructed all the men to keep a close eye on her. They will report back if she wanders anywhere she shouldn't or asks any pertinent questions.'

Ross grunted belligerently. In response, John smirked and picked up a letter-opener from the desk to toy with. 'She does appear to have put you in a bit of a mood—although I dare say accusing you of cheating in order to steal Barchester Hall would probably put me in a bit of a mood too. If it is any consolation, though, she does feel bad about that. Even more so now that I have put her straight on the subject—although why you never even attempt to defend yourself against such slander is beyond me.'

Ross huffed, but continued to pace. 'People will think what they want to regardless. I do not need to justify myself to them.'

He was done with all that. It was much easier to walk away from it than show people how much their disgust wounded him. He would not be pathetic and court good opinions. He would never give anyone that power over him.

'Perhaps not,' his friend mused, tossing the letter-opener back to the desk, 'But when you continually fail to defend yourself with the truth, as you have done for so many years, you give them the opportunity to make even worse assumptions about your character. The very fact that you allow the newspapers to print all that drivel unchecked gives the blighters free rein to write whatever they want to. I know that bothers you.'

'My dastardly reputation benefits us more than it hinders, John. We get left alone.'

Carstairs did not argue. 'I just wish I could remember who she is. Perhaps it will come back to me if I spend more time with her. Do you have any objections if I come back with you today?'

'You would be doing me a favour. I do not relish the prospect of another hour alone with her in the carriage. I thought I might die of frostbite on the way here.'

'Shall I go and chivvy Miss Prim, then?' John asked with a wicked gleam in his eyes, 'Seeing as she likes me much more than she does you.'

Ross pinned him with his stare. 'Thank you, but no. I shall do it.'

Chapter Fourteen

Hannah wandered to the carriage and stood waiting nervously next to it. At some point she was going to have to apologise to Jameson for her outburst. He had not stolen Barchester Hall—of that she was quite sure. Her stupid brother had practically handed it to him on a plate, and if Ross Jameson had not been the lucky beneficiary that night then somebody else certainly would have been. That did not mean she did not want it back, however, it just meant she was less angry with Jameson than she had been.

After a full five minutes of waiting for him to arrive, she decided to grab the bull by the horns and go and find him herself. She turned back into the warehouse and headed towards the door of the back office she had seen him disappear into. She turned a corner and slammed straight into the hard wall of his chest.

'Hello, Prim,' he said flatly. 'Are you having a good nose around?'

Sensing that he was still rightly annoyed at her, she steeled herself for the humiliation of having to apologise. 'I was looking for you, actually. I feel terrible about what I said in the carriage. I overstepped the mark and I am truly sorry for it. It is not my place to criticise you.'

He assessed her for a moment coldly before he pinned her with his mossy gaze. 'That is a very pretty apology, Prim, but I am not sure that it cuts to the chase. You say that you are sorry for the words, and that it is not your place to criticise, but you still have not acknowledged whether or not you believe me to be a cheating thief.'

This cold, stiff man was somebody she did not recognise and it made her uncomfortable. 'I believe that the Earl of Runcorn was an idiot to gamble away his home,' she finally admitted. 'It was hardly your fault that he did so. So to answer your question, no—I do not believe you to be a thief. I cannot honestly say what to make of you sometimes, but I am certain that you did not go into that card game with the express intention of cheating a man out of his property.'

After an interminable age he finally nodded curtly. 'Then I will accept your apology on this occasion, Prim.'

His unspoken message was implicit in his eyes: this was a final warning about her behaviour towards him and he would not tolerate it again.

'Thank you. I will do my best not to make unfounded judgements in the future. I truly am sorry.' He appeared unmoved by her apology so she tried to change the subject. 'I have taken the liberty of having the silk loaded onto the coach,' she offered quietly. 'It is ready to leave as soon as you are, sir.'

'Then I shall inform Captain Carstairs of that fact. He will be accompanying us back to Barchester Hall once we have collected his things from his lodgings.'

This was the first time he had ever spoken to her like a servant and she found herself bobbing slightly in acknowledgement. Then he turned on his heel and went to find him, leaving Hannah alone with her guilt and confusion.

Fortunately the two men discussed business for much of the journey home, so Hannah passed the time by watching the scenery fly past the carriage window. Her wool-gathering was interrupted by Captain Carstairs.

'What do you think of that, Miss Preston?'

Hannah blinked at him dumbly. 'I am sorry—

I was not listening. Would you mind repeating the question?'

Carstairs shared a brief look with Jameson and then smiled. 'I asked what you thought about the concept of free trade, Miss Preston. Are you for or against it?'

She considered the odd question for a moment. 'I have to confess, Captain Carstairs, that to answer your question I would need some clarity on what the term "free trade" actually means.'

Jameson sighed in exasperation. 'Free trade would mean that goods could be imported and exported around the world without government interference and tariffs. For example, at the moment government-backed companies like the East India Company have a monopoly over certain trade routes. That means they can fix prices and have the backing of Parliament to prevent other companies from trading in the same places.'

'If they fix prices, does that mean they can charge a higher price for those goods than is fair?'

Both men nodded vigorously at her question. 'And they are able to significantly line their pockets in the process. Sometimes the price of tea or silk is doubled or tripled by the time it goes on to the English market,' Captain Carstairs clarified.

'Well, in that case I am *for* the concept of free trade. I do not see why I should be forced to pay double or triple what something is worth just because I do not have a choice in the matter.'

Her answer seemed to please them, because they shared a knowing smile and then silence fell for a few minutes.

'How do you like Barchester Hall?' Captain Carstairs asked her, and she smiled in response. At least this was a topic she was knowledgeable on.

'I think the house is beautiful. And once all the renovations are finished it will be as lovely on the inside as it is on the outside.'

'It was sadly neglected,' Jameson chimed in. 'I do not think it had seen a bit of paint in decades.'

'I cannot say I am surprised,' Carstairs added. 'Runcorn threw away his entire fortune at the gaming tables. I never liked that man.'

Hannah's nerves prickled at this casual talk of her brother but she remained resolutely silent.

'I cannot say I got to know him,' Jameson replied. 'Why didn't you like him?'

Captain Carstairs leant forward a little in his seat and a pained expression crossed his handsome face. 'He was reckless and quite pompous, as I recall—too full of his own inflated importance than he should have been. Nobody was fooled. We all knew that he was in debt up to his eyeballs.'

It was obvious that Captain Carstairs had moved amongst the ton, but Hannah could not place him at all. 'Did you move in the same social circles as the Earl of Runcorn? I thought that you were a sea captain, sir.' She tried to make her enquiry sound casual.

It was Jameson who laughed at her question.

'Once upon a time John, here, was one of them—then his father disinherited him and he had to get an honest job. Oh, look—we are coming up to Barchester Hall now.'

As they turned into the long driveway Jameson pointed out how dilapidated some of the grounds were and their shoddy state embarrassed her.

'I don't think the Earl of Runcorn did a single bit of maintenance to the old place for well over a decade. It's criminal, the way he left it to rack and ruin,' he said disparagingly.

Hannah refused to be annoyed at his words. He spoke nothing but the truth.

'By all accounts the whole family were a bad lot,' Captain Carstairs interjected, and Hannah experienced an ominous sense of foreboding.

'Were they?' The comment had piqued Jameson's interest and he was watching his friend intently. 'How so?'

'The sister had to leave society after an enormous scandal. It was all over the newspapers and all anyone could talk about for months.'

Jameson snorted. 'Really? All over the newspapers? They are not exactly famous for printing the truth, John.'

'In this case I am afraid they *were* telling the truth, old boy. I know because I was there the very night it all happened.'

The bile began to rise in Hannah's throat while her heartbeat leapt into a gallop. There was no escaping it, she realised. The whole sordid tale was about to be told again for entertainment.

Captain Carstairs sat forward with barely contained excitement. 'The lady in question—I forget her name now—was engaged to be married to Viscount Eldridge and was attending a ball with her betrothed. She had done rather well for herself—Eldridge is good ton, and well respected at parliament. We all assumed it was a love match, because it was widely believed that Eldridge had to marry an heiress and we all know Runcorn never had a pot to piss in.'

Carstairs stopped and chewed his bottom lip. 'I am sorry for my language, Miss Preston.'

Hannah managed to nod and wave the expletive away, but tears threatened to fall. Eldridge had never loved her. At the time she had believed he did—but he had only been after the impressive sum that her father had left her in trust. She had realised that long ago.

'Anyway,' Carstairs continued, 'they were only a week or so away from taking their vows when Eldridge discovered something terrible about the girl. I have no idea who told him, but it all came to a head at the ball. He was so angry he marched straight up to her, right in the middle of the ballroom, and called her a whore!'

'That was not a very gentlemanly thing to do.'

Jameson's brows were furrowed and Hannah stifled the urge to thank him. Nobody else had even considered that on that dreadful night.

'Agreed.' Carstairs nodded. 'But Eldridge was furious. He accused the girl of deceiving him—of claiming she was virtuous and pure when in actual fact she had had a string of lovers. He said that he had proof she was carrying her lover's child and was hoping to fob it off as his.'

Hannah's stomach roiled at the lie and she feared that her breakfast was about to make a sudden reappearance.

'Still, he could have had it out with her in private.'

Jameson appeared to be outraged at her fiancé's deplorable behaviour.

Again Carstairs nodded. 'I do agree, Ross. I felt for the poor girl. She looked to be genuinely mortified at Eldridge's words. She pleaded with him—told him that it was all a pack of lies—but he would have none of it. He called off the engagement in front of everyone. It must have been true, though,' he added as an afterthought. 'Because her brother simply stood by and watched the whole spectacle without once going to his sister's aid.'

Hannah had not realised that George had been close by. He had certainly never mentioned that. Fresh hurt tore through her and she stared out of the window to cover the fact that her eyes were swimming with angry tears.

'What sort of a man does not defend his own sister? Regardless of what she had done, Runcorn should have stepped in to help her. I dislike the man myself now.' Jameson folded his arms in annoyance. 'What happened afterwards?'

Carstairs shrugged. 'She disappeared from society completely. I once overheard Runcorn telling one of his cronies that she had run away with her lover to the continent. I presume she is still there.'

That betrayal cut like a knife. Hannah had

been banished to Yorkshire by her brother until, as he had put it, 'the dust settled'. She had never been allowed back and had not seen hide nor hair of her loving brother from that day forward either. George had completely washed his hands of her.

Fortunately he had left her the five thousand pounds inheritance, which she assumed came from her dowry. It had always rankled George that their father had entrusted it to the family solicitor rather than to him. It was a good job he had, because otherwise George would have spent that as well before his death.

The carriage began to slow down and eventually came to stop. Captain Carstairs jumped out and proffered his hand to help her down. Hannah bolted to her feet to escape but Jameson stopped her.

'Are you all right, Prim? You look a little ill.'

His kindness was almost her undoing, but she managed to hold her composure briefly. 'I am not a good traveller, sir,' she muttered without looking at him. If she saw his concern she knew she would cry.

His large hand came up and rested gently on her cheek. 'Are you sure?'

Why did the blackguard have to be so thoughtful and considerate?

Hannah nodded numbly. 'I just need to lie down for a bit,' she managed to say, and then promptly climbed down the steps.

She did not wait around. Instead, she fled to her bedchamber and slammed the door behind her. Only when she was completely alone did she allow the bitter tears of humiliation to fall.

Chapter Fifteen

Hannah licked her wounds in private for the rest of the afternoon, but by six the heat was oppressive, and she feared she would go mad if she kept on staring at the same four walls, so she washed her face and headed out for a walk to clear her mind.

Even after all these years the horrible events of that evening still felt raw. She had not realised that it still had the power to wound her quite so deeply. In Yorkshire, it had never been discussed, and she had been in such seclusion from anybody from society that to all intents and purposes the whole affair might not have happened at all. Hannah had been able to squirrel it away in a part of her brain that her thoughts seldom strayed into.

Today she had been broadsided by the past and had been left with no other option than to think about it again. She had been so besotted with Viscount Eldridge, and so deliriously happy to be getting married, that she had overlooked many of the man's faults. He had kissed her once or twice, and the experience had been pleasant enough, but she now knew that those kisses had lacked the passion and desire that Jameson had introduced her to. That had been both intoxicating and dangerous.

Hannah crossed the gardens quickly and plunged into the meadow beyond, ignoring the beauty of her surroundings because she was too caught up in memories. To this day she had no idea where Eldridge had heard about her supposed lovers. When they had arrived at the ball they'd been happy and smiling. Two hours later he had hated the very sight of her. He'd claimed that he had irrefutable proof of her many affairs, that his information came from the most unquestionable of sources, but Hannah could still not fathom who had despised her so much as to have spewed such a pack of obscene lies into her fiancé's ears.

Aside from Eldridge, no man had ever even so much as kissed her—let alone planted a baby in her belly. To hear him, though, she had lain with so many men that she was little better than a lightskirt. The accusations had been so ludicrous they would have been laughable had she not been standing in a ballroom surrounded by two hundred people.

She had tried to reason with him, but he had turned his back on her and walked away. She remembered the deafening silence in the ballroom. The musicians had stopped playing and the great and the good had gathered around, listening intently to the scandal she had created.

When it was over, she'd had to suffer the indignity of her so-called friends turning their backs on her as she'd stumbled out of the ballroom in a state of shocked hysteria. In the strange and sudden absence of her brother, her only companion on that long walk to complete ruination had been the loud, thumping sound of her own heartbeat ringing in her ears and the silent condemnation of her peers.

Bitter tears came afresh, which surprised her. She had not realised she had more to spill, but clearly she had. With resignation she sank down into the tall summer grass and buried her face on her knees.

'Is everything all right, Prim?'

His concerned deep voice shocked her. Hannah did her best to scrub away the tears before she answered, but there was really no disguising the fact that she had been crying for the better part of the afternoon. Her face must be a fright.

'Y-yes. I am f-fine,' she stuttered unconvincingly as she stared in the opposite direction. She could hear Dog panting at his feet.

'Well, you don't look fine. I have a talent for spotting these things.'

She felt him sit down in the grass next to her but he did not say anything further—which was just as well because Hannah could barely stifle the sobs trapped in her throat. When a fresh white handkerchief was gently pushed into her hand she lost the battle and bawled into it.

To his credit, he did not run away as most gentlemen would have. Neither did he offer inane platitudes and say *There, there*, as if she was a silly child. Instead she felt two strong arms come around her shuddering shoulders and drag her into the solid comfort of his embrace. Bizarrely, just that made her feel so much better.

Without thinking, she burrowed against him and allowed herself to revel in his strength. She remembered how he had condemned Eldridge's actions in the carriage and realised that this man would never have turned his back on her in that ballroom. He was too kind-hearted to be that callous. He would have come to her rescue, as he had Reggie and his silly besotted dog, and helped her no matter what she had done.

Her despair was now tinged with shame. She

had spent the last month trying to see the worst in him, when in actual fact he had turned out to be one of the most decent people she had ever come across. That realisation made her cry even harder.

Ross let her cry, although it hurt to do so. The front of his linen shirt was soaked with her tears and still she kept going, as if her heart was breaking, and he had absolutely no idea what was wrong. If he knew what ailed her he would fix it—hell, he would slay dragons if need be.

When her loud sobs subsided a little, he absently stroked the top of her head. Her hair was soft and gloriously silky. He itched to pull out the pins and run it through his fingers—but it had nothing to do with desire and everything to do with the overwhelming surge of tenderness he felt towards her at this precise moment, and the need to bring her some comfort.

'I—I'm s-sorry.'

'Don't be,' he whispered into her hair, and then he absently kissed the top of it. 'My mother always says that women cry in the same way that men punch things. She says that it is better out than in. Is it all out yet? If it's not then the back of my shirt is still dry. You can grizzle on that. Or you could use Dog. He is quite clean now.'

He felt her laugh a little between hiccoughs

and tightened his arms around her possessively. There was something about her that made him want to protect her. It was odd. He had only ever experienced that emotion when it concerned either his mother or his sister before now—but he had never before yearned to kiss away another's pain.

'Now you are being too kind. I cannot destroy *all* of your shirt. Especially as your handkerchief is now quite ruined.'

He felt her take in a deep, steadying breath against his chest, then she sat up and idly scratched Dog between his pointed ears in an attempt to avoid eye contact. Ross allowed his arms to fall away, sensing she needed the distance, while she made a valiant if futile attempt to repair her face.

'Do you want to tell me what this is all about?' he asked.

She stilled before exhaling. 'It was the story Captain Carstairs told us in the carriage. It was a little too close to home for my liking.'

She chewed on the corner of her lip nervously, obviously considering how much she should confide, before her slim shoulders slumped and she worried at the sodden handkerchief that was balled up in her hand.

'It might surprise you to learn that I was

engaged once, Mr Jameson, and like the poor woman in the story my fiancé broke it off quite callously. I still have no idea why he did so.'

Anger flared on her behalf. Something about the way she'd admitted this convinced Ross that right now she was telling the truth. No actress could recreate the sheer pain he saw reflected in her lovely eyes.

'Then the man was a fool and never deserved you in the first place.'

The ghost of a smile briefly touched her lips and she shook her head. 'Maybe. But I was judged and blamed by everyone, regardless. That is the way of things. They all saw it as my fault that he had cried off.'

'In my experience people are always inclined to think exactly what they want to and there is absolutely nothing you can do about that. Unfortunately they usually think the worst.'

Her blue eyes lifted towards his for the first time. 'As I have with you?'

Ross wanted to nod, but he made an excuse for her behaviour instead, to make her feel better. 'We got off on the wrong foot, Prim. Your first meeting with me happened in my bedchamber, remember? And I was not alone. Or clothed. Under the circumstances you had every right to be shocked.'

'I disagree.'

Her hand rested tentatively on the back of his. He wanted to turn it and clasp her fingers in his, but resisted.

'You are making excuses for me that I do not deserve. I do agree that our first meeting was…unconventional…but since then you have been nothing but kind towards me. I am heartily ashamed of how judgemental I have been towards you. I know better than to behave that way. You are a decent man, Mr Jameson, and I have been judgemental and rude towards you from the outset. I hope you can forgive me for that.'

He smiled, because he did believe that she was being honest and it was nice to hear. 'I accept your apology, Prim, but please do not paint me as such a paragon of virtue. I did pretend to be drunk so that I could maul you in my bedchamber.'

He watched in fascination as her already blotchy red cheeks darkened with a blush, but she smiled too.

'I had just accused you of being a drunken debaucher, sir. So I suppose that we are equal.'

'That's very sporting of you, Prim. And please stop calling me *sir*. I don't like it. My name is Ross.'

He hoisted himself up from the ground and

offered her his hand as Dog bounced excitedly at his feet, but she hesitated.

'It is not proper for servants to call their employers by their first names.'

Ross rolled his eyes and glared down at her. 'I am no gentleman, Prim, and I thank God for it. I would hate to feel so superior and so self-righteous that I would turn my back on someone or look down my nose at them in judgement. I know what that feels like and it is not good. If that is what being *proper* is, then you can keep it, frankly.'

He held out his hand again and this time she took it. He pulled her to her feet with a little more force than was necessary. As he had planned, she came up against him suddenly, bracing her other hand against his chest and staring up at him a little startled.

'Call me Ross, Prim. That's an order.'

His face was inches from hers.

'Fine,' she whispered gently as she stared up at him with limpid eyes. 'Ross.'

It was his undoing. Without thinking, he dipped his head and touched his lips softly to hers. This kiss was not about passion or lust, although he was acutely feeling both, he simply needed the contact and sensed that she did too. It was brief and sweet and tender, and left him feeling a little dazed. When he drew his head back she made no attempt to move out of his arms but stared back at him, startled, her breathing a little ragged—much like his own.

For several seconds they stood like that, neither one of them knowing quite what to make of what had just passed between them.

Prim stepped away first. 'Thank you for the sympathy and the shoulder to cry on.'

She wanted to categorise what had just happened, he realised, to make it easier to accept. For a moment he was tempted to call her on it, sure that she would not resist if he hauled her back into his arms and kissed her again with more passion. She was rattled by what had occurred.

But he didn't—because he was rattled too. This maddening, untrustworthy and complicated woman was getting under his skin—perhaps worming her way into his heart—at a time when he needed to keep his head. She might well still be an enemy.

'I suppose, if we are now being informal, you should call me Hannah.' She offered him a shy smile and began to hurry towards the house.

'I prefer Prim,' Ross announced to her retreating back with a grin. 'Because I know that it riles you.'

Chapter Sixteen

Hannah was summoned to Ross's study the following morning and found him, coatless as usual, standing in the centre of the room with his hands planted firmly on his narrow hips. Captain Carstairs was seated at the desk.

'You wanted to see me, sir?' she asked, and was rewarded by a mock pointed stare.

His playfulness and proximity made her feel silly inside, and she only just stopped herself from giggling like an idiot.

'You wanted to see me, *Ross*?' she clarified, and was rewarded with a brilliant smile that displayed an impressive row of straight white teeth.

'I did indeed, Prim. The captain and I have decided to take the bull by the horns and sort out all my papers now that I finally have a proper place to store them. I have never felt safe, keeping them at the docks.'

The evidence of this was currently piled all over the floor of his study.

'I was hoping that you would agree to help. You have a knack for organising things.'

After all the hours she had spent secretly going through his chests, the fact that he was now inviting her to do so alluded to the fact that there truly was nothing sinister in them. She had been wasting her time all along. *Damn*.

'Where would you like to start?' she asked, surveying the carnage on the floor.

He scratched his head. 'I am not altogether sure. I am tempted to say let's shove it all in a cupboard, but I know that it needs to be properly ordered because I can never find things. I have started grouping things into piles.'

'I can see that,' she returned sarcastically, and watched his eyes dance with amusement. 'Would you please enlighten me as to the method with which they have been sorted?'

He slipped his arm through hers and led her in a circle around the mess while Hannah did her best not to revel in the contact.

'This pile pertains to current pressing business—letters, bills, agreements and such—and these need to be readily at hand. This lot is all correspondence. I have got into the bad habit of keeping everything, just in case I ever need it, so we should probably discard a lot of the rubbish and keep only the important letters. Over here…'

His arm slipped casually around her waist, sending a ripple of awareness shooting up her spine, and he led her across the room to the most enormous heap of ribbon-bound documents.

'These are business agreements, shares and investments.' He glanced towards the final pile and curled his lip in distaste. 'And I have called this pile the miscellaneous pile. There is all sorts here.'

Hannah stood and tapped her chin in thought, then pointed to the largest pile. 'If these are all investments, and such, then perhaps we should begin with these and organise them alphabetically. That way, when we go through the correspondence and other documents we can match them to a particular investment. Then everything will be in one place.'

Ross stared at her and then lifted one eyebrow, impressed. 'That is a splendid idea—it certainly makes more sense than keeping them all in the order they came in. I bow to your superior judgement, Prim.' He executed an exaggerated court bow and then turned to Captain Carstairs. 'Come on, John—get off your backside and start helping.'

The blond man stood half-heartedly and saluted. 'Yes, sir!'

To make the task easier, Hannah wrote the letters of the alphabet on squares of paper and laid them out on the sideboard and desk. Then the three of them took a pile each and began to sort them, as she had suggested. After little more than an hour they had completed it. Almost every letter had a small heap of legal-looking documents grouped beneath it.

'You certainly have made a lot of investments,' Hannah commented. 'Have they all been profitable?'

'In the main,' Ross answered cryptically, but made no effort to elaborate.

She supposed that he was entitled to keep his finances private, and it was considered vulgar to discuss money.

'Shall we start on the correspondence now?'

Carstairs rolled his eyes. 'Does it all have to be done today? I am all for helping out, but this is a terrible waste of my leave and I am starving.' He pulled out his pocket watch for emphasis and pointed to the dial. 'See here—it is already well past lunchtime and I had hoped to enjoy a little rest and relaxation during my visit. What do you say we continue this tomorrow?'

Hannah glanced at Ross and watched his eyes

slowly rise to meet hers. Wordlessly they communicated, and he gave her a secret look of exasperation before capitulating.

'The rest can wait till tomorrow.'

'If we leave all this on the floor Dog will chew it.' Oblivious to the bemused look that passed between the two men, Hannah began to load the remaining piles back into the empty chests.

'Why don't you let Cook know that we are ready to eat, John, and rustle up some tea?' Ross said to his friend. 'Prim and I can tidy all this up.'

To say that Carstairs bolted to the door in relief was a slight exaggeration, but he did not need asking twice.

As soon as he'd left Ross turned to her and smiled kindly. 'Are you feeling better today?'

'Much better,' Hannah murmured, feeling a little self-conscious. 'Thank you for being thoughtful and not mentioning it in front of Captain Carstairs.'

He brushed this off with a careless wave. 'He would only feel guilty for upsetting you inadvertently.'

She could feel his eyes on her but did not dare to look.

'Do you mind me asking how old you were when all this happened?'

'Barely nineteen. I was very young and very

green.' Hannah busied herself by plonking more papers in the chest. Now that they could apparently communicate without words she did not want him to see the vulnerability she felt. 'You probably think that I am very silly to let something that happened so long ago bother me still.'

'Not at all. Sometimes old wounds take a long time to heal. Did you love him?'

That was such a personal question to ask— and so typical of him.

'At the time I believed that I did,' she answered honestly as she felt her heart melt a little at his obvious concern. 'Although it was, as people are prone to say, a good match. He was from a well-respected family and could offer me a comfortable life.' That part was close to the truth as well.

'He broke your heart, then—no wonder you are so against the idea of marriage.'

He reached for a pile of papers and as he did so his hand brushed against hers for an instant. It was enough to set her pulse fluttering.

'I am not sure that I was heartbroken,' she countered quickly. Her soul had been crushed, and all of her girlish dreams had been cruelly shattered to such an extent she had not had the energy to think about her heart. 'It did leave me humiliated.'

He turned and leant his hips against the sideboard, looking thoughtful—and deliciously handsome. His thin shirt moulded to the muscles in his upper arms as he folded them across his chest distractingly.

'And that has no doubt put you off risking your heart again.'

Had it? In Yorkshire there had been no one to offer her heart to, but now that she thought about it it did make some sort of sense. She had certainly been adamantly against the idea of considering marriage ever since Eldridge's betrayal, although she had always thought that was because she did not want to be controlled by another man. Perhaps she *did* fear falling in love again.

'What made him call it off?'

'All he said was that he no longer thought me suitable to be his wife.'

Eldridge had called her a whore.

His perceptive green eyes regarded her with outraged sympathy. 'But he gave you no reason why?'

His scrutiny was too intense—he saw too much. So Hannah turned back to the task in hand before she answered. 'I never had the opportunity to ask. I have not seen him since.'

She reached for another pile of papers but his

hand stopped her. It felt reassuringly warm and solid on top of hers.

'And that does not bother you? You have the right to know the truth—especially when it has caused you so much distress. It would bother me a great deal. I would not be able to rest until I had got to the bottom of it and said my bit.' Gently, he caught his fingers to her chin and tipped it so that she faced him. 'Would you like me to give him a piece of my mind on your behalf?' His green eyes had hardened to flints. 'I think that I would enjoy that.'

Hannah's heart jumped to her throat. She was beyond touched by his reaction and his offer to be her knight in shining armour. Nobody had ever stood up for her before.

'There is no need. I am well rid of him. But thank you for the offer.'

He sighed, but did not let go of her chin. His large hand slid up and cupped her cheek. 'Then you are a better person than me, Prim,' he said vehemently. 'I would seek the scoundrel out and ask him what he was about. Then I would get my own back.'

The fierce determination in his voice excited her.

'It is so far in the past that it hardly matters now...'

But it did. She had not realised how much it still mattered until yesterday, when the memory of it had assaulted her and reopened the wounds.

'The past shapes us, Prim. It moulds us and affects all our future decisions. Sometimes it spurs us to change things and sometimes it holds us back. I think this is holding you back. It has certainly put you off marriage.'

His thumb was rubbing lazy circles on the underside of her jaw and it was making it difficult for her to concentrate.

'That is not the case. I am too long on the shelf and I value my independence too much. I have no desire to find myself a husband, nor to obey his commands.' She said this with less enthusiasm than she'd intended.

His thumb stilled and he gazed deeply into her eyes until she feared that she might actually drown in the intensity.

'You are assuming that all men will be like him. They are not. Ten years ago I believed that all aristocrats were nasty. I convinced myself that they were all untrustworthy and evil men who want to use and abuse those below them. But they are not. I have now met a great many of them, and benefited from their acquaintance because they have introduced me to possibilities that I had not previously considered. I soon came to realise that my prejudices were unfounded—that I had to treat each one as an individual rather than tar them all with the same brush. You cannot judge all men by your fiancé, Prim. That is unfair to them and you are denying yourself possibilities.'

Hannah felt a little unbalanced by his assessment—and by the fact that he was standing overwhelmingly close. Was he right?

'I prefer to be on my own.'

'From what I have seen you are not that sort of woman at all. You might try to act that way, but your true character betrays you. You are thoughtful. You make Reggie feel useful. You always ensure that there are sweet things on the tea tray without me having to ask for them. You are a nurturer, Prim. Look at how you have transformed this house already. You have not merely overseen the redecorating—you have made this house a home. I do not believe that you do not want those things for yourself—yet you have convinced yourself you do not want them because you are frightened they will all be taken away again. He has made you lose confidence in yourself. Don't give him the satisfaction. You are a beautiful young woman...'

He had inched so close that she could feel his warm breath on her face.

'A beautiful and desirable woman.'

Hannah had no recollection of standing on her toes, nor did she know the exact moment that she moved nearer to help him close the distance between them, but her lips appeared to be magnetically drawn to his of their own accord.

His mouth was soft as it lightly touched hers, but that soon changed. His fingers threaded into her hair and cradled her scalp, and with just that one hand he pulled her flush against him and plundered her mouth with his own.

Ross had not actually been trying to charm her. The kiss had happened naturally, as it had yesterday in the garden. One minute he had been trying to understand the cause of her sadness and the next he had felt a surge of protectiveness and had needed to make her feel better. Kissing her had not even entered his mind right up until the moment he had instigated it, and she had melted against him with a ragged sigh. Once that had happened he had been incapable of holding back—and apparently so had she.

What had started as a gentle meeting of mouths was now much more urgent and had taken on a life of its own. There was nothing prim or cold about the woman in his arms. She fairly pulsed with unspent passion and matched his ardour kiss for kiss. One of her hands was fisted in his hair and the other was splayed across his chest, exploring the shape of it brazenly. With a groan he turned, so that their positions were reversed and she had her back against the sideboard. Swiftly he lifted her to sit upon it, so that they were the same height, and cushioned his body between her legs while her tongue tangled with his.

The sound of rattling teacups had her pushing him away and scampering off the sideboard. Quick as a flash she busied herself by grabbing up a pile of letters and dumping them clumsily into the open chest, just as John sauntered into the room, closely followed by Reggie and a tray of clattering crockery.

He took one look at Ross, taking in the rumpled shirt and dishevelled hair, and raised one eyebrow in question. 'Tea is served,' he said with great ceremony.

Ross smoothed down his hair and made sure that his shirt was properly tucked in. He was not going to explain himself to John. Judging by the knowing grin he had pasted on his face, his friend had already put two and two together.

'Miss Preston,' John asked innocently, 'shall I pour the tea?'

Ross saw that Prim refused to turn around, and she still looked delightfully rumpled. A heavy lock of her hair had escaped its pins and bounced next to her cheek as she worked and the visible tips of her ears were bright pink. She scraped up the last papers and shoved them inside the chest.

'If you don't mind, Captain Carstairs. I have urgent things that require my attention.'

Without turning, she dashed out of the room and slammed the door smartly behind her.

'Was it something I said?' John drawled as he sat down on the leather chesterfield. 'Or something you did?'

Ross sat in the wingback chair and picked up his cup to avoid answering. He took a large gulp of tea that brought tears to his eyes as the hot liquid burned down his gullet, but pretended not to be in acute physical pain as a result.

The intensity of that kiss had bothered him. He could not remember when he had been so immersed in one—to the extent that he had not heard Reggie and John arriving. And Reggie was not known for being light on his enormous feet. If they had not been interrupted he doubted either one of them would have had the strength to break it. Hell, another minute and he would have had her skirts up around her knees and the falls of his trousers open.

He had never allowed himself to be so out of control before—he was not sure he felt comfortable with the lapse. Prim had a strange power over him that was unnerving. For the first time in his life Ross found himself feeling more than simple physical attraction for a woman—something he had the good sense to find worrying.

Prim had a mind. He could discuss things with her. He wanted to understand her vulnerabilities and he enjoyed her fiery temperament. She might be quick-tempered, but that trait made her passions rise quickly too. For the last ten years he had worked tirelessly to get where he was and not given two hoots as to what people thought of him, yet he did not want to be a disappointment to *her*. That was quite unsettling.

He looked forward to coming back to Barchester Hall too, and not simply because he now had a proper home to come back to. He enjoyed the comforting ambience Prim had created for him. He appreciated her thoughtfulness—even when it was camouflaged in irritation on her part.

Ross had always been the one who looked after people—his mother and his sister, Reggie, all the other waifs and strays he'd collected out of a sense of duty. But Prim looked after him. That was a lovely feeling. She might nag at him and tut—but she brought him tea to stop him from working too long and getting headaches. She had brought order and calmness into his life—which he realised he had been missing. And she could certainly rouse his passions quicker than any other woman had ever done before.

If only she would share his bed with him every night she would be the perfect wife.

Where the hell had that errant thought come from? Ross scowled and snatched up his tea in consternation. He was not ready to be thinking about wives. Not until his sister was settled. The woman was making him daft.

'I can see I have spoiled your mood.' John had the audacity to look rather pleased with himself. 'I must say, though, if she *is* a spy then she is a very good one. She never gave a single piece of paper more than a passing glance. Unless, of course, she is not interested in your investments. Perhaps she will tackle your correspondence with a bit more *vigour.*'

'You told me to soften her up. I was merely doing a bit of softening. Are you sure she did not pay any particular interest in anything?' He sincerely hoped his friend would drop it.

John shook his head. 'I kept a very close eye on her the whole time. She either reads very fast or only reads the first few lines of everything.' He took a sip of his own tea thoughtfully. 'Of course she could slip down here later, while we are not looking, and have a proper read. She has made everything much easier to find for herself as well as for you.'

'And she might not be a spy at all,' Ross added irritably, wishing that it was true. 'In which case we are both wasting our time.'

John stared at him for several moments before one side of his mouth quirked ruefully. 'An interesting point of view. Perhaps you are not the only one doing a bit of softening?'

Ross smiled tightly. 'Fear not, my friend, I am quite immune to that, I can assure you. You know that I am not interested in anything other than discovering the truth.'

It was a lie, and the possibility that such a thing might be the case worried him.

Chapter Seventeen

Hannah dunked her head under the cool water of the pond and then swam in another lazy circle. Even now, hours afterwards, she still felt hot and bothered after that kiss. Whatever had got into them both she could not say, and at some point she would have to tell him never to do it again, but for now she was content to revel in it and the sensations it had elicited.

His wise words had set her mind whirring. It was galling to think that Eldridge had damaged her to such an extent that she had been hiding behind their break-up all these years and wielding her independence as a shield to prevent herself from moving on with her life. How had he put it? Denying herself *possibilities*.

The problem was, lately the only possibilities she could think of involved Ross Jameson. She could dress it up however she wanted, but she felt more for him than simply lust. Her attempts at unmasking him had become increasingly half-hearted because, she realised with alarm, she had apparently lost the taste for it. In fact she really did not seem to actually *want* to find anything any longer.

She had done absolutely no digging at the warehouse. And today, when she had had the perfect justification to read through his private papers, she had barely given them more than a cursory glance. Instead she had been too busy enjoying his company.

When he had pulled her into his arms she had forgotten all the reservations she'd had. The seven years of loneliness, hurt and longing that she had buried ruthlessly inside had bubbled too close to the surface and had steadfastly refused to return to the neat box in her mind where she kept them. At that moment she had needed to feel beautiful and desired. She had wanted to be in those strong, safe arms again and to hell with the consequences.

Thank goodness they had been interrupted. Hannah was certain she would not have stopped the kiss otherwise. She had been too emotional and too raw, desperate to banish those painful feelings in the hot heat of his kiss. Her heart was already a little too engaged, and it would have been lost completely if she had succumbed.

Ross Jameson was best kept at arm's length going forward. He was nothing like any of the men she had known before. He was kind, generous, funny, self-effacing and quite noble. But also clever, ridiculously attractive, and so, *so* tempting. All in all, a very dangerous combination.

She caught a brief glimpse of her hands. Her finger tips had shrivelled up like prunes, and she realised that she had been languishing in the water for far too long. Reluctantly, she waded up the steep bank and collapsed onto the towel she had spread on the ground so that the heat of the early-evening sun could dry her skin.

Ross Jameson was a conundrum, and he had left her so confused that she really did not know what to make of him or her conflicting feelings towards him. But he was right about her former fiancé. It *was* grossly unfair that he had never had to answer for his appalling treatment of her all those years ago. She deserved the truth, if nothing else. Perhaps the lack of it *was* actually holding her back? *Was* she denying herself 'possibilities' because of what that man had done to her? Did Eldridge *really* deserve to wield that much power?

For the first time since that night in the ballroom Hannah decided that it was time to demand the answers that her brother had promised but failed to provide. Eldridge had accused her of all those terrible things. Had he made it all up to get out of his obligation or had somebody else deliberately sabotaged her chance at happiness? The very fact that the incident could still reduce her to a sobbing mess after seven long years made her want to draw a proper line under it. She needed to know. Hell—she had a right to know.

With a renewed sense of clarity she sat bolt-upright. Eldridge had robbed her of her place in society, her happiness, her future and her confidence. The very least he could do now was explain why that had happened. His house was less than an hour away. Why shouldn't she just turn up there and demand the answers that had never been forthcoming? If she left early tomorrow she would be there and back well before lunch.

Hastily she towelled off the rest of the water. If she got up before dawn she could saddle a horse and slip away unnoticed. Cook would make a suitable excuse if anyone asked.

Hannah twisted her hair into a knot and secured it with a few pins and then dragged on her clothes.

What would she feel when she saw Eldridge again? She knew already that she would not look at him with doe eyes any longer—but would she be angry? Or indifferent? She hoped she would be indifferent. That would wound the bounder much more than tears or regret.

The image of Viscount Eldridge confused and alarmed cheered her immensely. The sight of her would likely terrify him.

Hannah arrived at Viscount Eldridge's country home just before nine. She had only visited the house once before, and could not remember if she had considered it to be such a Gothic monstrosity then as she did now. The place did not hold a candle to Barchester Hall, and she was oddly thankful that she had been spared the ordeal of being its mistress.

As it did not seem proper simply to march up to the front door and demand entrance, she sat on a secluded bench that gave her a good view of the back of the house. Eldridge would likely refuse to see her if she was announced, she realised, and the element of surprise would keep her in control of the situation.

After an hour or so two young boys skipped out into the garden. From the genteel way they were dressed, they had to be his sons. Obviously he had married during the intervening years, and that made her angry. How typical that he should be allowed to blithely get on with his life while she had been left to suffer. A family had been denied her. Thanks to him.

Hannah was just contemplating sneaking in through the back door and confronting him when the man himself appeared through some French doors as if she had conjured him. Even from a distance she could tell that the years had taken their toll. His blond hair was much thinner than it had been, while the well-cut jacket could not completely disguise the beginnings of a paunch. The Viscount clasped his hands behind his back and began to stroll slowly around the lawn in what she assumed was his morning constitutional.

As luck would have it, he was inadvertently heading in her direction. She sat straighter on the bench as he turned the corner and inclined her head in greeting, ignoring the unmanly squeal that emanated from his thin lips the moment he set eyes on her.

'Hello, Charles,' she said casually, as if she had every right to be trespassing in his garden. 'It has been a long time.'

The Viscount's jaw hung slack as he blinked at her in confusion. 'H-Hannah! I hope you are well.'

The inane platitude made her smile. After all he had done, the best thing he could think of to say was that?

'Yes, Charles, I am well,' she responded dully. 'No thanks to you.'

Eldridge coloured immediately and stood rooted to the spot. It gave her an opportunity to look him over objectively. He was shorter than she remembered, and not even all the padding in his jacket could cover up his narrow, stooping shoulders.

The best adjective she could think of to describe his face accurately was *aristocratic*, and it was odd that she should consider such a word to be an insult—but it was. His pale eyes were too small; his nose was too long and prominent. It had a slight bump in it that added to his haughty demeanour, as did the fact that his chin was so nondescript that it was almost not a chin at all— merely an extension of his over-long neck.

Why had she never noticed that he appeared to be constantly looking down that nose at everyone? His eyes were humourless—she preferred eyes that sparkled with mischief—and his mouth was not the sort of mouth that she would ever consider kissing now.

'What do you want?' he asked furtively, his eyes flicking back and forth between her and the house. He clearly did not want his wife to find him in her company.

'Try not to panic, Charles. I would prefer *not* to cause trouble.'

He visibly gulped at the implied threat and

Hannah felt strangely empowered. This *was* therapeutic.

'I came here for some answers, Charles, and I will not be leaving until I get them. Why don't you come and sit down and then we can get it over with?'

Her voice dripped sarcasm, and for a moment she thought he might run away screaming, but after a few seconds of hesitation he did as she asked.

He sat primly on the furthest corner of the bench, with his knees pressed together like a maiden. Did he think that she was going to harm his male parts? His were the last male parts on the planet she would want anything to do with, but she smiled knowingly at him. Let him think that his jewels were in danger—it would serve him right.

'I thought you were abroad,' he muttered.

Large beads of perspiration had gathered unattractively on his top lip and prominent forehead.

'Clearly I am not. But that is by the by. I came here to talk to you about the night you called off our engagement.'

She watched his Adam's apple bob uncomfortably before he sighed. 'I am sorry for the... the public nature of our argument that night,' he said, not meeting her eyes. 'I regret not doing it in private.'

The very fact that he did not regret calling their engagement off was duly noted, and she narrowed her eyes. 'It was not your finest hour, but that does not concern me either. I am actually grateful that you broke our engagement. I cannot imagine how awful my life would have been if I had been saddled with such a spineless man as you. What I am more interested in is why you told everyone that I was a whore and pregnant with another man's child.'

All the colour had drained from his thin cheeks but he stared back at her indignantly. 'That was the truth. You cannot deny it!'

Hannah shook her head slowly. 'It was most certainly *not* the truth. I had taken no lover nor been impregnated by one. I was nineteen, for pity's sake, and had been out for just a year. Why would you think such a thing?'

Eldridge glared at her down his haughty nose, but withered under her level gaze. 'I was told it on good authority. I had no reason to doubt the source.'

Hannah felt a little queasy at the knowledge that another person had indeed deliberately destroyed her happiness so cruelly, but hid it. 'And who was the source of that vile lie, Charles?

Which person wished me so much ill that they would construct such a fable? I am curious.'

For a minute his expression closed and his shoulders stiffened, but then he turned a little green and deflated. 'I promised to keep his identity a secret,' he said finally, with a faint tremor in his voice. 'But as he is dead I suppose that no longer matters. It was your brother who told me.'

The words slammed into her like a punch in the gut, and she gasped and clutched at the bench for support. 'You are lying!' she whispered, sure that it could not be true.

He regarded her with righteous indignation. 'It is the truth. He had no reason to lie. He came to me during the ball and said that he could not in all good conscience allow me to be cuckolded by you. He told me about all your lovers.'

'All?' Hannah cried bitterly, still reeling from the betrayal. 'Pray tell me, sir, how many men did he accuse me of having when surely just the one was enough?'

Her own brother had sabotaged her wedding and banished her to Yorkshire on purpose. As soon as she got home she was going to jump on his grave.

Viscount Eldridge stood and smoothed down his coat. 'Your brother warned me that you would deny it,' he said, staring down his nose at her in disgust, 'But he said that he knew for certain that you had dallied with a number of your servants and that your own stable master was the father of your child.'

The only stable master they'd had had been eighty if he was a day. Hannah laughed at the ridiculousness of it all. Her life had been ruined by her own selfish brother.

'And you believed him?'

To her own ears she sounded a mite hysterical, and Eldridge was regarding her as if she were mad.

Hannah stood proudly. 'My brother was an idiot, Charles. Everybody knew it. He could not stay away from the gaming tables and he drank whisky with his breakfast. To think that you put more stock in what a man like that said than the word of your own fiancée says a great deal about you. You did not even ask me for my version of events. What is it about men of breeding and title that makes them believe they have the right to ride roughshod over a woman's feelings?'

The rhetorical question was meant more for her treacherous brother than Eldridge—but both men had wronged her. She could not help comparing them unfavourably to Ross.

'I had no reason to doubt your brother,' Viscount Eldridge said rather pompously. 'I still don't.'

At that, Hannah raised her eyes heavenward. Despite all the hurt he had caused, Hannah felt a wave of almost palpable relief. Her fool brother had actually done her a favour—not that she was inclined ever to forgive him for it. *This* could have been her life. *This* could have been her husband. She would have spent years being subservient to a man who was little more than an empty vessel.

There was no substance to Charles. He was a stuffed shirt with lead for brains and inherited opinions that were so rigid they formed a prison around him. She would have been truly miserable had she become his wife, she realised. Miserable and trapped with a man that she could never respect.

'Then Ross is quite right,' she said imperiously, 'You *are* an idiot and you certainly never deserved me.'

She would never shed a tear over the past again. Nor would she let it hold her back. With a flounce, she turned and sauntered back towards her waiting horse, strangely grateful that she had been saved from marrying such a pathetic man.

Chapter Eighteen

By midday Ross was quite ready to climb the walls, and Carstairs was not helping his mood.

'Why else would she have disappeared without warning?' his friend argued logically. 'She is obviously up to no good. Who knows what she could have stolen and given to the East India Company by now? You gave her carte blanche to go through all your documents yesterday and neither of us were here to keep watch last night. She waited until you let your guard down and then she pounced. I doubt you will ever see her again, old boy.'

The idea that his friend might well be right made him feel quite ill. It was not only the potential invasion of his privacy that bothered him, and the threat that placed on his shipping business, but imagining Prim going behind his back like that, when he had trusted her enough to let his guard down, felt like the worst sort of betrayal. He did not want to believe it of her.

Ross huffed and stalked out of the cheerful yellow morning room.

'Cook!' he bellowed as he rounded the kitchen door and spied his prey.

The older woman coloured guiltily and wrung the corners of her white apron in her hands.

'Tell me again where Prim has gone to.' He narrowed his eyes and glared down at her. 'I *know* that you know.'

'I told you, Ross—she has gone to do a bit of shopping, that's all.'

Cook was an appalling liar and could not meet his eyes. Something was afoot and he did not like it at all. Yesterday, Prim had kissed him as if she had meant it. And now she was gone.

Dog started to yap excitedly outside.

'Hello, boy,' came Prim's unmistakable tones. 'Did you miss me?'

By the sounds of rapture coming from the canine she had clearly bent down to rub the animal's ears. Then she sauntered through the back kitchen door—as if nothing at all was amiss and she had *not* left him climbing the walls with worry, fearing that John was right.

'Oh, hello!'

She smiled, clearly a little startled at the sight

of them. Two fetching spots of pink graced the apples of her cheeks and her hair was in wind-blown disarray. She looked so lovely that it took his breath away. Gone was the shapeless brown serge and severe bun. Prim was wearing a cheerful pale pink muslin gown that showed her trim figure off to perfection. Her hair had been dressed in matching pink ribbons but most of it was hanging loose around her face, mussed by the breeze. Instead of looking sheepish she grinned at him, her eyes twinkling.

'Prim—could I have a word in my study?' Ross muttered stiffly, and gestured towards the hallway.

'Certainly,' she said, breezing past him, wafting the seductive scent of flowers and fresh air in her wake.

Once inside the room, he slammed the door and rounded on her. 'Where the *hell* have you been?' he shouted, not wanting to admit that he had been concerned.

'Out,' she replied saucily, and then she walked directly to where he stood glowering at her. She smiled and stood on her tiptoes and then reached up and pulled his face to hers. The kiss was as brief as it was unexpected. 'Thank you,' she said as she released his head.

Bewildered, and more than a little off-kilter at

her bizarre response, Ross struggled to find the right words. None came, and he was forced simply to gape at her in complete confusion.

'I took your advice and went to see him and I gave him a piece of my mind. It felt marvellous.' She grinned giddily and spun a happy circle on the rug. 'To be honest, I am not entirely sure what I ever saw in him. He is weedy and cowardly and totally dislikeable.'

'I'm sorry…?' Ross was having trouble following. '*Who* did you go and see?'

Prim wandered over to the abandoned chests and began to pull out handfuls of correspondence. 'My former fiancé, of course.'

Instantly he felt a surge of pure, raw jealousy that thankfully she did not notice. He clenched his hands into angry fists at his sides and tried his best to look nonchalant.

'I thought about what you said and knew you were right. I *did* deserve to know why he called our engagement off and I am glad that I went. The man is quite odious. To think that I could have been married to *that* for the last seven years makes me feel…' She shuddered and screwed up her face. '*Eww!* He has beady eyes, no chin, and he pads out his jackets because he has absolutely no shoulders.'

She deposited a big pile of papers on the sideboard.

'*And* he was pompous,' she added for good measure. 'He was totally unremorseful about the whole thing—but he was absolutely *terrified* to see me. It was quite exhilarating, actually. I enjoyed watching him squirm.'

'I can see that.'

She positively radiated joy, and a new confidence he had not seen in her before. It was infectious, and his irrational jealousy faded away. 'I was worried about you,' he admitted, coming up next to her, 'I thought you had run away.'

'Why on earth would you think that?' Now it was her turn to look confused as she finally turned and faced him. 'I told Cook I would be back by lunchtime—and here I am.'

Ross did not bother fighting the urge to touch her hair and wound his finger around one fat curl. 'I thought you might have been upset about what happened between us yesterday.'

She blushed prettily, glanced at his lips and then looked down at her feet. 'Er…about that… I think we should forget that it happened.'

'I don't think I can do that. In fact I was rather looking forward to doing it again.'

She tried to dart away, but stopped short as soon as she felt the tug of her trapped hair in his fingertips. 'Ross—it is not proper,' she murmured half-heartedly.

He gently tugged her a little closer. 'Why ever not? My eyes are not beady, I have an *actual* chin and I have quite broad shoulders, if I do say so myself. Those were the main objections you had about your former fiancé, were they not?'

'It has nothing to do with your superior physical attributes,' she said a little breathlessly. 'It is simply a fact that employers do not fraternise with their servants. It is just not done.'

But she tilted her head so that he could freely nibble her neck, he noticed with delight.

'Next I suppose you are also going to tell me to behave like a gentleman?' he whispered between nips.

'On the contrary,' Hannah responded without thinking, caught up in the sensations he was creating, 'After this morning I am done with gentlemen. They are a pathetic lot.'

'I am pleased to hear it. Is that why you kissed me first this time?'

'I did not!'

'Yes, you did.' Ross buried his nose in her hair and inhaled her perfume greedily. 'You came into the study, grabbed me and kissed me. On the lips too. It was a blatant invitation, Prim.'

She looked delightfully flummoxed by this

logic. 'That…that was merely an expression of my thanks,' she stammered breathlessly as his lips found the underside of her ear. 'It was certainly not meant as encouragement.'

Ross chuckled against her neck. 'Mmm-hmm? I am certainly feeling your encouragement now.'

Only then did she brace her hands against his shoulders and gently push him away to arm's length.

'I am not ready to be a dalliance, Ross. My heart is not up to it.'

Her blue eyes looked so troubled. He could see the turmoil she was feeling. It matched his own.

'What if this is more than a dalliance, Prim?'

Ross was not exactly sure what he was offering, but he could not shake the thought that there was meant to be more between them. An uncomfortable knot of fear formed in his chest as he waited for her reply. Part of him wanted her to reject him. A bigger part didn't.

After an age she turned away from him. 'Sometimes I wish that…'

The noisy arrival of Dog in the hallway, closely followed by John and Reggie, prevented her continuing. She whipped her hand out of his grasp and stepped away.

'Tea's up,' Reggie announced from the doorway, and Ross actually growled.

She had been about to say something profound about their relationship, he just knew it, and now the moment was gone.

'I swear I am going to take that blasted tea tray and batter someone with it!' he bellowed to a stunned Reggie.

'They is just papers, Ross,' the big man placated, missing the point entirely. 'They ain't worth getting angry about.'

Chapter Nineteen

A few evenings later Hannah stood staring at the huge pile of documents that still needed sorting.

'When you said that you had got into the bad habit of keeping everything, I had not realised that you meant it literally,' Captain Carstairs uttered in disgust, shaking a letter in his friend's face and interrupting her thoughts. 'This is a receipt for *sugar*, for pity's sake! Why did you keep this?' He dropped it onto the enormous pile of paper that they had consigned as rubbish.

Hannah watched Ross wince. 'I put Reggie in charge of my post,' he admitted. 'Once I had read it I told him to put away anything important.'

'But the man cannot *read*,' Carstairs whined in exasperation. 'Did you know that when you gave him the task?'

'Of course I didn't,' Ross lied, quite convincingly.

Of course he had. Thoroughly charmed, Hannah quickly averted her gaze and felt a smile touch her lips. He had wanted to give Reggie a job so that he felt useful. Ross had a kind streak that was a mile wide, which he tried his hardest to hide. He grumbled constantly about Reggie and Dog, yet he had taken them both in and given them homes. Even now, when he thought nobody was looking, he was tickling the besotted mutt behind the ears.

She turned her head slightly and he caught her eye. His hand dropped and he curled his lip in a facsimile of a snarl and glared at the beast instead. Dog simply rolled onto his back and offered his master his rounded belly, his pink tongue lolling out of his mouth in sheer delirium.

She knew how the stupid animal felt—Ross had much the same effect on her too. There was no point denying the fact that she was seriously tempted by him. When he had suggested that there might be something more between them for the briefest of moments she had come close to capitulating and surrendering to the feelings that she was struggling to deny.

At the last minute she had realised that she was too frightened to risk it. She had given her heart once and it had been crushed. It had taken seven years to recover—if indeed if had fully. The thought of going through all that pain again, of entrusting it to another man again… It was too much.

'Look at this!' announced Captain Carstairs with great excitement as he unfolded a large piece of parchment. 'This is our first agreement with the Siamese silk merchant, Ross.'

Hannah did not notice the look passed between Carstairs and Ross, and nor did she see how they watched her to gauge her reaction. That was because she had just found something that looked suspiciously like a gambling marker. At the bottom, in barely legible writing, she was certain it was signed 'Tremley'. Carelessly she tossed it onto the rubbish pile and hastily picked up another piece of paper.

'Goodness,' continued Captain Carstairs in the background, 'I had forgotten how cheaply we bought that first shipment. No wonder the East India Company are worried about the competition. We seriously undercut them then.'

Hannah rose carefully, picked up the small pile of rubbish and walked it towards the chest that they had designated for burning. She surreptitiously slipped the marker into her hand and pocketed it.

'With any luck we will finish this tomorrow—but I fear I am all done for today. Goodnight, gentlemen.'

'She was not even remotely interested,' said Ross with an air of resignation after Prim had left the room. 'I don't think she *is* a spy from the East India Company.'

'She is just a good actress,' Carstairs countered. 'Spies have to be. I will wager my entire fortune that she comes back and reads this when she thinks we are in bed.'

Ross laughed. The whole business of trying to catch Prim in the act of industrial espionage was becoming a bit ridiculous. Carstairs kept dropping clues and leaving strategic things lying around but so far it had all been to no avail.

'I am not spending another evening with you hiding behind the chesterfield,' he said adamantly. 'Last night we waited for three hours. *Three!* And all to no avail. I can think of better ways to spend the night—sleeping immediately springs to mind.'

Carstairs nodded sagely. 'I agree. But I am still going to keep an eye out.'

'You are wasting your time.'

Ross knew in his heart that the woman was not a spy. Prim did not wish him any ill. In fact he was becoming rather hopeful that she was coming to see him in an altogether different light. All day she had been peeking at him shyly through her lashes with feminine interest, and blushing profusely whenever he caught her doing it. He found it quite sweet and touching.

He had also found himself doing exactly the same thing back. He was not altogether sure what had come over him. In the last few days he had started to feel very sentimental, and there was an odd ache bothering him in his chest. Perhaps he was finally ready to enter into more than a dalliance with a woman after all?

'Oh, stop mooning!' Carstairs said in disgust. 'It is quite pathetic to watch. You are supposed to be softening the woman up—not falling in love with her.'

Ross opened his mouth to argue and then stopped himself. *Was* he? He certainly had become quite fond of Prim. Ever since the day she had come back from visiting her idiot fiancé things had definitely changed between them. She was certainly less frosty, and had stopped glaring at him when he flirted, although he had not managed to steal another kiss. She smiled more frequently, laughed more.

In some ways it was almost as if a weight had been lifted off her shoulders. It was like watching a caterpillar slowly being transformed into a butterfly before his very eyes. Prickly Prim had almost disappeared. In return he had actively sought her company, and he did everything he could to earn the reward of one of her smiles. When he did he felt as though she had given him a great gift.

He became aware of his friend watching him.

'I knew it!' John said with irritation. 'First you lose interest in your mistress, then you move into a house, and now you are seriously thinking about settling down.'

'Hardly,' Ross countered, with less force than he had intended. 'I am not mooning. I am just tired. Thanks to your continued insistence that we keep guard every night I am simply exhausted. To that end, I bid you goodnight, Carstairs.'

With as much dignity as he could manage, Ross sauntered from his study and closed the door behind him.

In the privacy of her bedchamber Hannah pulled out the yellowed and dog-eared slip of paper and read it properly. It was indeed from Viscount Tremley, but made out to a Viscount Denham—not Jameson, as she had hoped—and it was a promise to pay the princely sum of three thousand pounds.

Hannah was astounded by the amount. But how had it fallen into the hands of Ross? Tremley's letter had stated that he intended to pay off his marker in full, so was this huge debt now owed to Ross instead? Was it some form of extortion?

She sincerely hoped not. The more time she spent with Ross Jameson, the more she liked him. She had not wanted to find this gambling marker, she realised, because its very existence justified all her former suspicions about him. Well, not entirely, she conceded with a sigh. At the moment it was the only evidence she had found that Ross might not be the thoroughly decent, kind and heart-stopping man she had come to know. He made her smile, set her pulse racing and kissed her mindless. Surely she would not have such tender feelings for a man who was capable of extortion?

Ever since she had confronted Eldridge she'd felt as if everything was up in the air. On the one hand she was still reeling from the discovery of her brother's betrayal. Only the worst sort of man did something like that to his own flesh and blood. Perhaps Ross was right and gambling had become an addiction and turned her brother into a monster. It was still no excuse for his treachery. She hoped he rotted in hell, so raw was her anger.

But on the other hand, bizarrely, she found herself beginning to hope. Perhaps love *was* in her future. She was certainly not as averse to the idea as she had been. It had started to feel like a just revenge on both her brother *and* Eldridge to move on despite them. Why should their influence still prevent her from living her life to the full? But could she really risk her heart again for a man like Ross, no matter how tempting that might be?

Hannah had suffered through one heartbreak which had taken years to mend, and she had never even truly loved Eldridge. She had convinced herself that she had at the time, but she had been young and lonely. Eldridge had never made her pulse flutter nor her heart melt with tenderness. He had never made her laugh. She had certainly never longed for him or dreamt about him.

Her sleep was frequently interrupted, of late, by those green-eyed cherubs—and that had nothing whatsoever to do with lust and everything to do with possibilities. Somehow she just knew that Ross had the power not only to break her heart, but to shatter it to smithereens. The problem was Hannah had no idea if she was brave enough to take the chance.

The bed suddenly felt too warm and too uncomfortable. Hoping that some hot milk might encourage her eyelids to close, Hannah slipped downstairs and tiptoed down the hallway.

Then all hell broke loose.

The shouting woke him up. Ross did his best to ignore it, but even with his head shoved underneath his pillow he could still hear the uproar in the hallway below. By the heavy sounds of footsteps on the landing he was not the only person who had rudely been snatched from the loving arms of Morpheus. He ripped back the sheet, pulled on his breeches and stomped out to see what all the furore was about.

'What the devil is going on?' he roared as he stomped past a confused-looking Reggie on the stairs.

The scene that confronted him was not at all what he had expected. A bleary-eyed footman was standing next to the open door while his gamekeeper stood menacingly over the two men who were lying prostrate in the middle of the hallway, a fearsome-looking flintlock poised in his hands, ready to shoot. Prim was standing close by in a billowing nightgown, her eyes wide as she watched the gamekeeper with obvious alarm. Dog was barking and bouncing up and down as if his life depended on it.

'What the blazes…?' Ross came to a halt next to Prim. 'Will somebody please explain to me what the hell is going on?'

The gamekeeper eyed him triumphantly. 'I got them! Caught the blighters red-handed, I did.' He motioned to the men on the floor with the butt of his rifle. 'They're lucky I didn't shoot the pair of them.'

As he looked back at Ross the barrel of the gun waved wildly in his direction.

'For goodness' sake, man, put that blasted gun down. Somebody could get hurt.'

Ross stalked towards him and took the weapon from his hands. Noticing that John had also made it down the stairs, he handed it to him. As he had hoped, his friend knew how to make the thing safe, and he leaned against the banister casually, clearly enjoying the unexpected entertainment.

'But they might run!' the gamekeeper exclaimed, glancing nervously back towards the open door. 'Shut that bleedin' door!' he shouted to the footman. 'And then go and fetch the constable.'

The footman slammed the door and then merely gaped at Ross like a fish.

'There will be no fetching of constables until I say so!' he shouted, at nobody in particular. 'Let's all calm down.'

He said this mostly for his own benefit, because absolutely everyone appeared to be looking to him for direction.

'Can somebody please tell me what is going on?'

The gamekeeper pointed to the floor. 'I caught them red-handed! These two are nothing but *vile poachers*.'

Chapter Twenty

Ross stared at the twin piles of quivering dark rags on the carpet. Their arms were raised, fingers laced on the tops of their heads, and their faces were obscured because they were lying face-down. It seemed to him to be the most humiliating position the gamekeeper could have put them in.

'Stand up, gentlemen,' he said, in his best commanding voice, and pinned the gamekeeper with a no-nonsense stare when the man tried to argue.

The two poachers stood and he got his first proper view of them. One was considerably older than the other, and both of them had clearly gone to great pains to avoid being seen at night. The whites of their terrified eyes glowed in the candlelight in stark contrast to their soot-blackened faces and dark clothes. Despite this, it did not take a genius to work out that neither of them was out to make a profit from their labours. Both were painfully thin, and filthy bare feet poked out of the bottom of their ragged trousers. These poachers could not even afford shoes.

'What have you got to say for yourselves?' he asked flatly, although he already suspected that he knew the answer to his own question.

'Who cares what they have to say for themselves?' the gamekeeper ranted. 'They were caught red-handed. There's a brace of pheasants and a baby deer dead outside. I say we get them arrested right now.'

The man spoke mostly to the other people assembled, Ross noted, in an attempt to get a majority agreement.

'Poaching *is* a capital offence,' John whispered quietly, in case he had not realised the ramifications of the charge.

Ross nodded curtly and glared at his gamekeeper. 'Everyone has the right to defend themselves. I will hear these men and then *I* will decide what is to be done with them. Do I make myself clear?'

The gamekeeper stepped back, affronted. 'I saw them with my own eyes. Do you doubt my word?'

Carstairs stepped between them smoothly. 'Of

course not, my dear fellow—but it is only fair to allow these men to speak and tell their side of the story.'

The gamekeeper, still disgruntled, nodded once and stood to one side.

Ross turned back to the two sorry fellows in front of him. 'Can I assume, from the peculiar way that you are both dressed, that you *did* come here tonight intent on killing those animals?'

The younger of the two looked about to burst into tears. Under all the soot Ross determined the lad to be little more than sixteen.

The other man stepped forward. 'My son had nothing to do with it. I am to blame. If you have to arrest someone, then let it be me.'

He stood proudly, his thin shoulders so straight that Ross could see the shape of the bones sticking out.

'Why did you do it?' Ross asked quietly, and he watched the man look at his own filthy feet for a moment before he stared back at him in defiance.

'I was trying to feed my family.'

'And the only way to do that is stealing?' Ross countered.

The man looked at his feet again. 'Now it is. Ain't no work around here any more.'

Ross scraped a hand over his face and sighed.

He knew the desperation of poverty too. 'What's your name?'

'Tom Farrow.' The older man's voice shook, but he looked Ross square in the eye.

'If you want honest work, Tom, for both you and your son, get yourselves cleaned up and report back here at six in the morning. My housekeeper will find you something to do.'

The poachers stared back at him, dumbfounded, but the gamekeeper could not hide his disgust.

'If you let them get away without proper punishment word will spread and we will be overrun with poachers!'

Ross ignored him. 'Reggie—help these men to carry their dinner home. Get one of the footmen to go too.'

The big man nodded and lumbered towards the door.

'Th-thank you, sir,' the older poacher stammered, his eyes filled with grateful tears. 'You won't regret this. I swear it.'

Ross waved away his thanks. 'Six o'clock sharp. My housekeeper Miss Prim runs a tight ship and I will expect you to earn your wages.'

'Yes, sir! Thank you, sir.' Both men nodded and scurried after Reggie.

'I'll go too,' offered John, casually hoisting the gun under his arm. 'Just in case.'

'You should have called the constable and thrown the book at them,' the gamekeeper squawked as he pulled roughly on Ross's arm. 'Proper justice needs to be done!'

'Don't lecture *me* about "proper justice",' he hissed, directly into the gamekeeper's face. 'If there was proper justice in this world then those people would not be starving!'

The man cowered back as if struck. 'I cannot work for a man who refuses to listen to me.'

'Then I suggest you pack your bags,' Ross said in annoyance. 'Because I do refuse to listen.' He saw Cook and Prim were watching him warily. 'And what the hell are you lot staring at?' he bit out unreasonably. 'Go back to bed.'

Ross did not wait to see if they all complied. Instead he stalked towards his study and slammed the door behind him, ashamed of his own roiling temper. He stalked over to the window and looked out onto the black midnight sky in an attempt to calm down.

After a few minutes he heard a knock on the door.

'I have brought you some tea.'

Prim did not wait for him to answer. She was already heading across the floor with the tea tray when he looked round. She deposited it on the little table and sat down to pour.

'Please don't lecture me on the proper order of things,' he said, when he could stand her silence no longer.

She stirred a spoonful of sugar into his cup and held it out to him. 'I have no intention of lecturing you. I came to give you some tea. You appear to be a little out of sorts.'

'I am sorry for shouting,' he responded, feeling more than a little guilty. 'I don't like to lose my temper.'

'We all lose out temper sometimes...'

He could hear the amusement in her voice.

'After that circus, it was hardly surprising. I cannot say I have ever been confronted by guns and prisoners in the small hours before. It was all quite exciting.'

Her good humour calmed him better than staring at the sky ever could.

Ross wandered back towards the window. 'I suppose I have given every poacher in the county a good reason to come here now,' he said after a while, and then sighed heavily. 'But I am not prepared to send two men to their deaths for a few birds and a deer. I know that is what is expected of me, now that I am a landowner and because of some silly gentlemen's code, but I won't do it. Did you take a good look at them? They were *starving*, for God's sake. I know how awful that feels.'

As a child he had not been able to sleep sometimes because of the hunger pains in his belly.

He heard the soft rustle of her voluminous nightgown as she came up alongside him and placed her hand on his bare arm in comfort.

'For what it's worth, I thought you handled the situation perfectly. Cook says that she recognised Tom Farrow. He used to be a tenant on this estate—although all the old tenants were displaced from here a long time ago, when the Earl of Runcorn raised their rents. She said that the Farrows were a hard-working family. They are clearly desperate. I am glad that you showed them some lenience.'

'Then you don't think me a soft touch?' he asked, facing her for the first time. Her golden hair was secured in a single loose plait that fell over one shoulder, and his fingers itched to undo it.

It slid sideways as she tilted her head and smiled at him. 'I'm afraid that I *do* think you are a soft touch. We all do.' At his pained expression she chuckled. 'If being a soft touch means that you rescue washed-up boxers, or feed a stray mongrel scraps from your own plate when you think nobody is looking, or show mercy to people who need it the most, then I think being a soft touch is quite admirable. Most of the maids are in love with you because of it. Even Cook goes a little misty-eyed when she talks about you, and she's old enough to be your grandmother.'

Ross smiled wickedly. 'That is because of my dashing good looks and abundant charm. I am amazed that you can keep your hands off me.' He tossed her a smouldering look, but ruined it by laughing.

She regarded him with amusement. 'There you go again—I have never known a person so unwilling to take a compliment as you are. You constantly try to deflect or joke your way around it, but you cannot conceal the truth. Accept it, Ross Jameson. You are a nice man—and all your charm and humour cannot disguise that one simple fact.'

It secretly pleased him that she had seen that side of him when so many didn't—but he scowled out of habit. '*Nice* sounds so bland. I deserve a much better adjective than that. What about charming?'

She shook her head, smiling. 'That's what you want people to see. How about kind?' she countered. 'Or loyal?'

'Now you make me sound like a dog,' he muttered as he crossed his arms over his chest belligerently.

He enjoyed flirting with this woman, he realised, and perhaps a little too much—because now that his temper had evaporated he wanted to peel her nightgown off and have his way with her.

Her eyes briefly flicked downwards and he remembered that he was wearing nothing but his breeches. By the guilty look on her face Prim had only just realised that as well, but she quickly dissembled.

'I shall leave you to your tea and your bad mood,' she said, turning towards the door.

Ross caught her hand and spun her back to face him. 'You're in your nightgown—I'm practically naked. It would be a terrible shame to waste such an opportunity.'

'You are incorrigible,' she muttered, with no real conviction.

'I like that better than *nice*,' he said, and he pulled her into his arms.

As usual, she braced her hands against his chest and regarded him warily. Ross sighed and let go of her.

'It seems ridiculous that we are behaving this way. We both feel this compelling attraction for each other. Why bother fighting it?'

'Because I am not sure that it is sensible.' She moved behind the chesterfield and out of his reach again.

'You are just running away again. Do you believe that I might turn out to be as worthless as your idiot fiancé?'

Hannah shook her head and sighed. 'You are nothing like him, Ross. I know that. That is the problem, I suppose. I certainly feel a great affection for you, and I am sorely tempted, but...'

Hannah desperately wanted to be brave enough to walk over there and give in to her feelings. It was not as if she seriously now believed him to be the rogue she had once sought to expose. He *was* a good man. Much better than her treacherous brother, Eldridge, and every other former friend she had thought she'd had in society. She felt it in her heart. Ross Jameson was decent and honest, and she did have affection for him.

More than merely affection, she realised. It was quite possible that she was already a little bit in love with him.

'But what?' he asked.

'I don't want to rush into anything that I might regret...and you *do* frighten me.'

'I frighten you?' His laughing eyes danced as he spoke. 'I think your reaction to me frightens you more. Be brave, Prim. Don't let that idiot from the past hold you back. Take a risk.'

'I am not a gambler, Ross. I do not take risks.'

'Life is one big gamble, Prim. If you do not take any risks you do not reap any rewards.'

'But you still might lose.'

And such a loss was too unbearable to contemplate.

His lips curved into a wry smile. 'I never gamble anything that I am not prepared to lose. Even if that is my heart.'

He circled her slowly, his gaze locked on hers intently, and she realised that he was nowhere as confident as he pretended. There was uncertainty and hope swirling in those tempting green eyes.

'I cannot predict the future, Prim, and I cannot promise you that this will all work out perfectly, but I do think that these feelings we have for each other are worth exploring. Will you give it a chance?'

She swallowed nervously, but let him slide his arms around her waist. He was offering more than a brief affair, her heart argued, she *should* give him a chance.

He saw her waver and raked her with a hot look. 'Is it my dastardly reputation that puts you off?'

Hannah felt her resolve beginning to fade as

he bent his head and kissed the tip of her nose. 'I am starting to believe that your reputation is ill-deserved—I cannot understand why other people do not seem to see it. If only someone from the newspapers had seen you earlier... They would have had to have published something positive about you for once.'

He nibbled on her neck and she was powerless to prevent herself from arching against him.

'Does it bother you that they say the most terrible things?' she asked, to stall him and by default to give herself time to consider the ramifications of what was happening almost too quickly.

He groaned against her skin. 'I can think of much better things to do than talk about the newspapers.'

He went to kiss her again but she tilted her head away and looked up at him. '*Do* they bother you?'

'Terrible things make good stories. Good stories make people buy newspapers. There is no point in trying to change that. It is basic commerce.'

'Are they all lies—or is there a grain of truth to some of them?' Hannah was trying to take her mind off the clever things he was doing with his lips and doing a very poor job of it.

'There is the odd grain of truth,' he admitted between kisses. 'But that is about it.'

'So you did *not* once cavort naked with two opera dancers on the stage at Covent Garden?' Hannah asked playfully.

He shook his head solemnly. 'I wish I had, though. I think I might have enjoyed it.'

'And you deny seducing that vicar's daughter?'

He chuckled and shrugged dismissively. 'Surely they have accused me of worse than that?'

'One story said that you regularly deflower virgins,' she stated boldly, and that earned her a shocked look.

'To the best of my knowledge,' he said carefully, 'I am not aware of ever deflowering even one. I think I would have remembered.'

If he carried on making her feel quite so wanton and wicked as he was right this minute, that might well change, she mused—and quite soon. She did not have the capacity to resist him tonight. Not any more.

'I also read that you have ravaged a few of the wives of the aristocracy.'

He struggled to meet her eye. 'I might have done that,' he conceded. 'Once or twice. But I was invited to do so by the wives in question and they were very happy about it.'

His lips found her neck again and she sighed happily.

'We already know that you win things in card games—this house and that ship you bragged to me about—but the newspapers say that you cheat. How do you plead, sir?'

'I do not cheat. I just have a talent for re-membering numbers. I see patterns…track the probability of things. It keeps my mind sharp—although to be honest it is much more of a challenge to lose.' He was looking quite pleased with himself.

'You expect me to believe that somebody who has such a talent with numbers *deliberately* goes out of their way to lose? I won't believe it.' She snuggled against him.

'That is the fun of it. I know exactly how to win—but to *lose* takes real skill. You have no idea how hard it is to lose a game when your hand is infinitely better than your opponent's. It takes a great deal of strategy. You have to throw away all your good cards at just the right moment or it becomes obvious. Also, you have to save enough atrocious cards to lay down when your opponent has nothing better than mediocre. It is the very best feeling in the world to see a man sitting smugly in front of you, gloating at his skill and good fortune, when secretly you know that *you* created it for him. I promise you I lose as much as I win—not that I ever let on, of course.'

He was so handsome when he was grinning—it made her feel quite dizzy.

'Where would be the fun in that?' she said sarcastically. 'Remind me never to play cards with you.'

She knew he was no cheat. She would not have given her heart to a scoundrel.

'One newspaper even said that you surrendered your own father to the authorities for a reward!' She giggled against his chest but he had stiffened instantly.

'There was no reward,' he said bluntly, and allowed her to push him away.

'I'm sorry...?' Hannah was both outraged and horrified at his admission. Deep down, she had believed that those rumours were as ridiculous as all the others. She had to have misheard. 'You are not denying the validity of the story, then?'

When he shook his head, she stalked across the room with her arms wrapped around her, suddenly chilled to the very bone.

'What difference does the lack of reward make?'

He regarded her calmly, his eyes for once inscrutable and cold. 'I think it makes the world of difference. To suggest that I did it for financial gain makes me appear mercenary.'

It was as if the ground had been cruelly ripped from under her. 'But you *did* do it? You surrendered your own father to the authorities?'

What was that if it was not mercenary?

He nodded.

'And he died as a result?'

He nodded curtly again.

'Do you feel no guilt whatsoever?' Hannah spat, not caring how disgusted she sounded at this revelation.

Just when she had finally started to see him as a decent person—had harboured some faint hope that they might have a future together—he had decided to show her his true colours. It was a crushing blow. He was no better than her treacherous brother after all. Everything had been a sham.

'How do you sleep at night?'

Ross regarded her coldly, then shrugged his shoulders. He raised his eyes to the ceiling, shaking his head with disappointment at her reaction, and then regarded her levelly.

'I sleep surprisingly well. True blackguards always do.'

His green eyes had frozen to ice and his lips had thinned into a flat line of disdain. It shocked her that he had the audacity to be angry at *her* when he had been the one to bring his own father's life to an abrupt end.

'What sort of person does that to their own flesh and blood? Why did you do such a terrible thing?' she cried, desperately wanting him to make it all right. There *had* to be a good reason.

'That is none of your business, Prim,' he answered flatly.

Then he turned on his heel and walked out of the room.

Chapter Twenty-One

Ross had little appetite and toyed with his breakfast. He had often heard people claim that words had cut them to the quick, but had not fully realised exactly what that phrase meant. Until today. Hannah's complete disgust, and her harsh judgement without first asking him for the facts or his side of the story, had almost literally cut him to the quick. There was now a tiny ache somewhere close to his heart that simply would not go away, no matter how much he willed it to.

One minute she had been all giggly and compliant, exactly as he imagined a siren who swam naked would be, and the next she had recoiled from him as if he were something nasty that had attached itself to his shoe. Even after he had told her he was prepared to risk his heart she had still chosen to believe all the rot written about him.

What hurt most of all—although he realised

that he was more devastated than hurt—was the fact that she had been so quick to judge him. After everything. She had not given him the benefit of the doubt.

There was no way in hell he was going to beg and plead with her to trust him now. He deserved better than that.

John snapped his fingers directly in front of his nose and it shocked him. 'Sorry. I did not get enough sleep last night.' That was almost the truth anyway. 'You were saying…?'

Ross turned his full attention back to his friend, determined not to think about his naked siren and his bruised, aching heart. He was a fool for ever letting his guard down.

'I was saying,' John said wearily, 'that I am beginning to think that your Miss Prim is not a spy after all. I have left all manner of interesting documents lying around to tempt her, and despite my best efforts she does not pay any of them a blind bit of notice. What sort of a spy does that?'

Ross idly glanced at the morning's post on the table in front of him. He had not noticed anything funny about the seals on his letters recently either. 'She's not a spy,' he agreed. She was judgemental, changeable and callous, but he was certain that she was not working for the East India Company.

Ross had obviously said the wrong thing, because his friend scowled at him. 'Then how do you explain the fact that all her references are false and nobody has ever heard of her?'

Ross sighed. 'Perhaps she did it to get this job? We have certainly told a few white lies in order to get contracts that might otherwise have gone elsewhere. You used to claim to be commodore of a fleet of merchant ships, when in actual fact you only had the one—and we would not have had that if I had not won it in a card game.'

'Yes,' John spluttered, 'but we managed to do the job well enough.'

'And Prim has proved herself to be an excellent housekeeper despite her lies.'

How pathetic was he that even now he could not help giving her the benefit of the doubt?

John grunted and attacked his eggs. 'Are you saying that we should give up?'

Ross nodded. He could hardly condemn the woman for being enterprising when he was guilty of the same. If only she had been so benevolent last night…

Hannah found herself spending the entire morning alone with Captain Carstairs, sorting through the study. Ross was nowhere to be seen and Captain Carstairs was not really much help in telling her where he had gone. The man had been waffling on about 'the thieving East India Company' for the better part of an hour now, and her ears were ringing.

In a way, she was glad that she did not have to face Ross just yet. She was bitterly disappointed in him, and in herself for letting her guard down. A man who would betray his own father was capable of anything—and she would do well to remember that fact. He was no better than her idiot brother in that regard. Both of them prepared to betray their own kin.

She had not slept after she had finally gone to bed. Her mind had been swirling with so many contradicting thoughts that she had not known quite what to make of it all. In the end, it all boiled down to one simple truth. Ross could be kind, thoughtful and charming when it suited him—and hard, cold and manipulative when he needed to be. He was not a man she could entrust her heart to.

The very fact that she almost had... Well, frankly that made her livid. She should have trusted her instincts. She had known he had a talent for charming people for his own gain and yet had still allowed it to happen to *her*. She had to give him credit for being persuasive. He had known exactly what to say to weaken her resistance—and like an idiot she had fallen into his honeyed trap.

You have lost your confidence. Open your-self up to possibilities. You are a beautiful and desirable woman. Who will put flowers on your grave?

Ugh! Just thinking about it made her realise how contrived it had all been. And she had almost succumbed. Silly, stupid, needy fool that she was.

A stray letter had slipped inside the pile of bills that she was going through and she snatched it up in annoyance. They had finished all the correspondence days ago. With an air of frustrated resignation she opened it, to see if it was worth keeping or one of Reggie's 'specials'—the name as she had come to use for all the rubbish. Why Ross had entrusted all his filing to an illiterate man she had long since ceased to find amusing.

To begin with it appeared to be a brief thank-you letter, but something made her look at it twice.

It was her brother's name.

Automatically she slipped the letter into the pocket of her apron. It was probably a coincidence, but it would not hurt to read it later.

When Carstairs toddled off in search of tea she finally had her chance. The letter had come from their old family solicitor. She remembered Mr Compton-Lewis as being a humourless and forthright man who had visited Barchester Hall occasionally when she had been growing up. Once her father had died she had not seen him again, but she had received correspondence from him after her brother's death. George had left everything in such a muddle that the solicitor had struggled to unravel it all.

The last time she had heard from him had been several months ago, when he had informed her of the unexpected five thousand pounds. He'd told her he had placed the bequest in a London bank, on her behalf, and had wished her well now that her brother's estate was finally settled.

She had assumed the solicitor had transferred funds from the trust set up by her father. It was the one and only thing that she was truly grateful to her father for. He had kept that safe from George, at least.

This missive was brief.

Dear Mr Jameson,
Thank you for your recent and very generous offer to my clients. Unfortunately I must decline it on their behalf. The remaining family of the late Earl of Runcorn are not in a financial position to take over the enor-

*mous burden of Barchester Hall at present,
nor are they likely to be in the foreseeable
future. As I am sure you are aware, such a
great house requires significant investment
and good stewardship.*

*The three Steers spinsters are quite con-
tent to stay in Yorkshire, and are not up to
the enormous task that such a benevolent
bequest would require.*

Yours sincerely

G.J. Compton-Lewis Esquire

The dreadful words made her feel light-
headed. Captain Carstairs had been telling the
truth. Ross *had* offered the house back to the
family but their solicitor had taken it upon himself to keep that pertinent fact from her. Why
would he do that?

Hannah should have felt anger, and she supposed that would come soon enough, but instead
all she could think about was her own shame. All
this time she had been so convinced that her family had been wronged—and they had. But not by
the person she had originally thought.

She had been so quick to see the worst in Ross
again last night. He was not a thief. Nor even a
particularly ruthless opportunist, if this letter
was to be believed. In the eyes of the law he was

the legal owner of Barchester hall, and yet it now appeared he had been quite happy to give it away after all, because it was the right thing to do.

Why was she always so quick to blame him for her predicament?

Ross was not malicious or cruel. In actual fact she knew in her heart that he was not capable of being either of those things, and bitterly regretted thinking the very worst. *Again.* There had to be a good reason why he had betrayed his own father. She owed him an apology. And the truth.

Ross had taken the ledger up to his bedchamber because he wanted to be able to work on it undisturbed. That was the lie he was trying desperately to believe. The truth was even more pathetic. He could not face Prim when he was this upset. He needed time to harden his heart and hide his wounded feelings before he faced the woman again.

With any luck Carstairs would miraculously catch her in some form of espionage and throw her out unceremoniously on her dimpled arse, and then he would never have to face her again. That thought made the little ache close to his heart throb again, and he rubbed it in irritation.

As if he had conjured her, Prim burst through

his bedroom door and stared at him dolefully with her blasted big blue eyes.

'What do you want?' he said harshly, and then remembered his pride and pretended to work on the ledger.

'I know that you have refused to see me but I have to apologise,' she whispered. 'I am so very sorry for the way I behaved towards you. It was unforgivable.'

Ross scratched a total in one of the columns and forced his features to appear neutral. 'I have come to expect it from you, Prim. You are a constant source of disappointment to me.'

She recoiled as if he had slapped her, and fat tears gathered in her limpid eyes. 'You are right.' She sounded completely despondent. 'Would you like me to leave?'

'No!' That blasted ache spread under his ribs and filled his chest with pain. 'I should like you to stay. At least until the renovations are complete. That is the one thing you are good for.' He hated the fact that he was being spiteful and looked back down at his numbers. 'If that is all, then we are done.'

She stood rooted to the spot for a moment, then turned and quietly closed his bedroom door behind her.

Hannah stumbled down the stairs blindly. She

deserved that, she knew. He had every right to be angry at her. Every right to dislike her.

When she got to the bottom she collided with Captain Carstairs. He took one look at her and his eyes widened in alarm.

'Are you quite all right, Miss Preston?'

'Oh, Captain Carstairs,' she wailed, 'I have been such an idiot!' Then she promptly burst into tears.

Chapter Twenty-Two

It was Reggie who next interrupted him. He shuffled into Ross's bedchamber as the afternoon sun was at its hottest and then slumped heavily onto the bed.

'Well, I hope you are proud of yourself. Poor Prim has been crying for hours.'

Ross tried to suppress the pang of guilt that came at this announcement and shrugged as if he did not care. 'She only has herself to blame. How dare she stand in judgement of me when she knows nothing about it?'

'And whose fault is *that*?' the big oaf said reasonably. 'You could have explained yourself but you didn't. You never do. Look at it from her point of view. One minute she thinks you're her prince and the next she thinks you killed your dad. Me and the Captain want to know why you didn't tell her what a bastard he was.'

'Because she didn't ask,' he replied with a touch of belligerence.

She had. Eventually. But by then he'd been riled and wounded and angry, and had felt foolish for offering her his heart, so he had lashed out in his customary fashion.

Reggie had the nerve to look at him if he was stupid. 'The Captain thinks you didn't tell her because you were frightened she'd disapprove. You have to tell her. Sometimes women like to be confided in.'

He nodded sagely after his final point, to make sure that Ross understood it was important. The fact that Reggie had given so much consideration to it made him feel even worse.

Ross stood up and began to pace in exasperation. 'She'll get over it. And then everything will be back to normal.' But would he get over it? Right now he sincerely doubted it.

Reggie rolled his eyes and stared down through the mess that had once been his nose. 'She won't get over it, Ross. You've really hurt her feelings.'

'And she's hurt *mine*!' His irritation grew when he saw Reggie smile knowingly, as if he understood better than Ross did.

'That's precisely the point—I ain't never known you to be so upset by a girl. Me and the

Captain both think you've got a soft spot for her. Go and find her and make it up.'

'I most certainly do *not* have a soft spot for her.' Yes, he did. He could not stop thinking about her. He wanted to kiss her more than strangle her, at least. 'What did you mean when you said she thought I was her prince?'

It was a sad state of affairs that now he was actively seeking Reggie's romantic advice, but he was just a tiny bit curious.

'To hear her speak, you're a bleeding saint. 'Course, I couldn't make out the half of what she was saying, on account of all the grizzling, but that was the gist. That girl has strong feelings for you.'

'Did she cry a lot?' Ross was feeling more miserable by the second. He had been uncharacteristically cruel.

'If you call hours and hours a lot. Even Cook couldn't get her to stop. She just kept saying that it was best if she left Barchester Hall for good.'

Now Ross felt truly wretched. She had asked him why he had done it and he had clammed up and sulked. He had behaved like a lion with a thorn in its paw. When she had tried to apologise he had called her a disappointment. He had been a cad.

'Where is she now?'

'No idea. She said she was going for a walk to think about things. We haven't seen her since.'

Ross had a pretty good idea where he might find her, though.

Twenty minutes later his suspicions were confirmed. Prim was floating on her back, eyes closed, as naked as the day she was born. The sight of her made his groin harden and his blood heat.

Before he could think better of it, Ross skirted around to the opposite side of the pond and stripped off his clothes. What better way was there to make things up than this? She was sorry. He was sorry. They didn't need to waste time talking about it. He had a strange desire to hold her in his arms.

'Hello, Prim.'

The sound of his voice startled her and she sank under the water with flailing arms. When she spluttered, coughing, back to the surface he was swimming towards her with a wicked glint in his eyes.

'Don't come any further,' she shrieked, while simultaneously trying to cover her naked body with her hands and trying to stand. Unfortunately the water in the centre of the pond was a few inches too deep, and she was forced to tread water one-handed instead.

'Why ever not?' he said innocently. 'Don't tell me you are naked under there?'

Like an otter, he suddenly dived under the water to have a look, and when he surfaced close by he was grinning.

'You *are* naked! I am scandalised. Too shocked for words. Guess what?' he whispered as he stealthily came towards her. 'So am I.'

Hannah tried her best to swim out of his reach, but with one hand clutching her bare breasts staying vertical in the water proved to be quite difficult. 'Ross—please,' she pleaded. 'Stay back. This is not… Oh…!'

Her voice trailed off as his arm grabbed her around the waist and pulled her tight against him. His skin was warm and slick against hers.

'You were going to say not proper, weren't you? You are absolutely right, Prim. This is not the least bit proper.'

His face was creeping closer to hers and she was forced to brace one hand on his shoulder or drown.

'Are you going to move that arm?'

He stared pointedly at the arm in question. It was sandwiched between them, still covering her bosom. Hannah blinked in shock.

'I see that I must resort to more dastardly means.'

With one hand still wrapped around her waist, he used his free palm on the back of her head to pull her mouth onto his. Like an idiot, she let him.

The kiss he bestowed upon her was achingly gentle. His lips slanted slowly over hers until her own began to respond. Little by little her resolve melted, until she finally succumbed fully to it. Goodness, the man could kiss, she thought fleetingly, before he tangled his clever tongue with hers. Hannah could do little more than cling one-armed onto his strong shoulder as she floated, helplessly suspended, next to him.

He pulled her hips flush against his own and she felt the hard length of him press into her abdomen. Did this mean that he had forgiven her? She closed her eyes and tried not to hope. The man confused her so very much. One minute he was generous and noble, and the next he could coldly hand his father over to the authorities and seemingly not feel guilty for it. But the more she knew him, the less likely it seemed that he could be that cruel and callous. Should she trust her instincts?

As if he'd read her mind, he kissed her softly. 'My father was not a nice man. I *will* explain myself. But please don't make me do it here. Kiss me, Prim.'

Hannah saw the truth in his eyes and did as he asked. She arched against him and he groaned. Emboldened by his obvious desire, she finally relinquished her hold on her modesty and wove her fingers into his slick wet hair, matching the movements of his teeth and tongue urgently. For long moments they clung together like that, until both wanted more. He wrapped her legs around his waist and lifted her so that her breasts came clear of the water and were level with his face.

Initially Hannah felt exposed, and embarrassed to be so intimately displayed, but then she saw the admiration reflected in his eyes and felt his hardness jut against her insistently. When his hungry lips finally sought her puckered nipple and drew it into his mouth she cried out and undulated her hips against his urgently. Her body wanted him inside her.

'Please...' she heard herself moan. 'Please, Ross.'

He tortured her other breast first, worshipping the hard tip with his tongue until she made a guttural sound that she had never made before, and reached between their bodies to touch him intimately.

Now it was his turn to growl in pleasure. With her legs still wrapped around his waist he began to carry her out of the water, kissing her neck, face, breasts—anything he could reach. Only when they were safely upon the bank did he carefully lower her body to the ground.

He knelt beside her and allowed his eyes to slowly take in everything. 'You are beautiful,' he whispered in wonder, and she believed him.

'So are you.'

It was the truth. Naked, he was magnificent. The dark hair on his chest clung wetly to his muscles and wove its way over his flat abdomen, stopping at the base of his large and rigid manhood.

Shame flooded her again and she thought she would cry. 'I am sorry—I feel wretched about my behaviour last night.'

One side of his mouth turned up in a smile. 'We were both in the wrong. I should have explained, but I have got into the habit of never explaining. Let's not talk about it now.'

Hannah sighed at the sight of the raw emotion shimmering in his eyes. It was more than desire. She held her arms open shyly and he gratefully fell into them. Once again when their mouths met they forgot about everything except the moment they were in and the sensations they were eliciting from each other.

His hand cupped her breast and his thumb brushed over her nipple until she thought she would die from the pleasure. He eased back a little so that he could stare down into her face, watching her as his fingers brushed over her ribcage and her tummy and then slowly drifted into the soft, downy hair at the top of her thighs, then lower still. He carefully parted her flesh, touching her in a place that had never been touched before, and watched her shudder. Over and over he circled that sensitive spot until she could stand it no more.

'Please, Ross...' Hannah had no idea what she was asking for, and did not care that her legs had fallen open, allowing him to see her most private place. She wanted him to touch it. Her hips rose impatiently into his hand until eventually he positioned his body there, poised to push inside. Her breath caught and he saw her nervous swallow.

'Am I your first?' he asked, suddenly concerned, and she nodded. His eyes closed briefly. When they opened he was smiling. 'Good,' was all he said, and slowly pushed inside.

Inch by glorious inch his hardness filled her. It felt a little alien at first, but the moment he started to move Hannah felt the discomfort ease as pleasure built. She allowed her palms to roam freely over his back and buttocks, revelling in the solid weight of him on top of her. Once again she wrapped her legs around his waist at his encouragement, and he moved her hips to meet his thrusts until her body picked up the rhythm. By then conscious thought had gone, and all she could think of was where their bodies joined and how wonderful it felt to have him sliding in and out of her.

His eyes were locked on hers. She saw affection, tenderness, desire and wonder in their depths.

Even when she shattered and her muscles clenched around him it felt natural. It was as if she had been created to be joined with this remarkable, beautiful and complex man. A few seconds later his own climax rocked through him and she revelled in the beautiful moment when he finally collapsed upon her—fully spent. Their hearts beat together furiously against their ribs until eventually he withdrew from her body and pulled her wordlessly into his arms.

She curled against him instinctively, contented, until she happily drifted off to dreamless sleep.

Ross did not sleep. He couldn't. Making love to her had turned the world on its head and he was still trying to sort out exactly how he felt about it.

He had always enjoyed sex. It was a pleasant

way to pass the time and after a healthy bout of it he usually felt invigorated. But, frankly, the woman in his arms had disarmed him. Granted, she was his first virgin. That might have something to do with it. But the peculiar ache around his heart had got worse and he was overwhelmed with the most enormous feelings of tenderness and possessiveness now that he had had her. Already he wanted her again.

Prim had been no meek virgin. She had writhed and moaned and undulated against him with such untutored but such honest passion that he had lost his head somewhere in that pond. Even now he was not certain that all his wits had returned. For want of a better word, he was stunned. And perhaps bewitched. He was certainly besotted.

She had been so trusting it had humbled him, and it was very satisfying to know that he had been her first. No other man had ever seen her or touched her as he had. He suspected that she would be his last lover. He could not imagine wanting another woman ever again, and hell would freeze over before he allowed her to lie with another man.

She stirred against him and smiled sleepily. 'Hello, Prim,' he managed to whisper, sounding reasonably normal, and kissed the top of her head.

She rolled onto her back and stretched like a cat in the early evening sunshine, giving him a totally unencumbered view of her nudity. 'Hello, yourself...'

She smiled seductively up at him and he realised that the stretching was a deliberate ploy.

'There is nothing Prim about you,' he muttered, running his palm over her breast. 'I should have realised that the first time I spied you swimming in this pond.'

Her lovely eyes narrowed suspiciously. 'The first time?'

Ross chuckled and kissed her. 'I followed you here once.'

Her mouth hung open in shock, so he kissed her nose instead.

'Don't look so outraged. I did warn you that I am not a gentleman.'

'Obviously not,' she replied, half smiling, half still aggrieved. And then she kissed him in forgiveness. 'I suppose ladies do not swim naked in broad daylight either.'

'I think I might be in love with you, Prim.'

The words had just tumbled out, but he realised that he meant them. He was not risking his heart—he had lost it to her long ago. He had no control over how he felt about her and there was no point in pretending otherwise.

Her blue eyes blinked back at him. 'I think I might be in love with you too. And that terrifies me.'

The ache near his heart lessened. 'Well, that is a good start.'

'But I still feel awful about the way I reacted last night.'

'You hit a sore spot and I reacted badly. My relationship with my father is...was...complicated.'

She rolled on her side and faced him silently. Perhaps Reggie was right and women did want to be confided in. If they were destined to be together she would expect it. He exhaled and gathered her close to his chest so that he would not have to see her eyes when he spilled out all the sordid details.

'My father had little to do with us when I was growing up. He was a forger and a drinker. When I was younger he turned up from time to time like a bad penny...' she chuckled at his inadvertent pun '...but after my sister was born we saw him less and less. By then he was in with a very bad crowd. When he wasn't drunk he gambled. Badly. Mum used to say that he would bet the shirt off his back if anybody would take it. He regularly lost the rent money, and more often than not we all had to sleep on the streets. When I was about fifteen, Mum kicked him out for good. Things improved then. She got a job serving in a tavern, and I was old enough to bring in some money too—that's when I started to load cargo at the docks. I don't think I saw him again for years.'

Those years had been tough but happy, he remembered.

'Then one day he turned up again. We would have nothing to do with him but he kept loitering, kept asking for money. Sarah, my sister, was thirteen by then, and she always was a pretty thing. By then I was busy trying to better myself, and I did not spend as much time protecting my family as I should have.'

Prim snuggled against him and rested her hand on his heart. It made him feel a little better, but he would never truly forgive himself for his absence during that awful time.

'My father was in a lot of trouble then—not that we fully understood it at the time. It turned out he had been passing counterfeit money to the particularly nasty owner of a gaming hell to pay the huge debts he had racked up there. The owner gave him a week to find real money to repay those debts or face death. He asked us for money and we sent him packing. One night Mum came to the docks in a state. Sarah had gone missing and somebody said that she had been seen with my father. I searched everywhere but couldn't find her. But I found him. He was roaring drunk, as usual, and claimed he had not seen Sarah at all. I knew he was lying. He was happy. And he was never happy so I knew something wasn't right. I got frightened. London can be a dreadful place for a young girl on her own.'

Ross wondered if he should censor the rest of the story but decided against it. It was best if she knew the whole truth.

'I grabbed him and shook the bastard. I kept asking him where my sister was, but he just kept laughing and telling me that it was none of my concern. He repeated the same phrase over and over again. "She'll be home tomorrow night—they've promised". In the end my temper got the better of me and I beat it out of him.'

He felt bile rise at the memory. He had nearly killed his father when he had found out the truth.

'He had sold Sarah to a brothel.'

Hannah's eyes widened. 'What happened?' Without thinking she wrapped her arms around him. He looked so utterly distraught she wanted to protect him from the memory more than she wanted to hear the truth.

'It was a special brothel. High-class. Any and all perversions were catered for—at a price. Fancy gents paid big money for virgins—the younger the better. My father had sold Sarah's virginity for one hundred pounds.'

At her sharp intake of breath he kissed her.

'It never happened, thank God. I broke in and stole her back. Fortunately the Viscount who had paid for her had not yet arrived, and the brothel keeper had locked her in one of the bedrooms.'

For the first time during the tale she saw a smile touch his lips.

'My sister is blessed with a fine pair of lungs. I could hear her screaming and carrying on a mile away, so it was easy to find the room she was locked in. Sarah was shaken, but thankfully unharmed.'

'Thank goodness you found her.' Hannah kissed his cheek and he sighed.

'After that I went to the magistrate. I couldn't risk my father doing something like that again, but I didn't want to drag Sarah's name through the mud either. So I told them all about his forging. He was arrested and tried. I testified against him—so did Mum. We celebrated when he was sentenced to twelve years' transportation. I can't say I felt anything when I heard that he had died of typhus on the ship. If that makes me a bad person then so be it.'

Hannah kissed him hard. 'You are the best man I have ever known. I am *glad* your father is dead.' To think of that young girl, abducted, frightened and potentially violated, made her blood boil. 'What sort of a man does that to his own daughter? Now I understand why you have them living in Kent.'

'They are safe there,' Ross said quietly, turning to face her. 'It has made it easier to do what I've had to, knowing that they are safe. I always intended to make something of myself—right from a young lad. I did not want my entire life to be as hard as those early years were, but what happened gave me more of an incentive to do it quickly. And probably spurred me on to aspire to more. Bad things like that do not happen to people with money. Money gives you power and security. It gives you control over your own destiny. I started dabbling in buying and selling. I told you I have a knack with numbers—that helps— and I have an eye for things that sell well. It has taken about eight years to get where I am now. You don't think badly of me?'

His green eyes were more vulnerable than she would have thought possible.

'Never again,' she promised, ignoring her niggling doubts about Tremley's gambling marker and rolling on top of him to stare lovingly down into his face. 'I have never met a man like you.'

This time it was she who made love to him.

He needed her understanding and absolution and she wanted to give them to him. She kissed and explored every inch of his body with her hands and mouth while he watched her lazily through hooded eyes and let her do whatever she wanted. He taught her how to ride him and she did so shamelessly, feeling beautiful—buoyed up by the way his eyes devoured her and his body trembled under her touch.

When she felt him pulse inside her she cried out joyfully, not caring if she was heard. All that mattered was that she was in love and was loved in return.

Chapter Twenty-Three

Well after the sun went down the pair of them crept back into the house, giggling like naughty children, and rolled around in his big bed enthusiastically until just before dawn.

Exhausted, Hannah slept until mid-morning and the wretch let her. When she finally did awaken the late morning sun was streaming through the window.

She opened her eyes to find him propped on one elbow and smiling down at her with a very satisfied expression on his face. The tangled sheet barely covered her legs, and she realised with a start that she was displaying everything to him.

Instinctively she grabbed the sheet's edge and dragged it over her naked body, only to have in unceremoniously snatched away.

'Too late, Prim,' he said with a triumphant

smile. 'I have already seen everything. If you recall, I think I have kissed most of it too. Just to be sure, I should probably do it again. It's important to be thorough.'

Before she knew it his lips had descended on to hers.

'Wait,' she said, staying him with her hand. 'There is something important I need to talk to you about. I wanted to tell you yesterday, but we got a little carried away.'

The distinct sounds of the maids going about their usual morning duties floated through the bedchamber door. It was like being doused with a bucket of ice water.

'What time is it?' Hannah sat bolt-upright in alarm. 'Everybody is up and about! I should have been up hours ago.' In a blind panic, she scrambled off the bed and scurried around the room, looking for her clothes.

'Don't worry about all that. I hear your employer is very lax about such things. Come back to bed.' Ross was reclining against the pillows, his hands braced under his head, proudly displaying another impressive erection and looking like sin.

'I can't,' she wailed tearing her eyes off him reluctantly. 'I have to get to work. No matter what I do, everyone will know that I have spent the night in here with you!' There were tears of anguish in her cornflower eyes. 'What is everyone going to think?'

Seeing that she was genuinely upset, Ross groaned but sat up. She was hardly a fallen woman, after all, because he had already made up his mind to marry her. Assuming she would have him, of course. But after last night he was hoping that tiny detail was nothing more than a technicality. However, he did understand that she would not want their dirty linen washed in public.

'If I create a diversion you should be able to sneak out and get back to your own room,' he suggested calmly. 'I'll go downstairs and pretend to be looking for you. When you finally make an appearance you can claim to have been unwell. People will understand, especially as you were so obviously upset yesterday. Nobody needs to know that you have been thoroughly ravished and completely ruined.'

He could not help feeling smug about that.

This seemed to placate her, so he pulled on a fresh shirt and combed his hair while she dressed herself.

'Will you come swimming with me later?'

Ross saw her lips curve at the question. 'I would like that.'

He kissed her loudly and smiled down into her lovely face. 'Come on, then—let's break you out of jail.'

She hovered close by as he poked his head out of the bedchamber door. 'The coast is clear.' He turned and winked at her and watched, amused, as she dashed out of his bedroom and disappeared behind one of the servants' doors while he engaged one of the maids in a rambling conversation about the weather.

He found Carstairs and Reggie at the kitchen table, eating. 'Have you seen Prim?' he asked as he carved off a huge slice of bread for himself. 'I cannot find her anywhere.'

He should be on the stage, he thought smugly, so convincing was his delivery. Both men exchanged an amused look, which he ignored. It was only when Cook slammed a cup of tea down in front of him and sniffed her disapproval that he realised something was amiss.

Cook pinned him with her glare. 'Well, as she is not in her room—which was the first place I checked this morning, when I wondered the very same thing—I was rather hoping you might be able to answer that question for me.'

She was looming over him with her hands planted solidly on her wide hips.

Ross acted ignorant and regarded the woman

with concern. 'Prim is missing? Where on earth can she be?'

It was worth a try, but he could tell by her disgusted snort that she did not believe him. All thoughts of a career on the stage vaporised when she swatted him around the head with a towel.

The ghost of a smile played on John's lips as he tapped his chin thoughtfully. 'You saw her last night, Reggie. Where *was* that again?'

Reggie did not bother reciprocating with subtlety. 'I believe, Captain, I last saw her kissing Ross on the landing—just before he carried her into his bedroom.'

Oh, dear, thought Ross guiltily, Prim was not going to like that. By the ferocious look on her face, neither did Cook.

'Don't look at me like that.' He gave her his best roguish grin and held up his hands to ward off another threatened swat. The towel hung poised in Cook's chubby fingers. 'We both lost our heads.'

And all of their clothes. That thought made the corners of his mouth turn up.

Ross lowered his hands in defeat and grinned at her boyishly. 'There is no need for you to be so protective. I promise. For once my intentions are completely honourable.'

'You mean to marry her?' Carstairs dropped

his cup with a clatter and blinked. 'Good grief! I never thought I would see the day. Congratulations, old boy.'

'It is as much of a surprise to me as it is to you, I can assure you, but I find myself rather smitten.' Ross inadvertently rubbed the spot on his ribcage that refused to feel normal. 'But I have not asked her yet. I know women like a man to do that properly.'

He wrapped one arm around Cook's stiff shoulders cajolingly.

'I don't suppose you would rustle up a delicious evening picnic for me? Think how romantic that would be. The sunset, meadow flowers, your lovely food...'

The towel bludgeon dropped and she began to smile a little. 'Don't think that I have completely forgiven you, you scoundrel, but if you are going to make it right... Well, I suppose I *could* make a nice picnic.'

Ross grinned soppily at John and Reggie. 'I would be grateful if you two refrain from telling Prim that you know about last night. She would be mortified. She likes things to be proper.'

'Mum's the word,' said Reggie, rising.

As soon as he had shuffled off John spoke softly. 'Are you completely sure that she is not up to no good?'

Ross sighed and sat down opposite his friend. 'Prim is no spy, John. We both know that. I think that I am a pretty good judge of a person's character, and Prim is kind and caring. She is not capable of true deception. I just know it.'

'Good grief!' John glared at him in disgust. 'You are just smiling to yourself—all wistful and sighing—it is quite nauseating to witness. You look positively lovesick.'

Ross smiled sheepishly in return and heaved a winsome sigh for comic effect.

'You've got a visitor, Ross,' Reggie said, poking his head back into the kitchen. 'He's waiting for you in the hallway.'

Both Ross and John stood and followed the big man out, intrigued.

'Tremley!' Ross strode towards him with his hand outstretched. 'What are you doing here?'

Viscount Tremley met him halfway and returned his friendly handshake enthusiastically. 'I did write to you and tell you I would come—but as I am on my way to London I thought I might beg lunch from you rather than going to an inn. Especially as you were so gushing about this place when I last saw you in town. It has been very lax of you not to offer me an invitation to visit sooner. I thought we were friends.'

His amused eyes scanned the newly decorated hallway before they rested back on Ross.

'I must say, it does look very impressive.'

Ross beamed back with pride. Thanks to Prim, the hallway did now look impressive. So did the morning room and a goodly number of the upstairs bedrooms. It was just as well that he had had the good sense to delegate all of that to her—especially as she would soon be the mistress of this house.

'I shall give you the guided tour later. Come into my fancy new morning room. Reggie—get some tea, would you?'

A sixth sense made Ross turn around. He just knew that she was nearby, and saw the back of her golden head at the top of the staircase.

'Prim! Come here. I have somebody that I would like you to meet.'

She glided down the stairs, smiling, looking lovelier than he had ever seen her in a pretty pink dress that he knew she had donned just for him.

'Viscount Tremley, may I present…' His voice trailed off as Hannah's jaw dropped and she stopped mid-step, halfway down the stairs.

Tremley grinned and rushed up the stairs to greet her. 'There are no need for introductions. We are already acquainted.' Tremley grasped

Prim's limp hand and pressed it to his lips. 'It is lovely to see you again, Lady Hannah.'

The hallway became a blur. But she could recall with great clarity Ross's shock at hearing her honorific. Captain Carstairs gaped in stunned silence, and then stood rigidly and glared at her in accusation. At that moment she knew that he had also recognised her. Then an oblivious Tremley made it all even worse, if such a thing was possible.

'Your generosity continues to surprise me, Ross. It is so kind of you to let Runcorn's sister live in this house.'

Pain flashed briefly in his green eyes before they hardened to sharp emeralds. Other than that, his face was a flat mask. 'Indeed. If you will excuse us for a moment? I need a brief word with *Lady* Hannah.'

Hannah watched Ross stalk from the hallway to his study and could do nothing but scurry after him, feeling sick to her stomach. She had wanted to tell him the truth this morning, but once she'd realised the time she had not. It had been a cowardly decision, she realised now.

He held the door open stiffly and she trailed into the room behind him. Then he slammed the door shut with more force than was necessary.

Anger shimmered off him although he held his body rigid when he finally turned to face her.

'*Lady* Hannah? Runcorn's sister? I think you owe me an explanation.'

'I know that this looks bad—' she started, and then shook her head. This was not the time for excuses. 'This *is* bad—I realise that—and I have wanted to tell you but I could never seem to find the right words to explain—'

He interrupted her with a snarl, his face inches from her and his breathing heavy as he fought to control his emotions. 'You have lied to me. Every step of the way you have lied to me. Why, Prim?'

'You must know that we were desperate. My aunts and I were left with nothing, initially, and I wanted to make everything that George had done right again. I wanted to fix it all. I did not know that you had offered this house back to the family, I swear it.'

There was a hint of hysterical desperation in her voice.

'The solicitor kept it from me. Why he did that I have yet to find out—but he took it upon himself to inform you that the family did not want the house. Had I known that, I never would have deceived you. I thought that you had taken the house by foul means. I believed all the lies printed about you in the newspapers and I suppose that I hoped you were a villain. It made my brother's betrayal so much easier to bear.

'I came here hoping to find some evidence to prove that George had been duped or pressured into handing over the deeds. I was trying to get Barchester Hall back, and perhaps a little piece of my pride as well. You have no idea what it is like to be exiled in the middle of nowhere for something that was a complete lie. Please believe me when I tell you that my opinions began to change rapidly as I got to know you... Everything that has happened between us since—'

'Stop!' He turned his back on her and stalked to the window. 'So you *were* spying on me? I should have trusted my instincts and thrown you out when I first suspected it.' Bracing his arms on the frame, he stared unseeingly into the garden. 'When you accused me of stealing Barchester Hall I should have thrown you out. What did you hope to find, Prim? Evidence of blackmail or fraud? You think so very highly of me?'

She came up behind him and touched his shoulder gently. He snatched his body away as if he had been burned.

'It started like that, but for a long time I have realised that you are not capable of being that devious. I know that I was mistaken. When I found a letter from my brother's solicitor I realised that you had tried to give me my home back, even though you did not have to. You had tried to be decent. Had I known that...'

She touched him again and he did not pull away. Emboldened, she slid her arms around his waist and rested her cheek on his shoulder.

'I fell in love with you, Ross. You are the best man I have ever known.'

The taut muscles in his abdomen relaxed a little before they bunched again under his fine lawn shirt. 'Just to be clear—' his voice became clipped '—you came here to find enough evidence to have me thrown in jail in your attempt to regain Barchester Hall and when you could not find that evidence you simply gave up? Just like that? You expect me to believe that?'

Hannah breathed in his comforting masculine scent and nodded against his back. 'I stopped looking. As time went on my feelings for you grew.'

Callously he prised her arms from around his waist and stepped out of them. 'You're a liar, Prim. And I'm a fool.'

He laughed bitterly and dragged a hand through his black hair in agitation.

'You expect me to believe that what has happened between us is a coincidence? That it never entered that pretty, scheming little head of yours that you could have more? That there was another way of getting your house back? As my wife you would have complete control over it— and I can afford to keep you in *such* comfort. You would get your home back and become a wealthy woman overnight. Don't you think your sudden change of heart is just a little too suspicious to be believed? One minute you sniff and look down your oh-so-proper nose at me—the next you go out of your way to seduce me? It is all just a little too convenient.'

Hannah's mind was reeling at his reading of the situation. 'I never tried to seduce you!' She had not really been averse to it, but she had never gone out of her way actively to pursue him— until now.

'Of course not!' His tone was sarcastic. 'You just happened to wander down to the pond, strip yourself naked and cavort there right in front of me. And like a fool I fell for it. You knew damn well I was watching you.'

'I have been swimming in that pond since I was little girl and I had no idea you were watching me!' Hannah could not understand how he was coming to such preposterous conclusions.

'You suddenly opened your legs for me because you hoped that I would do the right thing by you!' he bit out cruelly. 'That was an even better scenario than having the house to yourself. You'd get to benefit from my fortune, knowing I have to spend a great deal of my time in the city on business. How perfect. You would be the lady of the manor again in return for a few well-timed and convincing sexual favours. It's only a shame that you would have had to have married so far beneath you. But after your own scandal I don't suppose any self-respecting gentleman would touch you. Better to settle for someone who is not a gentleman but who has a fortune to lavish upon you. No wonder you welcomed my touch so enthusiastically.'

'What happened between us happened because *you* instigated it. I am in love with you, Ross—that is why I allowed things to develop the way they did. I wanted you as much as you wanted me. For goodness' sake, I gave my virginity to you. You have to believe me.'

'You gave me a false name, wore a disguise, forged your references.' He counted each of her crimes off on his fingers. 'You opened my mail, broke into my trunks and accused me of cheating, stealing and of being a drunk. So, no, *Lady* Hannah, I do not have to believe you!'

He closed the distance between himself and the door in three quick strides and tore it open.

'I cannot bear to look at you, Prim. You disgust me... I want you to pack your things and go.'

Ross slammed the door behind him, leaving Hannah to stare blankly at it, wondering what had just happened.

It took several moments for the horror of what had transpired to sink in fully. When it did all she could do was slump onto the chesterfield in shock. She had no strength left to do anything else.

Over an hour ticked by as she stared helplessly at the wall. Everything he had accused her of had been true—apart from his dismissal of her feelings for him. Under the circumstances he had every right *not* to believe her. Viewed through his eyes, her actions must appear callous and calculated: when one plan failed she had simply switched to another. A woman cold like that would think nothing of using her innocence and her body as bait if it got her what she wanted.

The worst part of it was that she had only herself to blame. She should have told him the truth and fallen on his mercy the very moment she'd found the solicitor's letter. If she had things might well be very different.

How was she ever going to make this right?

Hannah tried to think of how she should approach Ross again. There was no point in trying while he was so angry, but she had to make him realise that she did love him. Even if he could not bear to look at her again, he had to believe that her feelings for him were true. Perhaps when he was calm he would be more inclined to listen.

Then again, in only a few minutes his clever, strategic brain had created a terrible scenario that was so plausible he had believed it instantly. The longer she left him to stew, the more damage might be done. It was probably best to hunt him down now and beg, plead and reason with him until he had no choice but to listen.

The door opened quietly and Captain Carstairs stepped in. Without acknowledging her presence, he walked stiffly to the bank of cupboards she had had installed and rifled in one of them for something. They were now so well organised that he found what he was seeking almost instantly, then stood and walked towards her, doing very little to conceal the disappointment he felt at her cruel betrayal of his friend. He held out a ribbon-bound document.

'Ross has instructed me to give you this.' He thrust the parchment into her hand and she stared at it blankly.

It was the deeds to Barchester Hall.

Hannah had not thought it possible to feel any more wretched. Even now, when he was so convinced of her guilt and manipulations, he was still trying to do the decent thing.

'I don't want it,' she said, her eyes suddenly filling with tears.

A few weeks ago she would have grabbed them with both hands, but now they meant nothing to her. Without Ross she did not want the house. She pushed the deeds back but Carstairs refused to take them.

'Neither does Ross. You have ruined this house for him.'

The tears fell then. Hannah covered her face with her hands and let them fall.

'We will ensure that all his personal belongings are removed within the week, Lady Hannah,' Carstairs continued coldly, indifferent to her tears. 'After that, you will become responsible for the financial upkeep of Barchester Hall, including paying the wages of the staff. Ross was going to continue doing so until the end of the month, but I cannot in all conscience see his good nature abused like that. You have made enough of a fool of him already. Congratulations, my lady, things could not have turned out better for you.'

'I beg your pardon?'

The Captain's words cut through her despair like a blade. Hannah shot to her feet and launched

herself like a banshee. He was not expecting her
to push him squarely on the chest and stumbled
backwards into the chair behind him. She braced
both her hands on the arms of the chair, caging
him beneath her furious glare.

'Captain Carstairs, you may say what you
want about me. I deserve every one of your petty
insults—and probably more—but if you ever
refer to Ross as a fool again I will knock every
one of those pretty white teeth of yours down
your throat. Do I make myself clear?'

He stared at her, dumbfounded, and then his
expression turned curious. 'Interesting...' he
said, tilting his head to one side. 'Perhaps you
are not a dead loss after all.'

Hannah snatched up the deeds. 'I shall save
you the bother of giving these back to Ross—I
will do it myself. If he thinks he can just benevolently foist this house on me because he is such a
decent, nice and honourable person—and expect
me to accept it—he has another think coming.'

She turned on her heel and marched out.

Several minutes later she had searched the
entire house and found no sign of Ross. She
stalked into the morning room and found Captain Carstairs with Viscount Tremley.

'Where is he?'

'He has taken the carriage and gone back to

London,' Carstairs replied. 'It is a good thing that he kept his bachelor quarters, isn't it? Although I dare say you would have preferred to see him homeless.'

Hannah sat down heavily at this news. 'Oh.' So much for having it out with him here and now. 'What time will he be returning?'

Carstairs shook his head. 'He won't be.'

She should have been upset to hear this, she supposed, but in actual fact the information fed her temper more. What *was* it about men that they just did things without first listening to her? Her former fiancé had called off their engagement without listening to her, their solicitor had tossed away her home without asking her, her father and brother had never, ever consulted her and now Ross was preventing her from having her say.

How typical of him to avoid confrontation. That appeared to be his stock answer to everything—just walk away and leave all the badness festering until it turned to poison. Hannah was sick and tired of it all.

'Then I am going to London,' she declared to the room in general. 'And he will deal with me there.'

Viscount Tremley smiled. 'I would be happy

to drop you there in my carriage, my lady. We can leave within the hour.'

Carstairs glared at him in warning, but Tremley laughed. 'Don't look at me like that, John. If Ross had not intervened in my shambolic life then it would be a mess right now. If he had not won back my marker from Denham then I would be ruined. But he did—and then he made me go home and face my responsibilities while I paid the debt back. Had he not intervened I would still be in London, penniless and feeling sorry for myself. At the time his interference annoyed me, but it did not take long for me to see that what he was doing was for the best. It turns out he was right. There are much more reliable ways of making money than at the gaming tables.

'Now I have become quite the farmer, thanks to Ross. Of course that first year I had to plough, sow and harvest the crops alongside the few paltry labourers I could afford, because I had less than nothing to my name. Oh, how I hated him then! But the second year I was able to hire a few more hands and plant even more. Three years on and it appears I have a knack for growing the right things and selling them at a profit, just as he showed me. I have not played a game of cards since that night...

'He might not thank me right away for interfering now, but I saw how upset he was. He obviously has deep feelings for this lady or else he would not have reacted so badly—so if there is even the slightest chance that they can be happy together then I think she deserves to be heard. I quite like the idea of repaying him in kind. It makes me feel almost noble.'

'Thank you.' Hannah beamed gratefully at Tremley. 'I shall gather my things and I will meet you at the front of the house.'

Chapter Twenty-Four

Thankfully they were on the road within fifteen minutes.

'I have something that belongs to you,' said Hannah as they turned out of the drive, and she handed Tremley the gambling marker she had found. 'I originally thought that Ross had ruined you—*and* my idiot brother—but I cannot help thinking there is some link that binds us all together.'

Tremley turned the small, yellowed piece of paper over in his hand and smiled wistfully. 'Three years ago I was well on the way to completely ruining myself. I lived quite carelessly then, and gambled away far more than I had. I was down to my last few pounds that night, and yet still I did not have the sense to stop. I kept thinking that I could win everything back if only my luck would change—a ridiculous notion, I know, though at the time I believed it sincerely.

'Viscount Denham actively sought me out and offered me odds that were too good to be true. For a stake of two and a half thousand pounds on my part he would double the pot if I beat him. I should have realised that I did not stand a chance—Denham is never beaten at cards—but I was desperate. Needless to say I was trounced. Denham took my marker and demanded that I meet with him on the morrow to discuss how I would pay it. Ross was there.

'I did not know it then, but there is bad blood between him and Denham. It goes back years, and Carstairs has suggested that it has something to do with Ross's sister, but other than that I am none the wiser.'

Hannah knew instantly, but kept her own counsel. It was not her secret to tell, but it was clear Viscount Denham must be the vile aristocrat who had paid for his sister.

'Anyway,' Tremley continued, 'Ross wandered over and threw a ridiculous amount of money in front of Denham against my marker. Denham happily accepted, because Ross has a reputation for losing more games than he wins. Much to Denham's disgust, Ross won every trick. He saved me. If Denham had kept my marker I would have lost everything. That man is completely ruthless and he preys on the foolish, weak and desperate.'

He said this with such venom that it was a surprise when he coloured and apologised.

'I am sorry, Lady Hannah, I did not mean any offence.'

'Why on earth would I be offended?' she asked, genuinely confused.

Tremley regarded her quietly. 'I thought you knew. Ross only played against your brother that night because it was Viscount Denham who was going to take the house. Ross stepped in and took it instead. There is no way that he actually *wanted* the house. He just wanted to beat Denham. I know Ross would have wanted to help your brother see the error of his ways, like he did me.'

Hannah felt a rush of love. 'My brother was indeed foolish, weak and desperate. Had he not been such a pathetic coward then I know Ross would have helped him regain his life just as he did you. But George never gave him the chance to do so—and that is entirely his fault. Not Ross's.'

When the carriage pulled up outside her solicitor's office in the heart of the city, she said her goodbyes to Tremley. He had offered to stay with her on her quest, but she had refused. Whatever happened between her and Ross, she did not want to spoil the friendship the two men had.

Steeling herself for her first confrontation of the afternoon, Hannah marched up the three short steps to the door of Messrs Compton-Lewis and Stroud, Attorneys at Law. Before she faced Ross it was high time she knew the real truth.

A bespectacled clerk greeted her sedately and bade her to wait while he enquired if Mr Compton-Lewis was in. Moments later, the clerk asked her to follow him into a dark and austere office, where the solicitor greeted her with his usual pompous disdain.

'Lady Hannah. I thought you were still rusticating in Yorkshire?'

'I was never rusticating, sir, as well you know. I was banished to Yorkshire by my brother after a scandal. It was all over the papers, if you remember, and I was painted very black indeed.'

She watched him blink in alarm at her bold statement, but she could not find it in herself to be remorseful. She had come here for answers and there was no point beating around the bush.

He motioned for her to sit, and only after she had done so did he follow suit. He rested his elbows on his desk and made a steeple out of his fingertips. 'To what do I owe the pleasure of this visit, my lady?'

'I wish to know why you refused to accept an offer to restore Barchester Hall to the family on my behalf, and why you wilfully neglected to inform me about it in the first place.' She stared at him levelly. 'It should not come as a great surprise that I am not very happy about your decision. Tell me, on what authority did you begin making my decisions for me?'

Mr Compton-Lewis had the nerve to be affronted. 'I have looked after you family's legal affairs for over thirty years, my lady. I can assure you that I had only your very best interests at heart.'

'How would you know what was in my best interests, sir? To the best of my knowledge we have not met since my father was alive.'

He bristled at that, and peered imperiously over his spectacles. 'Your brother entrusted me to handle *all* arrangements in the event of his death, and under the circumstances it was prudent to turn down the offer. Three spinsters would not have possessed the wherewithal to manage the estate. You did not have the money to take on such a burden. I know because your brother left the coffers empty.'

'Apart from my inheritance!' she countered

angrily, annoyed at his arrogant male attitude. 'You knew that was still intact because it was held in trust. My father kept it away from George.'

He glared at her as if she had gone mad. 'Your brother withdrew those funds many years ago, upon the announcement of your engagement— as was his right as your legal guardian. He did so, he assured me, in order to give them to your fiancé as part of the marriage settlement. When the wedding did not take place he did not return them. I have always assumed that he spent the money himself, as he was wont to do. That would not surprise me. He had been trying to unlock your dowry for several years. I was reluctant to pass it over to him, but I had no choice in the matter.'

This did not make any sense. The old lawyer was clearly losing his marbles. 'But I received the money only a few months ago,' she explained irritably. 'You yourself informed me of the bequest.'

He coloured and clenched his jaw. 'That money did not come from your brother's estate. And at no point did I suggest that it did. I merely said that you had come into the money. It was a bequest from a benefactor who preferred to remain anonymous.'

'A benefactor?'

Why on earth would somebody send her five thousand pounds so swiftly after her brother's death? Unless...

'Did the bequest come *before* or *after* Mr Jameson offered the house back?'

She knew from Cook that Ross had initially expressed no intention of living at Barchester Hall. Had he changed his mind after the solicitor had refused it on her behalf?

'I am not at liberty to say, my lady.' Compton-Lewis became very tight-lipped, stood up and walked towards the door to his office. 'I am bound by client confidentiality and the man was adamant that the transaction remained anonymous. I wish you a good day.'

It was a curt dismissal.

'You said "man"—not gentleman,' she said, mortified, as it all suddenly began to fall into place.

'I am sorry?'

Hannah stood and walked to the doorway. 'Why would you make such a distinction—unless he was *not* a gentleman, of course?'

Men like Compton-Lewis would always look down their noses at somebody like Ross. He would never be considered good enough to be one of them.

Hannah felt numb. It was all too much to take in, and yet it did not take a great deal of imagination to fill in the blanks. Her brother had taken her dowry and spent it—lost it at the gaming tables, more likely. Unable to pay her marriage settlement, he had concocted a terrible lie that had meant the marriage would have to be called off. Eldridge—the spineless, arrogant fool that he was—had believed him without question and done exactly that.

To add insult to injury, her brother had then banished her—either so that she would either not discover the truth or so that he would not have to live with the constant reminder of what he had done. Knowing her brother, the truth was likely to be a bit of both, and neither made her feel particularly charitable towards him. Then, being an idiot, he had lost the house.

It all made perfect sense.

Ross had offered the house back to the family, because he would have thought it the decent and honourable thing to do, and when that offer had been rejected he would have insisted on paying for it. She had five thousand pounds sitting in the bank because Ross had actually *bought* Barchester Hall from her. In his mind that would have been the right thing—and Ross always did what he thought was right.

The deeds to the house felt suddenly heavy in her reticule. All along he had behaved like a true gentleman and she was a fool—no better than her idiot brother—ever to have doubted him. Ross Jameson was unlike any man she had ever known and thank God for it.

As soon as she was outside she hailed a hackney. She demanded that the driver take her to her bank. 'And be quick about it.'

White's was full, and frankly Ross was in no mood to be in a crowd. But Carstairs had sent a message that Prim had come to town looking for him, and the gentlemen's club was the only place he could think of where she would not be able to bother him. They might let guttersnipes-made-good into their marbled halls, but they would draw the line at a woman. Even a titled woman.

If his heart had not been broken he would have laughed at his own stupidity. She had only wanted the house. Not him. Never him. She had been so determined she had seduced him to get a stake in it—especially if her story about her solicitor was to be believed and she had not known that he had tried to give the thing back to the family first.

The more he thought about it, the more plausible that explanation became. To start with she had been so hostile and then, just like that, she had been all friendly and gushing and telling him that he was the best man she had ever known. What a joke!

She must have realised he would follow her down to the pond. Prim had planned it to perfection. He had to give her credit for that. Every splash, siren stretch and casual bit of naked hair-brushing had been a deliberate ploy to seduce him so that he could not think straight. And all for her precious Barchester Hall.

At least his arrangement with his former mistress had been based on honesty. She had wanted money, he had wanted sex, and both of them had benefited. He had known where he stood. He had never really known where he had stood with Prim.

He did not want the house now—it would be a constant reminder of her. She had decorated all the rooms, chosen the colours and fabrics, with her own future comfort in mind. Hell, the blasted woman had turned the place into her home and made him pay for it! If he even sat in his study he would have to remember her in it—making him tea, pretending to be thoughtful, making him think that she cared about him. She could keep the house because he was done with the place—and he certainly did not want her either.

No matter how much that irritating spot on his chest ached.

The fact that he was still dwelling on it this late into the evening annoyed him. With no better plan, he headed listlessly towards the card tables. The familiar pattern of numbers and strategy might be just the ticket. He would need to lose big to do that—but it would be worth it if he could forget about her for a few hours.

The hackney pulled up outside White's and Hannah practically broke into a run as soon as she had the door open. She marched towards the uniformed doorman. 'I am looking for Mr Ross Jameson,' she announced imperiously. 'Please take me to him.'

The doorman gave her a bored look. 'Sorry, miss, ladies are not permitted in the club.'

'I am well aware of that fact—but this is a dire emergency. I am Lady Hannah Steers, daughter to the twelfth Earl of Runcorn.' She pulled herself up to her full height and tried to appear affronted.

'It makes no difference who you are, my lady. I cannot let you in. I can pass a message to him for you if you would care to wait?'

Hannah huffed in annoyance. Ross was rightly furious at her. If he knew that she was waiting for him outside he would likely never come out. 'No, thank you. I shall speak to him later. In person.'

Hannah made her way down the short steps and loitered under one of the gas lamps. This was a good spot to watch the entrance in the hope of seeing him when he finally decided to leave.

After leaving the bank, it had taken her hours to track him down. She had been to his warehouse and his bachelor lodgings. As a last resort she had bribed the doorman at his lodgings and thankfully, with a few shillings in his hand, the man had suddenly remembered Mr Jameson telling his driver to take him to White's.

Now that she knew exactly where he was she did not want to have to start again from scratch because he had disappeared out through the back door to avoid her.

That was an idea! With fresh purpose she hurried down the street and then turned into the mews behind. It was easy to discern which building was the back of the gentlemen's club. A few coach drivers were sitting around a makeshift table, playing cards.

She edged as close as she dared to the rear entrance. It appeared quiet, but she could not make out whether or not there was a doorman inside, guarding it. In desperation, she crouched down and hid behind a low wall and bided her time.

After the better part of five minutes the coast appeared to be relatively clear and a servant finally opened the door to inform one of the drivers that he was needed. Like a flash of lightning, Hannah shot up the narrow steps in front of the door, squeezed underneath the man's arm and emerged into the passageway beyond. Guessing that the centre of the club was upstairs, she headed to the servants' stairs. At least she assumed they were servants' stairs...

'Oi!' came an ominous cry. 'You shouldn't be in here!'

Hannah quickly looked behind her to see the uniformed servant charging up the stairs after her. She did not bother stopping and trying to talk her way out of trespassing. If the man caught her she would be unceremoniously kicked out on her ear. Instead she picked up her skirts and broke into a run.

Two flights up, and the raucous noise coming from behind the panelling signalled that she was close to the right place. She followed the noise, dashing down the narrow servants' corridor until she found a door. She managed to burst through just before her pursuer grabbed the back of her dress.

'*Now* I have got you!'

She was yanked backwards with a jolt. Hannah swiftly brought her right elbow back. It landed satisfyingly between the man's ribs and his firm hold loosened enough for her to wriggle free.

'Take your hands off me! I will leave as soon as I have done what I came to do.'

By now she was attracting quite an audience. Gentlemen in varying states of inebriation eyed her with open curiosity.

'I am looking for Ross Jameson,' she announced defiantly, daring anybody to try and stop her.

One gentleman answered, obviously highly amused by her antics. 'He is at the card table.' He jerked his head over to the left of the large, well-lit room and intercepted her would-be jailer with a smile. 'Give her a minute. It might be entertaining.'

As she began walking the crowd parted as if they were the Red Sea and she were Moses, Hannah could hear murmurs of speculation and outrage from them. A woman in White's was a great scandal. Her antics tonight would likely make it into the newspapers, and Ross would not like that at all. However, as he had given her no choice but to come here and root him out, he could hardly blame her for that tiny detail.

As she turned into a small ante-room she spotted him straight away. He was dressed formally for once. The well-cut clothes made him look more dangerous, and she realised she much preferred him in just his shirt. Or nothing at all.

The buzzing around him must have alerted him to the fact that something was amiss, because his green eyes flicked up and met hers. Apart from the smallest twitch of an eyebrow he managed to disguise his shock at seeing her. Here. In his club.

She took a steadying breath and walked slowly towards him, aware of at least a hundred male eyes watching her intently. He made no move to stand or to speak to her. He simply looked back at the cards in his hand with a bored expression on his face and waited for her to do her worst.

She pulled the papers and the banknotes out of her reticule and threw them on the table. The crowd gasped to see such a vast amount of money.

'I came to challenge you to a game of cards,' she said loudly, so that everyone in the room could be left in no doubt. 'My stake is five thousand pounds and the deeds to Barchester Hall.'

Chapter Twenty-Five

'That is a significant bet, my lady,' he drawled, gathering the cards in his hand and placing them neatly on the table, the very picture of complete indifference. 'What do you expect me to wager against it?'

'I would have thought that would be quite obvious,' she challenged. 'If you win, you take the house and all the money you paid for it without my knowledge. If I win, all you have to do is marry me.'

Hannah ignored the gasps from the crowd behind her and focussed solely on Ross. He gave nothing away, but she could see his clever brain whirring away.

Two more uniformed guardians of the club skidded into the room. 'Madam,' said one, in his best authoritative tone, 'we must insist that you leave immediately. Ladies are not permitted in the club under any circumstance.'

The other man grabbed hold of her arm roughly.

'Let go of her.' Ross's casual delivery did nothing to hide the veiled threat in his voice. The man backed off instantly and both men stepped back reluctantly.

'Let her play!' This came from the same man who had directed her to the card tables. 'I will wager one hundred pounds that she beats Jameson.'

He motioned for her to sit and picked up the deck of cards. 'You know you cannot beat me. By the end of this game you could leave here with nothing.'

Hannah shrugged. 'A very sensible man once told me that you should never wager any more than you can comfortably afford to lose. As it turns out I have walked in here with nothing of any significant value to me. I am quite happy to lose it all.'

She watched him for any signs that he believed her, but he merely placed the neat deck of cards on the table and sat back in his chair, nonchalant.

'I suppose the reality of managing a big estate is that it requires a significant amount of money to do so. A husband with a large fortune would come in handy in such a situation. It would certainly make your life a little easier.' He picked up the cards again and began to deal them out.

Hannah rolled her eyes in exasperation. The stubborn man still believed the only thing she would ever want him for was his money.

'It must be a wonderful thing, to be born a man. You take so many freedoms for granted. We women are subject to the whims and edicts of the men in our lives. For example, according to English law if I marry everything I own becomes my husband's property, to do with as he wants. That would mean the house would be yours again. And as to your suggestion that a wealthy husband would make my life easier— need I remind you that my husband could banish me back to the wilds of Yorkshire quite legally as soon as we leave the church? He could dally with a succession of mistresses or gamble away all his money and I would have absolutely no recourse whatsoever.'

Hannah picked up the cards in front of her and fanned them out, because that was what people who played cards did.

'What game are we playing?' Not that it really made much difference. She had played slapjack in the nursery, but apart from that her knowledge of cards was woeful.

He gave her a disbelieving look. 'Piquet—that is why you have been dealt twelve cards.'

He began to sort through his own hand, then sat back and waited for her to start.

'Just the one hand, then. The winner takes all.' Hannah turned towards the gentleman in the crowd who had so far been the most helpful. 'Excuse me, sir, I wonder if you could give me one or two pointers about the rules? I am a little out of practice with Piquet.'

The crowd began to buzz at this. Behind her there were snorts of disbelief and frantic wagering.

'One hundred pounds on Jameson!' one man shouted gleefully.

'She's bluffing,' said another, 'Fifty pounds on Lady...?'

The voice trailed away, so she turned helpfully and smiled. 'Lady Hannah Steers—you might re- member me. I was involved in the most terrible scandal a few years back.'

This started a furore of excitement as the gruesome details of her past were bandied about in hushed tones by one and all. If he wanted her total humiliation as proof of her sincerity she was perfectly happy to give him that too. With- out him she had nothing.

The kind gentleman gave her a brief rundown of how to play, then glanced at her hand. 'Those first, my lady.'

She thanked him and laid the cards down face-up on the table.

'If you would prefer to play a different game we can start again,' Ross offered, looking bored.

She shook her head cheerfully. 'This game suits me well enough, thank you.'

Ross stared at his own hand to give him time to think, but his heart was hammering so hard in his chest it threatened to burst out of his rib-cage at any moment. He was like a swan, gliding effortlessly across the water. Nobody saw how frantically his feet were paddling to achieve such serenity. On the outside he might appear to be calm—but inside he was a complete mess.

A tangle of conflicting emotions warred within him. Anger, hurt, lust and hope swirled in his gut and made him feel decidedly off kilter, while the ache in that spot close to his heart was worse than ever. Without thinking, he laid down some cards and won the trick.

What she had said about English law was something he had not considered. Win or lose—he got the house and the money back either way. Which meant that she had a greater scheme in play or... Or she actually really wanted him.

He watched her lay down more cards. Her teeth worried at her plump bottom lip nervously. She knew that she did not stand a chance against him—was she seriously hoping he would lose the game on purpose?

And why the hell had she told everybody who she was? As if a woman forcing her way into White's and challenging him to a game of cards for his hand in marriage would not cause enough of a scandal already. Was it a calculated risk, to incentivise his compliance, or was she making a completely different point entirely? He was beyond confused by it all.

Testing the former theory, he easily took the second trick as well and stared at her coldly, waiting for her to spew apologies and dramatically throw herself on his mercy, or cry for the benefit of everyone watching. If she was trying to manipulate him that was exactly what he would expect her to do.

She did neither, and carefully studied her hand again before laying down three more cards.

'You cannot beat me,' he whispered harshly. 'You do not even understand the rules of the blasted game. That is plainly obvious.'

Her blue eyes lifted to his briefly before returning to her cards. 'I know that.'

'Then what do you hope to gain?'

She mulled this over for a moment and then shrugged. 'At worst, justice will be done. I have wronged you grievously and it is only right that you get your property back.'

'And at best?' His heart was hammering vigorously now, so he had to fight to keep the anxiousness out of his voice.

Her eyes sought his and held them. 'The man I love with all my heart will forgive me for ever doubting him.'

It was just a pretty speech, he cautioned himself, and he would be wise to keep his wits about him. She had made a fool out of him too many times already.

Ross quickly scanned the cards she had laid. He could easily trump them. Then again, he could just as easily not. Deciding to truly test her mettle, he took the points anyway. She smiled ever so slightly at this, but he saw it waver a little at the corners.

A hush settled over the crowd as they greedily ate up the scene playing out in front of them. If he purposely won, in front of an audience, knowing full well that she was a truly atrocious card-player, then this would be the second callous and humiliatingly public rejection she would have received from a man. The fact that she was already braced to accept it stoically touched him.

She laid down her last trick and then squared her shoulders bravely. The nine, ten and jack of clubs stared up: a mediocre selection for the final rubber, and no match for the queen, king and ace of hearts in his own hand. In one fell swoop he could ruin her...

And then he would make them both miserable.

She looked at him levelly and he saw her fear, doubt, hope and acceptance.

'I went to Barchester Hall in order to expose a despicable rogue, and I did—except it wasn't the man I thought it would be. It was not the man who had hauled himself out of the gutter but one who had thrown himself into one. It was my own brother who betrayed me. He stole my dowry and sabotaged my wedding, all the while hiding his actions, before he banished me to the middle of nowhere and doomed me to a life of spinsterhood. You have every right to hate me, Ross. I accept that. I did not know the true facts—they were kept from me. But I know them all now. You are a shameless flirt, an opportunist, a rogue and certainly no gentleman—but you are decent and honest and noble. You deserve to have Barchester Hall, Ross. The house is a better place with you in it.'

She was trying to make him feel good about the outcome, he realised. She knew she was beaten.

His eyes locked with hers. Past the bravado and the pride and the hope he saw the one thing that mattered the most. Possibilities. She had not simply fallen into his arms. Prim had resisted and resisted. He had been the one to push and push. But was she worth the risk?

With a sigh, Ross tossed his three remaining cards face down on the table. 'I concede.'

The crowd were in uproar, and for a few moments he watched her blink in confusion, uncertain of the outcome. When several gentlemen suddenly gathered behind her and began to pat her on the back she finally plucked up the courage to smile at him. Tears shimmered in her lovely eyes, and then she launched herself out of the chair, in front of everyone, and threw herself onto his lap and kissed him as though her very life depended on it.

When she finally came up for air she was grinning, despite the tears streaming down her face. Ross brushed one away with his thumb. 'Such a scandalous display is not proper, Prim.'

She wound her arms possessively around his neck. 'I think that the rules of propriety can be relaxed a little when two people are engaged to be married. And besides, I am already ruined. To the best of my knowledge a lady can only be ruined once—so who cares?'

Ross did not bother to argue, because she was kissing him again.

'I am sorry I spoiled your plans for a sunset proposal,' she whispered, for his ears only. 'I was looking forward to going swimming with you today.'

'I have a good idea how you might be able to make it up to me.' He chuckled wickedly. 'If we leave now we can be home as the sun rises. I think an early-morning dip will be just as enjoyable.'

He felt her smile against his lips. 'Are you not worried that the water might be a little bracing at that hour?'

Still cradling her in his arms, Ross stood and started to carry her towards the door. White's, the noisy onlookers and everything else faded into insignificance. He was so absorbed with the woman he loved that he did not even stop for a moment to consider what the newspapers were going to print about them tomorrow.

'If it is…' Ross began to march with some purpose '…I will know just how to warm you up.'

* * * * *

MILLS & BOON®

& HISTORICAL

AWAKEN THE ROMANCE OF THE PAST

A sneak peek at next month's titles...

In stores from 19th May 2016:

- **The Many Sins of Cris de Feaux** – Louise Allen
- **Scandal at the Midsummer Ball** – Marguerite Kaye & Bronwyn Scott
- **Marriage Made in Hope** – Sophia James
- **The Highland Laird's Bride** – Nicole Locke
- **An Unsuitable Duchess** – Laurie Benson
- **Her Cheyenne Warrior** – Lauri Robinson

Available at WHSmith, Tesco, Asda, Eason, Amazon and Apple

Just can't wait?
Buy our books online a month before they hit the shops!
visit www.millsandboon.co.uk

These books are also available in eBook format!

0516/04

MILLS & BOON®

The Irresistible Greeks Collection!

2 FREE BOOKS!

You'll find yourself swept off to the Mediterranean
with this collection of seductive Greek heartthrobs.
Order today and get two free books!

Order yours at
www.millsandboon.co.uk/irresistiblegreeks

6_IG

MILLS & BOON®

Mills & Boon have been at the heart of romance since 1908... and while the fashions may have changed, one thing remains the same: from pulse-pounding passion to the gentlest caress, we're always known how to bring romance alive.

Now, we're delighted to present you with these irresistible illustrations, inspired by the vintage glamour of our covers. So indulge your wildest dreams and unleash your imagination as we present the most iconic Mills & Boon moments of the last century.

Visit **www.millsandboon.co.uk/ArtofRomance** to order yours!

0516_AOR

MILLS & BOON®

The Billionaires Collection!

2 FREE BOOKS!

This fabulous 6 book collection features stories from some of our talented writers. Feel the temperature rise with our ultra-sexy and powerful billionaires. Don't miss this great offer – buy the collection today to get two books free!

Order yours at
www.millsandboon.co.uk/billionaires

_BR

MILLS & BOON®

Why shop at millsandboon.co.uk?

Each year, thousands of romance readers find their perfect read at millsandboon.co.uk. That's because we're passionate about bringing you the very best romantic fiction. Here are some of the advantages of shopping at www.millsandboon.co.uk:

* **Get new books first**—you'll be able to buy your favourite books one month before they hit the shops

* **Get exclusive discounts**—you'll also be able to buy our specially created monthly collections, with up to 50% off the RRP

* **Find your favourite authors**—latest news, interviews and new releases for all your favourite authors and series on our website, plus ideas for what to try next

* **Join in**—once you've bought your favourite books, don't forget to register with us to rate, review and join in the discussions

Visit **www.millsandboon.co.uk**
for all this and more today!